LIFE GOES ON

TRANSLATED FROM THE GERMAN BY DAMION SEARLS

FARRAR, STRAUS AND GIROUX   NEW YORK

Life Goes On

HANS KEILSON

Farrar, Straus and Giroux
18 West 18th Street, New York 10011

Copyright © 1933, 2005 by S. Fischer Verlag GmbH, Frankfurt am Main
Translation copyright © 2012 by Damion Searls
All rights reserved
Distributed in Canada by D&M Publishers, Inc.
Printed in the United States of America
Originally published in 1933 by S. Fischer Verlag, Germany,
as *Das Leben geht weiter*
Revised German edition published in 2005 by S. Fischer Verlag, Germany
Published in the United States by Farrar, Straus and Giroux
First American edition, 2012

Library of Congress Cataloging-in-Publication Data
Keilson, Hans, 1909–2011
    [Leben geht weiter. English]
    Life goes on / Hans Keilson ; translated from the German by
Damion Searls. — 1st American ed.
      p. cm.
    ISBN 978-0-374-19195-5 (alk. paper)
    1. Keilson, Hans, 1909–2011—Fiction. 2. Germany—History—
1918–1933—Fiction. I. Searls, Damion. II. Title.

PT2621.E24 L413 2012
833'.912—dc23

2012012326

Designed by Jonathan D. Lippincott

www.fsgbooks.com

1 2 3 4 5 6 7 8 9 10

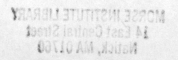

LIFE GOES ON

The landlord walked into the store. He was fat and moved with the gestures of a woman.

"I would very much like to speak with you, Herr Seldersen," he said pompously.

Father was sitting behind the counter by the shop window, reading. That is what he usually does when he is alone with no customers. In the past few months, he has had a lot of time to read; sometimes he reads the whole newspaper three times in a single day. When he heard footsteps, he jumped up as quick as he could and said, in a punctilious voice, "How may I help you?" Then he saw it was his landlord, and his face relaxed. He laughed.

"So sorry to bother you, Herr Seldersen. It's only me. My wife said I should drop by and see if you were alone, so I came over. Actually it's not urgent, but I would like to speak with you." He expressed himself in a roundabout way, with everything veiled in obscurity.

Father came out from behind the counter to the front of the store, next to the high stack of linoleum rolls. The landlord's ambiguous words have made him a little anxious. Who knows what's happening now? he thinks.

"Here's the situation, Herr Seldersen," the landlord begins, suddenly strangely abrupt and to the point. "The corner store next door is opening up. The jam business's lease is up in six months."

The landlord does not want to renew the lease, even though he has received an appropriate rent for the place for many years and has made a handsome profit from the store. But his own shop, selling paper, writing supplies, and newspapers—where he has been for twelve whole years—has now become too small for him. He wants to expand, he is feeling the pressure. Fine.

You wouldn't believe what I have stuck in storage, he brags, I could fill a whole warehouse! Pictures, books, pens, stationery, souvenirs. In addition, the newspaper publisher that he represents here in the city wants him to expand to a branch office; it'll have a big green sign outside listing the names of all the newspapers and journals he stocks, and a large display window where he can hang the latest issue for passersby, all cosmopolitan and generously furnished. So he wants to expand into Herr Seldersen's store, which is located next to his own. He'll tear down the wall between the two and convert the two small spaces into a large business. Herr Seldersen, then, would move another door down in the same building, to the corner location, and otherwise everything would stay the same. That's his plan. What does Herr Seldersen think? Isn't it splendid? Just think, a corner store, on the main traffic street along the market; how many people have had their eyes on that corner! There's no better location.

Pause.

Herr Seldersen stood there the whole time the landlord was talking, as though listening to a speech, but he knew everything as soon as the landlord started. Now it was his turn to say something, and he said:

"Yes, well, I have to talk to my wife first."

Nothing more. No contradiction, no refusal, he just had to talk to his wife first.

The landlord hadn't dreamed it would be so easy. "Of course, go ahead and talk to your wife; there's no hurry, it's six months away. Of course, I'd set everything up for you, repaint, new floors, anything that needs doing. We'll come to terms on everything; first you should just think it over."

Father said nothing—he leaned against the counter, reached his hand back to support himself on the countertop, and said nothing. Then Frau Seldersen walked into the store and saw the two men. The landlord or his wife come over often; they and the Seldersens visit each other, they are on good terms. When the landlord and his wife had their last child two years ago and the doctor and midwife needed additional help, they called Herr Seldersen. Whatever anyone wanted, he could do—fix watches, sole shoes, wire doorbells, polish floors, take down curtains and put them back up again—he knew everything. And on that occasion too he put on a big apron and ten minutes later a bouncing baby boy was born. They never forgot what he had done.

"It's good that you're here, Frau Seldersen," the landlord said. "I've just been talking to your husband."

"What's wrong?" Mother asked anxiously. The landlord started over from the beginning. Frau Seldersen listened and felt a terrible shock. She kept calm at first, but soon her nervousness started to show; her gaze moved from the landlord to Father standing there with a blank look as though not wanting anyone to guess his thoughts, then back to the landlord. After only a few sentences she understood what was happening. Father is like a child in a situation like this, she thought, awkward and helpless, and if she hadn't come in just in time he would have accepted it all in silence, not answered anything, and kept his thoughts to himself.

"Really, that's asking a bit much," she began. "We've been here in this store for more than twenty years and now you want to throw us out."

"Throw you out? How could you think such a thing, no one's throwing anyone out! You would move to the corner store next door, isn't that a good location?"

Mother was agitated; this was all so unexpected. "Yes, but why this change right now when no one knows where we're heading?" They still had a few years left to work—not another twenty-five years, by God—and they had known things would change, but at least they would be in the same place.

"Why put up such a fight?" the landlord suddenly asked in a sharper tone. "It doesn't matter if you're here or next door, anyone who wants to shop in your store will walk the three extra steps to the corner. Three steps, no more, in the same building, it's ridiculous . . ."

Mother shook her head. These last comments bounced off her as though she didn't hear them at all.

". . . when you yourself say that you don't plan to stay very long anyway, that you're going to retire soon."

"Yes, retire," she repeated bitterly.

"All the same," the landlord continued, "I have to worry about myself too. My children are still young, while your son will be done with school in a few years and your daughter is already in Berlin." What about me, what about me?

"But you do own the building," Mother interjected. He laughed. Yes, true, the building, she's right, the building does belong to him. Pause.

Can she see the gray hairs on his head? They belong to him too. Ha-ha, he owns the building, if only she knew the worries he had she wouldn't say that so casually, no; the building brings him nothing but cares and worries. Here the roof leaks and workmen have to come to fix the ceiling, there a pipe bursts and he has to call the plumber, there's the garbage disposal, and then property taxes on top of it all. . . . He held his head in his hands. No, just recently he had told his wife: Little Mother, he said, the building is nothing but a huge headache, it has never brought me a minute of happiness. He had inherited it from his mother and he hadn't wanted to accept it, he resisted it to the end, but finally what else could he do? (The mortgages were paid off during the inflation, before they were revalued.) He gave a heavy groan.

"But the corner location is so much smaller," Herr Seldersen said, resuming the conversation after a while.

Not too small, definitely not too small, and it'll be easier for you to have everything within easy reach. And it's bright, the light is significantly better, you'll save a lot of money on lighting.

"And the display window around the corner will also be no good to us," Frau Seldersen added. "Who's going to go around the corner to look at the window? And both windows are a lot smaller too. Is this how it's going to be?" she asked finally.

"Not right away, not for six months," the landlord said. "I said that at the beginning." He was not in the mood to continue the conversation, it might turn into an argument after all. What's the point of their arguing, if he wants to . . .

Pause.

Mother broke the silence, trying to put on a carefree tone: "We'll think it over, and you can think it over too," she said, as calmly as she could. "You'd lose the rent from one of the businesses, after all, that's something you need to think through pretty carefully."

"For the few years we have left here," Herr Seldersen said in all innocence, "let us stay in the old location. I've been here twenty-four years; we won't be here much longer, hopefully we'll be done soon. Talk it over again with your wife."

"I've told her everything already," the landlord answered. But he promised to go over the whole situation with her again. Then he left.

Father and Mother stayed where they were. He stood with his back resting against the counter; she paced restlessly back and forth. "No good will come of this," she said, "just don't touch it, I'm not setting foot in the new shop. No, no. . . ."

Father said nothing. He thought about how much of his life he had already spent standing in this store, day after day, except during the four years of the war. Mother has her own way of thinking, he makes fun of her superstitions, but deep down he is not free of them himself. He groans. Of course it wasn't a simple matter of just moving next door, as the landlord had so casually presented it. And in the end, time was a powerful factor too: its traces could not be erased so quickly. Herr Seldersen remembered exactly how he had first come to this city as a traveling salesman, so many, many years ago. A small two-story building with ladders and scaffolding in front stood on the market square. When he visited again some time later, the construction was nearing completion. It was actually only a renovation, but you couldn't recognize the old building in the new one: a small, dilapidated building had turned into a towering corner building visible from far away, with four shops set into the ground floor, including eight big shop windows. Herr Seldersen saw here the fulfillment of his dream to be an independent shopkeeper in his own shop, responsible to no one but himself. For three more years he continued to travel, without a fixed residence, just an employee like so many others. He earned good money and had no one but himself to spend it on; he worked hard and people treated him with respect and goodwill, but he was tired of that wandering life and wanted something for himself. He had saved up three hundred thalers. . . . Without a moment's hesitation he went to see the owner and found a short, hunched-over craftsman, who had bit off more than he could chew with the construction and was now deep in debt. He stared at him and said, "I still have one shop free, on the main street, next to the corner. You can have it. I like you." So they came to terms. Herr Seldersen opened his store six months later and hung a sign with his name on it over the door; his wares were laid out tastefully in two display windows and Herr Seldersen stood in the store himself, indefatigably selling whatever a person needed by way of clothing, from shoelaces to suits. You could buy everything there.

Time passed, the owner died, but Father stayed standing in the same place in his store. It was unthinkable that it would ever be different. Conditions had changed dramatically, though. He could certainly tell you a thing or two about that.

Punctually on the first of the month, he took the rent to the first owner's son, the same one who had just shown up with his suggestion.

"We'll wait and see," Father said to Mother after a while. Wait and see, she nodded in agreement, yes, that was their only hope.

She didn't say anything else—she knew that however hard she resisted there would be no other choice for them.

Albrecht, their son, came home from school and the three of them went upstairs to the apartment to eat. The apprentice shopgirl stayed downstairs alone. It was always empty in the store around lunchtime.

Father's plates went back to the kitchen untouched. He sat mutely at the table, with a serious look on his face, as though something terrible had happened. Mother kept asking him to have just a spoonful of soup, a bite of meat—but in vain. He didn't touch his food.

"It doesn't taste good?" she asked.

"I'm not hungry," Father answered. His face stayed rigid.

"You won't change anything by not eating," she said at last, but she went along with it.

Father said nothing. Albrecht, the son, sitting at the table with them, found this all very mysterious. What couldn't Father change? Albrecht had unsuspectingly come home from school and now was made to witness this conversation. It occupied his thoughts for quite some time afterward. He paid close attention to the words his parents said, surreptitiously observed their behavior, tried to interpret and explain everything to himself, but he couldn't quite manage it. He was sixteen years old, a thin boy of average height, the youngest in his class and a bit dreamy, with a delicate, almost girlish sensibility. He already showed certain talents, but it was impossible to tell what direction life would take him in later.

"At least have a few vegetables," Mother began again. She passed Father the serving bowl.

Her constant questions were too much for him: Oh, stop tormenting me, can't you see I'm tormenting myself enough already? (But he no longer said such things; you could only tell by looking at him that he thought them.) He immediately stood up and went back down to the store, skipping his short midday nap. But downstairs, sitting in his chair, he felt such overpowering exhaustion come over him that he visibly collapsed in on himself, leaning his head on the hard armrest and nodding off in that ridiculously uncomfortable position.

Mother and Albrecht stayed upstairs. She could no longer control herself; too many thoughts were running through her head and she fell into sorrowful memories.

Albrecht timidly asked her to tell him what had happened while he was at school. At first Frau Seldersen thought she could put him off with excuses, but since the boy persisted, she told him about the conversation with the landlord. Albrecht listened carefully. After she was done, he said frankly that he couldn't see a problem with moving three steps down to the corner shop, no more than the landlord could; the landlord would just have to come down on the rent a bit, since she said the new space wasn't as nice. Mother smiled slightly at his forceful words. "No," she said, "that's not the whole story, there's more going on here, but you wouldn't understand." That made Albrecht really want to hear from Mother whatever it was that he didn't understand, so she tried to explain to him what it meant to her to have to leave a place where she had spent half her life and had had such experiences. . . . "Twenty-four years, that's longer than you've been alive, don't you see that?" Albrecht rested his head in his hands and said thoughtfully, "Yes, I think I understand, but if there's no other way . . ."

To which Frau Seldersen said, much less calmly than before, that you have to resist every change for as long as you can. Especially now, when they've already lost everything. Now they want to force them into this too.

Albrecht did not understand the context that lay hidden in

her words. He looked her right in the face: when she said that about having lost everything; her voice sounded hard, masculine, as though the situation didn't concern her at all. In addition, he did not understand what it meant to possess something and then have to give it up—he didn't possess anything and didn't know much. He had heard Mother talk about having "lost everything" many times, almost as an apology, the way someone asks for special consideration when his eyesight is bad, but he didn't have any clear image of what it meant.

"Maybe the landlord can still be talked out of it," he finally said, magnanimously, to try to cheer her up. She shook her head. "No, I don't think so, we just have to prepare ourselves." Then she left. Albrecht stayed behind, alone in the room. He repeated her last words to himself and thought about how exaggerated and overemotional her way of dealing with things was, in his opinion. He felt that with a little energy and strength you could avoid a lot of unpleasant things, or at least make them less unpleasant. He didn't take the whole situation very seriously.

·

That summer, they finally finished the construction on Herr Dalke's building: two stories and a giant facade with tall windows. It had taken more than a year and a half; it had seemed for a while that it would never end. They had hit groundwater while digging the foundation, and for weeks and weeks all they did was pump out water—after finishing at night they would find another big lake there in the morning. Then there were the storms, making the ground soft and clayey: everything seemed to disintegrate into dampness, people shook their heads that the construction project wasn't coming along quickly enough, it made the city look unsightly, trucks were constantly stopping in front to unload stones and boards and ladders or load up with garbage and debris to take away, there was dirt and rubble on the street. But deep down, people were happy about the project; a lot of workmen had work for a long time and made money. The construction stretched out but Herr Dalke could sustain it, even if he did run around a lot in those days with a worried look on his face, saying how much he had taken on, if he had only known before he started. . . .

But now it was finished: a magnificent building, its appearance doing honor to the city as a whole. When you walked in, you felt like you had entered a large, airy hall where only good cheer reigned; when you looked at all the many things laid out for sale, you could think only happy thoughts. A staircase led up to the second floor, which was the domain of children and women: everything you could want for the house, and fashionable clothes. Now Herr Dalke was the undisputed leader, and Herr Wiesel didn't hide how worried he was—he was close behind, in second place, and actually had nothing to complain about, but he was a nervous type.

"We'll feel it, you and me," he said to Herr Seldersen. "How bad will it be for us, do you think? Or do you have plans to build a building like that any time soon?"

Father was thinking that now he was going to have to move to the new place on the corner, where everything was smaller and more cramped. But he answered in a relaxed voice that everything had always worked out until then, why wouldn't it work out in the future. "And Herr Dalke must have incurred incredible expenses," he continued, "he's outpaced all of us there too. He has to bring in a lot more per day than I do, for example, if he wants to break even, that's for sure."

Herr Dalke came by and invited Herr Seldersen to have a look at his new building. They were on good terms, even if they were competitors; they would drop in on each other's stores several times a day, and take day trips together with their families on Sundays. Herr Seldersen accepted the invitation and one evening, after closing time, Herr Dalke proudly led him through the lit rooms and showed him everything he had done. Herr Seldersen complimented and praised, didn't tire of expressing his admiration out loud, shook Herr Dalke's hand and thanked him for the friendly invitation, and went back home without a trace of envy.

In the fall, the Seldersens moved into their new store on the corner, three steps down. They had no other choice. The landlord kept his promise and redid everything—the walls, the floors. Everything was much smaller and more cramped and it smelled of paint. Mother and Father knew that they would never feel at home there, but they no longer said anything about it. At first Frau Seldersen followed through on her threat and never set foot in the new store, but eventually she could no longer avoid it. Everyone they knew came to visit, Herr Wiesel too. He looked very closely and carefully at everything and discussed the advantages and disadvantages with Herr Seldersen; things were going well with him, he owned a big store on Eisenstrasse and had nothing to worry about. Frau Seldersen said that he had come only out of curiosity, to see whether the shelves were fully stocked, but Father said she shouldn't be so suspicious. "We've all done fine up to now," he said, "and Herr Wiesel means well."

In the early days, the landlord often dropped in too. "So, now you've almost gotten all settled in, I told you it wouldn't be so hard." He sounded like he was consoling them.

Herr Seldersen didn't answer, only making a hand gesture that the landlord could interpret however he wanted. Then the landlord said that next spring the street was going to be torn up and repaved. Everyone in the city council was eagerly making preparations. "There'll be work," he added, "people will have money and will be able to go shopping again."

"In spring," Father answered. "Who knows what'll happen between now and spring? It's not even winter yet. And where will the city get the money for it? A loan, new taxes, who knows?" Anyway, they're only making preparations for now, that doesn't mean anything.

That winter was the first one when all the poverty and misery was out in the open. Unemployment was rampant, sometimes affecting both father and son in the same family, and people came by and told stories, complained about all sorts of things, and were all so discouraged. There were no signs of new hope anywhere.

The Seldersens stood in their new store just like they had stood in the old one, worrying about the immediate future without any wider desires or ambitions. The times had brought such changes already, you had to accept them without fighting it, with an almost pious calm, as though a god had had his hand in it. This too was only another link in the immeasurable chain; it would not be the last.

Seldersen the shopkeeper had never in his life wanted anything to do with people whose heads seemed to be bursting with big, boundless ideas. What he needed was right there next to him, in arm's reach at all times; his type is absorbed in everyday life, and he always kept his air of calm mastery, not without a certain restraint and reserve. He was a whole man, and behind him stood a whole age. He was past fifty by that time and his life up until then had been nothing but one long struggle. In retrospect, everything looked certain and firmly established, like the accounts in his books: it traveled a straight path, at the end of which stood old age, rest, and an end to work. He had survived the war on the front lines unharmed, even if those four years seemed like ten; he seemed blessed with enormous good luck and his strength was unbroken. His wife had run the business during those four years, while raising two children. Despite how hard she had tried, Herr Seldersen had found nothing but ruins when he came back: shelves empty, customers gone, a distressing outlook all in all. Father suppressed any unpleasant memories and pointless brooding. His credit was still good and he got down to work along with everyone else, rebuilding. At first things improved, everything looked promising. The city was growing, spreading out in all directions, with marvelous factories, companies doing good business; everyone had work, prosperity, and contentment, Herr Seldersen too. He had his views and his principles and he lived his life accordingly. If he had been more decisive and ruthless back then, a lot would be different today.

He lost all his money in the inflation and this time had to struggle hard to barely get back on his feet. He used to employ three salesgirls at busy times, with Mother helping out too. Now it was him and one apprentice. But he made enough to get by and was satisfied. So times were tough and there were signs of even more serious problems ahead—you just had to be a man and shoulder whatever burden there was. But there was no getting around old age.

·

On the night of Easter Sunday, the factory out by the alum mines burned down to the foundation. It was an awe-inspiring fire, filling large sections of the sky with blood-red light and bringing fire departments with old-fashioned fire hoses from far away, up from the villages of the marshes around the Oder River and down from the peaks of the Brandenburg hill country. They thought half the city was burning—but it was only a single factory.

The city, on the edge of the vast plains stretching out beneath the mountain range, was visible from a great distance. Untold years ago, in times of myth and legend, powerful glaciers had carried rubble, boulders and masses of earth, and deposited them there, squeezing the plain like a vise. Today there were rolling, gentle hills, covered with somber firs, slender birches, and severe beeches; healing waters flowed up from the ground and the earth offered itself up as a gift.

Where the hills gradually fell off into the flatlands, brickworks had sprung up all around, and occasionally you would run into one on the plains too, in the middle of the fields and meadows, near a half-silted, dried-out lake. Agriculture and industry existed alongside each other: the factories were big business, attracting a lot of people whom the farmers had to feed. This stretch of country was not prosperous—the soil grew potatoes, rye, barley, and turnips, just as it had for many years, just enough to eke out a modest daily life.

The factory workers were better off: they did their prescribed hours of work and were not dependent on wind and weather, only on the goodwill of their masters and the state of the labor market. But no one had to worry about those things until later, when everything started to go more and more downhill.

The night was cold, with good conditions for a fire. When the alarms sounded and the first firemen, still half asleep, were stomping through the streets in their heavy boots, the fire broke through to a second area, a storage shed packed to the roof with finished bricks. The sky overhead glowed like a fireplace.

The night's peace and quiet vanished from the city in an instant. Since the last period of fires, two years ago, when for several weeks a barn, or a stack of hay bales, or a stall would go up in flames every day, no one had seen such a mighty fire. Now the flames burst in on the sleepy security of the night. The night, the burning factory, the ghostly light on the forest behind it, the reflected glow in the sky: it all awakened fearful thoughts in the groggy men and women, thoughts directed at the future and seeming to sense here a first dark sign of it. The people who didn't run out to the site of the fire climbed up onto their roofs and looked out over a great lake of fire inset in the deep, dark woods that themselves gave off a beguiling red glow, as though the forest were on fire too.

That night, Seldersen the shopkeeper stood at the window for only a little while; the shrill alarm at the beginning, and the louder and louder street noise, had lured him out of bed. He leaned out, saw the firemen's preparations on the little square behind City Hall, and heard the excited cries of the people hurrying by.

"It's burning in the alum pits," he said to his wife. She was lying in bed, somewhere between sleep and waking. A steady stream of images passed through her mind.

"It's cold, shut the window," she asked in a soft voice.

Father lay back down and entrusted himself to the warmth of his bed. But sleep never came. He lay awake the whole night; the feverish excitement outside also forced its way inside. All sorts of thoughts tormented him. Nothing that ever happened had consequences limited to the event itself—everything was linked by fate, one way or another, and in the end no one could escape their share of responsibility for the whole.

In the alum pits, the fire kept burning. Many of the men who worked there were his customers. Every Thursday, when they were paid—either that day or the following day—they came into the city and shopped. When they came this week, they would have quite a story to tell, but what about their money and their shopping . . . ?

That night, around two hundred workers lost their jobs and would stay unemployed for a long time. The owner took the insurance money and moved on. People said that the fire had not come at an inconvenient time for him; he was going to have to cut back the size of his business in the foreseeable future anyway, it wasn't making enough of a profit. The burned-down factory was bought by another corporation and stayed empty for two years.

.

The fire had long since been forgotten, the sulfurous smoke that had hung in the air for a long time had dispersed, and the burned-out factory stood there, a sad image of abandonment, with children playing in the ruins. When the workers walked by, they averted their eyes.

Then, one afternoon, a man appeared downstairs in Seldersen's store. He was short, and still young, with a firm, decisive air—he curtly asked to speak to Father and did not seem shy about anything else either. His outward appearance was strange in certain ways: he wore a particularly high collar that looked almost like a neck brace or socket for his head, and when he talked his face twisted into a grimace in regular intervals. At each grimace, countless tiny wrinkles appeared on his smooth skin and he looked like he was grinning.

Herr Seldersen seemed to be expecting him. He picked up his account books, whispered something in his wife's ear, and went upstairs to the apartment with the stranger. He struggled a bit under the weight of the books, but the other man did not offer to help. Mother stayed downstairs alone, sat down behind the counter, and folded her hands in her lap. She was anxious and kept control of herself only with difficulty. That was how Albrecht found her when he walked into the store.

"Where's Father?"

"Upstairs," Mother answered. She was doodling interlocking circles on a sheet of paper and didn't stop. After a while: "Go upstairs, the man from the tax office is here. Listen to what they're saying."

Albrecht was shocked. "A man from the tax office? What does he want here? And he didn't even give any warning?"

"He made an appointment this morning, I didn't know, Father only just told me now. He wants to take a look at the books."

"At the books? Damn," Albrecht gasped. He had no great experience in business matters—his parents kept everything to do with all that from him. When he was down in the store during business hours, they usually sent him upstairs; he was no good at sales, he just stood around in everyone's way; it was better when he stayed up in the apartment.

Father, as a businessman, was obliged to keep his accounts in order. He could be asked to show the authorities his books and receipts at any time. Every night, after counting up the day's earnings, he made his entries, and at the end of every month, then every quarter, then every year, he added up the grand totals from which his taxes were calculated. Bookkeeping was an art and if you were good at it there was a lot you could do to pretty things up, trim a little here, add a little there. Albrecht didn't know for sure whether his father ever did such things. At the moment, he even felt a little doubt.

"I hope everything's in order," he said, worried.

"Of course it is," said Mother, who seemed very sure of what she was saying, "but that doesn't mean an audit is any fun." Albrecht went up to the apartment and settled into the side room to listen.

The stranger, the man from the tax office, picked up a large book and, before he opened it, said a few general, introductory words.

"As you know, Herr Seldersen, we are not convinced by your declarations. It seems to us that you are trying to evade a significant sum in taxes. The difference between this year and the previous year seems especially striking. Lots of people are trying to finagle things with the state nowadays"—he actually used the word "finagle," then and a few times later as well; "cheat" seemed to be too strong a word for him—he didn't have any actual proof, after all. "It's only natural," he went on. "So our agents are out every day, and they're bringing quite a few things to light."

Father leaned his whole upper body all the way across the table to be quicker with the passing of books back and forth. He calmly listened to the accusations. What could he say? Compared to the previous year? The books here would give the man all the information he needed. Albrecht, behind the door, strained to hear. But before the man started, Albrecht heard Father ask:

"How long have you been working for the tax office?"

"Nine months."

"I see, I see."

And why was he asking, the man wanted to know.

"Oh, only because I've known your colleagues for many years, but I've never seen you before."

Pause.

It was a harmless question, almost meaningless and out of nowhere, but Herr Seldersen had his reasons. He was crafty.

Ask your coworkers about me, he was trying to say—ask them who you're dealing with here, a crook or an honest businessman.

The tax official was not stupid. He understood the purpose of this question, but he had only just started looking things over. How he trembled, this old man!

"You mustn't misunderstand me, Herr Seldersen," he said. "As an officer of the state I am required to protect it from any finagling, and if I am here to see you today, that is in no way meant to cast aspersions on your honor. We merely need to ascertain that all the information you have given us is in order. I understand that it's a difficult time for you these days, as it is for businesses everywhere, for all of us. We hope that things will improve soon."

Father nodded.

Yes, it certainly was difficult, it couldn't go on like this for long. There wasn't much more to say, was there? He had worked and made money, then lost it and worked some more, even though he was past fifty and often longed for rest and relaxation. Everything here in the books was strictly correct and absolutely honest. His memories gained the upper hand and he picked up a book: "Here are the balances from the years before the war. Take a look, now those are numbers, don't you think? We'll never see those again, never. But of course that's not what we're asking for, things just need to get a little bit better. We want to know that things will slowly, eventually improve."

The man started paging back and forth through the account books, checking a sum here, comparing entries there, tracking an individual account, checking sample numbers everywhere. As he did so, he occasionally asked Father a question:

"You have two children, Herr Seldersen?"

"Yes, a girl and a boy."

"And your daughter is in Berlin?"

Father nodded. "She's found a job there, and is continuing with her studies on the side."

"I see. How much a month do you give her?"

"Nothing at all, nothing at all. She earns it all herself."

"She lives on her income and pays for her education too? That's not easy," the man pressed him.

Father explained how it was possible. The school bills were low, she got student discounts and other benefits, and "I can get her her clothes very cheap."

"And you don't give her a thing?"

Father shifted from side to side. "Do you consider it support if I slip five marks into her pocket or send her a care package?"

"Where do you log the sums?"

"They're just little expenses on the side, I don't enter them into the books," Father answered. He was getting embarrassed; his voice grew less and less sure of itself—a sign that Albrecht knew well. He kept listening, anxious to hear what came next.

"And your son's violin classes?"

Father hesitated. As it went on, this interrogation was starting to feel uncomfortable. What did this man want from him? He must have seen the violin in the corner, next to the piano. But still, this was turning into an interrogation, a real interrogation.

"Right here," he answered, picking up a little book where such expenses were recorded.

The man had more questions; for example, why Herr Seldersen didn't own a house in a city where he had lived for such a long time. Surely he must have had opportunities to buy a place?

"Thank God I didn't, something else to worry about," Father said.

Worry? On the contrary, it would have been a good place to put his money, he wouldn't have lost it all.

"Yes, I missed my chance," Herr Seldersen admitted, as though confessing to a sin. "But how could I know everything in advance?"

The man turned page after page; it took a long time. Albrecht eventually got bored in the next room and went downstairs, giving Mother an exact report: Everything's fine so far, Father is a little worked up, but he's giving clear answers, the man can't find any problems. She seemed satisfied.

Meanwhile, the man from the tax office was still working, adding, comparing. Suddenly he found two small mistakes and laughed.

These mistakes here are insignificant, they don't change the final totals, but a practiced eye can catch them right away.

Father's face flushed and he nodded heavily to one side. "When I started to keep the account books myself," he said, ashamed, "I wanted to spare the expense of a bookkeeper. I'm sure I made a few mistakes at the beginning."

"You calculated the annual totals yourself too?" the man asked in disbelief.

"I did, with my wife. It was hard at first, but later I could manage it."

"Good for you. I mean it, that's very impressive." He kept checking.

And then, suddenly, all the sums were smaller, the daily earnings lower and lower, you could see it in the books.

A whole history could be read in those numbers. No case study could have been better. Herr Seldersen sat there and stared at the pages covered with numbers. His tension had gradually disappeared and now he was filled with a sense of calm and control. "Believe me, that's the way it is, just as it says there," he said lightly.

The tax officer said nothing. Was he sitting next to Herr Seldersen every evening as he counted his money and entered the sums? He compared the income to the outlays. Bit by bit, he lost his initial stiffness and suspicion—he thawed, you might say, and grew chatty.

"Is your son going to go to university?" he asked Herr Seldersen.

The latter didn't answer for a moment; the question did not need an immediate response. How to decide what to say? After a while:

"There probably won't be anything else for him to do. We'll have to wait and see."

He already felt a slight discomfort when he thought of the time when his son and he would have to decide.

The tax officer said he had very much wanted to go to university himself. The war got in the way, and afterward he had to try to earn some money as quickly as possible. He often regretted it even today; he was passionate about botany.

"So you were out in the field too." Father steered the conversation into a new channel.

"Of course. I was wounded too, a ricochet in the arm, it went clean out the other side."

Herr Seldersen offered him a cigar.

In the end, the man had to take the books with him; he had not been able to get an exact picture of the state of things from this short look. As far as he could tell, the information seemed truthful; aside from a few minor errors, he couldn't find any irregularities. Herr Seldersen would receive his final determination in a few days.

When Father appeared downstairs in the store again, he laughed.

"Everything all right?" Mother asked anxiously. She had been worried the whole time.

"What could be wrong? Of course, everything's accurate."

After a few days, the man brought the books back in person. This time he was nothing but friendly and forthcoming.

"Here are your books," he said. "Everything is in order. I expected nothing less."

Herr Seldersen felt a sense of satisfaction. They stood there together for a long time and talked about prospects for the future. The man's name was Röllger.

"Money's tight and expensive to borrow too," Herr Röllger said. Herr Seldersen nodded in agreement.

"Where is it going to come from?" he wondered.

Röllger said, "Well, we lost, and that's why we're in this dicey situation."

"But the others," Herr Seldersen put in, "the ones who bring in all the money—are they really doing that well?"

Röllger gave a mocking laugh. "You couldn't say they're doing *well*, but they're getting by for now. They have enormous reserves. And then the debts and the reparations, when you add it all there's no relief. They'd rather all go down together than help out someone who desperately needs it."

Herr Seldersen felt sure enough of himself to say straight-out that these developments weren't all that clear to him, he couldn't make heads or tails of how it actually all hung together; granted, he never made much of an effort or worried that much about the situation as a whole. He had enough to do on his own—later, too, he would use this sentence many times: he had enough to do on his own—and that was that. Plus, that was why he went to the polls and voted, so that other people who had more time than he did could deal with it and, as it were, decide things for him. But he was almost afraid that these other people didn't have any more of a clue than he did! It's priceless, really, he said, and they both laughed. And then all the grand meetings and conferences, a new one every minute, they eat well there and talk a pretty speech, you have to admit, and naturally they always have legal advisors at the ready, and they find their legal precedents and justifications, but who knows how much any of it has to do with the law, with what's right? There's been peace for ten years now, but it's worse than the war was. But the time will come soon when everything turns around at last.

"Very true," Röllger said, "very true." When he left he shook hands with Father. They understood each other.

.

One month later, in the height of summer, Herr Seldersen cele-brated the twenty-fifth anniversary of his store. Twenty-five years! Early that morning, the landlord had sent his little daugh-ter over with a big basket of flowers that had twenty-five daisies wound around its handle. Congratulations! Later, the landlord and his wife came in person to congratulate him. They said how honored they felt that Herr Seldersen had had his business in their building for twenty-five years. The acclaim and honor being heaped upon him today spilled over onto them as well. They had gotten along with each other for twenty-five years . . . and may it last another twenty-five! they said, and heartily shook Herr Seldersen's hand. They didn't mean it literally, and probably didn't think anything about the phrase, but Herr Seldersen had silent thoughts of his own—in all honesty, he no longer had any great ambitions. Everyone stopped by and congratulated him, and there was something in the newspaper that afternoon: A short look back . . . a true member of the community . . . respected . . . a piece of history. Many congratulations and best wishes for the future!

There were some of his customers who had remained true to him through all those years—buying what they needed from him and no one else. They had started off as parents with young children, and Seldersen had watched the children grow up, go to school, take confirmation, get married. Now they dropped by themselves—maybe their father had already died, so they brought their mother, who sat on a chair, her head shaking slightly from side to side—and remembered the old days.

Herr Seldersen walked around and took it all in without a word, in happy silence. He didn't like being the center of attention, even briefly; he felt more comfortable when he could stay in the background; he hadn't rendered any great service, after all. But he could not conceal how moved he was. Thank you, many thanks! Tomorrow's another day. But he felt it—a day like this was certainly an event. You could look forward to it, look back on it later, it made up for a lot. It was impossible to deny, though, that the memories that day called up were not always pleasant ones—they'd had their share of unhappy memories too. Twenty-five years ago, you're just starting out, with plans and dreams, you're young and strong and you know how everything's going to turn out, oh, what high hopes you have. And twenty years ago . . . and fifteen years ago, and then . . . the war, four years, and then . . . and still you keep on, and then . . .

Father had been in the store all day when, early one afternoon, little Kipfer came by. He had been a cigar worker for a long time until his lung problems started. He was just on his way to City Hall to register an assembly for next week; when he came around the corner, Herr Seldersen was standing in the door, looking out at the street. Little Kipfer paid a call on his way back. He had always been interested in politics, even when he was healthy—especially issues around the economic restructuring, industry, rationalization, all those words that sounded especially strange coming out of his mouth. After his health condemned him to inactivity, he started working for a radical party that even sent him abroad once. He was well-read and clever, with a big old soldier's overcoat enveloping his short, thin frame. He often dropped in on Father and they always had things to talk about.

First, little Kipfer offered his somewhat belated congratulations. The anniversary was quite a while ago. Herr Seldersen thanked him.

Kipfer said he had been very busy, there's always a lot of running around to do before an election. He had had to organize and set up various things, receive instructions and pass them along, everything went through him. "We never see you at the meetings," little Kipfer started saying. "Now, you're a sensible man. . . ."

Father laughed. "Yes, well, if politics was my calling, but . . ." He was always so tired at night, he excused himself on the spot. At the moment he was not in the mood for a conversation.

"A worker shoving wheelbarrows of clay around for eight hours is tired too. If everyone said that, where would democracy be then?" He didn't let up.

Herr Seldersen frowned, looking sullen and disgruntled. "You don't need to tell me that," he said, in a tone that made his distaste fully clear. "I was out in the field for four years." After hours he wants his peace and quiet at least. He stands down here all day and hears enough of what people have to say—the last thing he wants is to go sit in a stuffy, overcrowded room and listen to speeches with all the bravos and other shouts. To a certain extent, this passionate participation strikes him as ridiculous, dilettantish, even unmanly. I don't see how you can really think it has any influence on events, either today's or in the future, he said. And anyway, I always stay informed about things, I read the newspapers, obviously, you have to know what's going on in the world. But nowadays I fall asleep half the time. So said Herr Seldersen: speaking reluctantly, sarcastically, and giving off an air of comfortable security.

Everything must be going well for you so far, the combative party functionary replied. You probably think that politics are only for people who have nothing better to do, but if you really knew what was going on in the world, you would think very differently about it. For example, you probably didn't know that enormous harvests of wheat and cotton are being destroyed while right here at home there are more than enough people who lack even the bare necessities. Or maybe your newspaper deliberately suppressed that story—that is one of the key reasons for the general ignorance.

Herr Seldersen had heard that. Yes, he remembered, someone or another had told him that recently. He couldn't believe it at first. But surely there was some reason for it?

"Right you are, there's a reason: keeping prices high."

Then it was good for him, Herr Seldersen decided. He saw things in very simple terms and quickly came to his conclusions, without much reflection.

"All right, but it still has to correspond to everyone else's income. What good are high cotton prices to you if you can't sell your products? The artificially elevated prices may seem good for you for now, but fundamentally it doesn't only affect you, independent of all the other things affecting daily life. It's one part of a system of many things that go all together, and that won't all bring advantages to you, Herr Seldersen." The truth is, it's so intertwined that everything is part of everything else. Today he might say that it's good for him, but it might go far enough, maybe sooner than he thinks, so that he too, someday . . .

Hmm, hmm. Father understood what he meant but played it cool, as though without a care in the world, as though he weren't having sleepless nights. Still, it made him uncomfortable. He could sense that this conversation did not reflect well on him and was not producing any particularly good results. He wanted to cut it off abruptly, not let it reach its natural end, but the consumptive little radical would take that as clear proof that Seldersen couldn't withstand his arguments. So he tried a different tack.

"It's different for me," he said deliberately.

"What do you mean, for you?"

"A businessman like me needs to use other tactics," he said with a certain self-importance. "I'm a businessman, Kipfer, I'm in the public eye, so to speak, out in the open. What I do is not just for myself, within my four walls or under my own roof, as it were. The inspector from the tax office comes by with his wife, the landlord descends from the heights, the worker comes in from the brickworks, you see? They all have their own political opinions, and I may well disagree with half of them, in terms of politics. But am I supposed to ruin things with them? Meet them in some council meeting and say, Good evening, Herr Inspector, I'm happy to sell you whatever you want every day, you have an account with me, but as for your politics, your party is nothing but scoundrels, crooks, and con men. What would he say to that? He'd say, My political views are none of your damn business, pardon my language, and I'll spend my money at Herr Wiesel's instead, thank you very much. That's the end of that customer. Or what if we started talking in the store, what should I say about his views? Maybe I'd say, Yes, you're right, but then the next customer walks in, and he has to be right too, and then the one after that. It's better not to say anything, just play dumb. No, anyone who's independent or can stand to lose his customers should openly say what they think. I certainly have my opinions, but I don't push them on anybody."

Of course, no one is asking you to, little Kipfer agreed. But that doesn't seem to be the whole story, Kipfer said, not when I really think about it. You said something before about "independent," Herr Seldersen, but who in God's name would you consider independent? Who in this day and age depends on himself alone? The farmer, the office worker, the laborer in the brick factory? They all risk getting fired if they attract any attention with their unwanted political ideas.

"So why are they so stupid?"

"Stupid?" Little Kipfer shook his head. "They're not stupid, that's for sure." More like courageous, in his view.

"Yes," Father said with a mischievous laugh, as though playing his trump card. "There are always the unions. . . ."

"That's right," little Kipfer replied, his face flushing, "there are the unions." But he didn't feel beaten; on the contrary, now he was really getting started. Herr Seldersen himself had put the weapon in his hand.

"And who do you have looking out for you, Herr Seldersen? Let's say you run into problems, let's say you go bankrupt tomorrow, what'll happen to you, who's in your corner?" He was feverish with excitement; now he had the fish in the net. "Look at your competition—Herr Wiesel, for example, or the big store up there; let's take him first, he's much more dangerous. He's finished his building, two stories, huge setup, his business is worth a quarter million at least, you can get anything you need there. You think that came from nothing, like he spun it out of himself, with no one standing behind him? If you have to shut down he can last three times longer, because he has backing, support, a lot of people behind him ready to jump in if things get serious for him. He'll only have to shut down if the big retail companies go under, and the banks. And the other gentleman on Eisenstrasse, Herr Wiesel, I was just in his store, and I know a thing or two about business but I have never seen such a big store, and it's all paid for. Say what you want about his way of doing business, maybe you know something I don't, but he owns a house and just bought a car too. He doesn't have to worry either. But you, Herr Seldersen—don't take it the wrong way if I speak openly with you; my mother was shopping at your store when I was still in school, you were still in the shop next door, I remember it perfectly—you are all on your own in your store here, you have to fend for yourself. It must have gone much better for you before, you've at least earned the right to call it a day soon, but if things start to fall apart now, you'll be among the first to go, and a lot of others with you."

Pause.

"But maybe I'm wrong, maybe you still have a lot of money, who can tell?"

"Yes," Father hurries to answer, "a whole crate full of money, from the inflation." Both men laugh.

Herr Seldersen was a respectable person. He kept his distance from any political activity, and in fact considered himself above it, since for him politics meant one-sidedness, dumbing down, and shouting, without seeing any significant effect or improvement or even the first signs of progress anywhere. He was not as dumb as he pretended to be—he saw what was going on around him and sensed that it would affect him, even target him—but he has not grasped it, not really seen it yet for what it is. All in good time.

"Herr Seldersen," little Kipfer said, stepping closer to Father, "in these times we live in, and the times we're facing, it's not good to be isolated and alone, and proud of it too. Everyone needs to know where he belongs. Whether it's you, as a shopkeeper, or me, or Dr. Reschke: anyone who doesn't know his place counts for nothing and will be left behind, out of the running, buried alive. Don't you see that?"

That was little Kipfer. Who knew where he got the words

from, but he talked like a book. He had a point too, even if it always ended up with his party, the only thing he cared about.

Herr Seldersen fidgeted with his key ring in his pocket. He was embarrassed and didn't know what to say.

"That's right, alone and proud of it." Silence.

Then little Kipfer again: "You're too apathetic, as though none of it made any difference to you. But you're feeling the effects, you personally. Lots of other people are too, but especially you. Or are you trying to deny it?"

Deny it? Not in the least. In fact he had all sorts of personal experience of it, Kipfer was right, but everything else he was saying didn't entirely fit the truth. He wasn't apathetic. Did he not faithfully carry out his civic duty and vote in every election? Even when they came three times a year? Doesn't he go to a meeting every now and then? But not anymore, and why should he, can he change anything? "Can you do anything at all at the moment to change conditions or stop them from getting even worse?"

Little Kipfer shakes his head. "Not at the moment. But for the future, I think so, together with others."

So, thoughts for the future—and that's enough to fill his belly?

Little Kipfer said nothing. That took the wind from his sails; now he was out of words at last. He stood there and stared at the floor, but he smiled to himself, invisibly. He knew he was right, even if he was going hungry at the moment.

Father felt sorry he had said the words almost as soon as they were out of his mouth. He truly regretted them, even felt ashamed of them, especially when he saw that little Kipfer couldn't reply. He hadn't meant to mock or hurt him; when it came right down to it, he admitted that little Kipfer was much better off because he had a vision that he shared with other people. Maybe that was what kept him above water, who knows? He, on the other hand, Seldersen the shopkeeper, was all alone. Yes. But now he had to go upstairs for lunch.

"Potatoes and herring today."

"We get that only on Sundays," little Kipfer called after him.

.

One night, when Father stood up from the table, Mother said: "Are you going out for a walk? I'll come too."

"Yes," Father answered, "but stay here, you're tired, I want to go by myself."

"No," Mother said, "I'm not tired, let me come with you."

But Father needed to be alone. He didn't dare say out loud: Yes, you are tired, you're exhausted, look in the mirror: you've got bags under your eyes. He just went out alone.

The evening was warm and sweet, with a lively hustle and bustle on the streets. The day with its work and toil was over, and people made use of the quiet hours to catch their breath and stroll through the darkness. Everyone relaxed in the warm, bright night.

Father ran into lots of people he knew. "Good evening, Herr Seldersen," they said, in the mood to stop and chat; "Good evening," Father said abruptly and without looking up. He had left Mother at home because he wanted to be alone. He hurried to get out of the city center, where it was brightly lit and everyone knew him.

A deep silence reigned in the park. The trees with their thick trunks cast wide shadows over the grass and the paths. There was a lonely bench. Herr Seldersen sat down and leaned his head against the hard wooden back. Silence. A pair of lovers walked past, holding each other tight, and after three steps they stopped and gave each other a long, fairy-tale kiss. Every three steps. They have been walking together for two whole hours, saying not a word the whole time. They slowly disappear into the deep shadows, their hesitant footsteps sounding in the distance.

Herr Seldersen sits on the bench for a long time, sunk in thoughts, then he suddenly rouses himself and everything is sharp and clear again the way it was before. He is an old man, life will soon be behind him; he has walked all but the last stretch of the road. But he casts a searching look back over the long path taken so far, and not a single tiny segment escapes his memory. That is my life, he thinks, and all at once the idea comes over him that he will soon have to think about death. But what does death have to do with him? Nothing for the time being, nothing yet.

A light breeze makes the trees sway, the branches clatter against one another, the sky appears through a little gap. The old man sitting on the bench breathes the scent of the flowers and the trees, and closes his eyes. Silence.

He has left the house not exactly morose but not in a totally happy mood either. His wife had wanted to come with him but tonight he wanted to be by himself for once, not saying a word. His head is pleasantly numb; a sluggish lethargy fills him, then sleep, and he nods off. When he wakes again, he startles and doesn't know at first where he is, but he quickly remembers. He feels as though he has slept for several hours; he can't say how many hours because he has left his watch at home, but it must be very late. There is not a sound in the park. He quickly walks home; he'll have to be back on his feet again early tomorrow.

Tomorrow . . . who knows what tomorrow will bring. He has no great hopes for it; over time he has learned not to expect much. Suddenly the conversation with little Kipfer comes to mind again. . . . The truth is, you've earned the right to call it a day, he'd said. Father clearly remembers the words and the whole conversation. Has he earned that, really? He groans softly and quickens his steps. Who asks after him, who is looking out for him, who? No, no, but now he has to think about it: how to gradually bring his life to a peaceful conclusion. He isn't old yet, he still feels young and vigorous, but the thought comes over him like a soft wind: What if he cannot bring it to a peaceful conclusion? He has a faint premonition: the way he thought it would be, the way he started life and led it all these many years, might not be the way he finishes it—he feels it slipping away from him, more and more, he no longer has any power over it. Maybe it is in the grip of some other, uncanny power now. But there is nothing more he can know about it, not yet.

Back in the city, he looked up at the clock on the church tower: two in the morning. He walked up to the apartment quietly, got undressed in the side room, and held his breath as he crept into bed.

"Where were you so long?" Mother asked. She had lain awake the whole time. "I was so worried. How late is it?"

"It's late," Father answered in a soothing voice. "We can still sleep for a few hours."

Soon he was fast asleep.

．

The days took their placid course, nothing important happened: everyone went about his business and it was more or less monotonous at school too. A new principal replaced the old one, there was a new wind blowing—you could tell from many little things that there was a new punctiliousness and precision in the whole institution.

At home, over lunch, Albrecht faithfully reported on events at the school; his parents asked questions and he eagerly answered. Every so often, he would notice that his father was not paying attention—he let Albrecht talk, even asked a question now and then, but barely paid attention to the answer. He held his spoon in his soup, bent forward over the bowl, and stared fixedly at the tablecloth; he forgot to eat, lost in thought. Albrecht stared at him and laughed. His father was not in a laughing mood—on the contrary, he seemed not to like being laughed at here at the table. Who would have thought he would be so sensitive? Sometimes at night he would leave the apartment, jumping up at the slightest difference of opinion and taking the key to shut himself up in the cold store for hours, even though there was nothing he needed to do downstairs. He locked the door behind him. Mother crept anxiously downstairs and listened at the door, leaving only when she heard him walking around or working. At first it would be completely quiet—he would sit on a chair and stare into space in the dark. Then he would stand up and turn on a single light, enough for his sad work. He took the fabric samples off the shelves, rolled them out, measured each piece, and piled them on the counter. Then he started to reorganize everything, putting the cambric next to the linens, the aprons next to the corduroy, switching the woolens with the notions. No one could find anything the next day. It gave him pleasure, a strange, bitter, stubborn pleasure, suited only to him: first to make a huge mess and confusion, strewing his goods over the tables, chairs, even the floor after he had spread out big white strips of paper to put them on, and then to create order once more, straighten up, smooth out. The work let him put things to rights—there was no other point to it, it was useless, just extra work. For hours he drove his rage and God knows what thoughts out of his head. It was late when he went back upstairs to the apartment. When he shut the door downstairs, the sound echoed through the nighttime quiet of the house. The next day, everything was back to normal. It was impossible to get anything out of Mother—she said not a word, just fanned herself when it got too terrible. Then she walked around the apartment as though in a church; she talked and acted like she was preparing a sacred offering. That exaggerated the whole situation and made it worse than it actually was.

"You shouldn't laugh when Father's sitting there thinking," she told her son. "He's worried about things. Try to cheer him up, not make fun of him."

"You're right," the boy answered, and his child's face grew serious; "tonight I'll play something for him on the violin, I know he likes that." Mother nodded and looked at him for a long time. He was still a little boy, even if they no longer called him by his first name at school. He played the violin, he was very musical; he was delicate but not mollycoddled, and held his own in games with boys his own age, and deep into the fall he went swimming in the lakes that ringed his hometown. In winter too he didn't hang around the house.

Fritz came by one night. Albrecht's friend was a year and a half older, with a much stronger build. They were classmates. His father owned a building on the main street, where he had a plumbing business.

Fritz invited Albrecht out for a walk and his parents had no objection—it was late summer, the night was warm and bright. It was just a little way up a steep street and a long, steep stairway before they were up in the forest. They walked farther, to a clearing with a bricked-in stone wall around it. There they lay on the stone wall and looked down.

Silence.

Night rose up softly from far behind the chain of mountains, with the wide and mighty river wending its way at their feet; it settled down into the basin of the valley and slowly crept toward the city. The little villages, scattered far and wide across the plains, nestled into the delicate white haze rising up from the ground. Everything was still; only the blinking lights on the church towers kept turning, showing the airplanes in the sky the way. Peace and quiet gradually came over the city.

The two friends lay there in silence for a long time, until it started to get too dark to see, but even then they were filled with the landscape and unspeakably grateful for their happiness. They knew how it looked in the morning too, when the sun rises through the mist and the workers walk to the brickworks down lonesome streets; or at noon, when the country lasses carry meals out into the fields and the apprentices sit on doorsteps in the blazing midday sun; or in the evening, when the automobile lights race through the quarry and the smoke from the chimneys blends into the darkness of night. They knew it in every season, and even though they often found themselves slinking around with everyone else down below, doing their part in the little city's important little life, they much preferred to spend their time up by the wall. That was when everything felt like it belonged to them, like they were all-powerful masters of the world. Life would take them away soon enough, and who knew where—they would live in other cities, meet new people, see new places, so many images and impressions—but this one image would stay fixed in place, reaching all the way down to the bottom.

On the way back, they stopped by Fritz's house. Fritz's parents were still awake, sitting in front of the door and talking to the neighbors.

Frau Fiedler said, "Where were you, getting back so late?"

"You know where we were," Fritz countered.

"We were just out for a walk," Albrecht added. Why was she acting so suspicious?

"Oh, today of all days. Right after you left, the von Arnims sent word that the lights were out in their stables. Erich had to ride out, there was no one else here."

Erich, Fritz's brother, had to go even though he worked hard all day and should have his peace and quiet in the evening at least. Fritz could hear the criticism in her voice.

"I see." He stayed standing there for a moment, as though he had something else to say, but not a word came out. Then they both went inside in silence. The radio was on a table in the corner. Fritz pulled up a chair and sat down in front of it. The lights blinked, he turned the knobs, and a soft hissing and whistling started up from the loudspeaker, then a clear voice. "Berlin," Fritz said, and he turned the dial farther; the voice disappeared. Albrecht sat down and listened eagerly. A mysterious music sounded, quiet and delicate, from a great distance; it swelled and filled the room. "Vienna," Fritz said. He looked at a chart and tuned the dial again.

"There's another one," Albrecht said.

Fritz just nodded: "Oslo. Next is Moscow." He knew what he wanted and he flipped switches, turned knobs, fine-tuned, producing a muddle of weird squealing and whistling.

"There," Albrecht said; he vaguely heard a hoarse voice. Fritz shook his head. "No, that's Warsaw or something," he said self-importantly, "it's a real art to get Moscow." Albrecht leaned back and waited patiently. He watched Fritz get tense: his face became rigid and the poise he always seemed to have disappeared.

Meanwhile, Erich had come home. It was only a little repair, not really worth the long trip out. He brought his bicycle into the room and when he saw the two friends sitting there, he said, "There you are! You could have saved me a trip, Fritz. I'm on my feet all day."

"We are too," Albrecht answered, laughing.

"Really? What have you two been doing?"

"Greek homework."

"That's not work," Erich said good-naturedly. "School is just lazing around. I went to school once too." He was only three years older than Fritz and had graduated from secondary school. He had already spent five years working in his father's business: working hard, saving up his money, doing a good job. His parents didn't know how lucky they were. This errand tonight hadn't come at a great time—he had had better things planned for his evening—but since there was no other choice he rode out, fixed the problem, and calmly turned around and rode back. He put his bike in the back of the room, washed up, made himself a sandwich, and sat down.

Fritz was still sitting in front of his machine: looking, turning, flipping switches, listening into the loudspeaker—nothing, nothing. He shook his head.

"This is getting boring," Albrecht said. "Put on some music or something, enough of this hunting around."

Fritz was in the grip of an obsession, but finally agreed and gave up on Moscow. Instead he went through all the other stations, rummaging through all of Germany and the rest of Europe, and every time he picked up another station he whispered its name like a magic formula. He luxuriated in the distances and didn't stay anywhere for long, always searching, ever farther—restless, foolhardy, like he was trying to get the whole world into this one room. Albrecht had long since walked over to Erich and sat down with him on the sofa. It was just too boring, sitting quietly next to Fritz and waiting for him to come to his senses.

"What does he see in it?" he said. "At least if he would listen to one piece of music straight through to the end, but all this endless twiddling. . . ." There was no pleasure to be gotten from that. Erich agreed: "I don't understand it either. All that squeaking and whistling would kill me, I don't know how he stands it—he's crazy about the radio." Erich said he knew a thing or two about circuits himself, of course, but he couldn't relate to Fritz's obsession.

Eventually most of the stations stopped broadcasting. Only some English stations were still there, ruling the airwaves. But Fritz had had enough. He stood up. "Yes, Moscow," he said, "that's a hard one." He was still not over it. Albrecht said goodbye, he was tired, but Fritz was still fresh and energetic—he seemed to have just then woken up. He could stay on the radio for hours, he bragged. Meanwhile, his brother's eyes closed; he was tired too.

The next day, in school, Mother's words came to Albrecht's mind: Father was worried about things. In the middle of his exercise he stopped writing and stared at his teacher for two minutes. When he got out of school he went straight to the store and asked Father:

"Why were you so absentminded yesterday?"

The question surprised and embarrassed Father. "Oh, it's nothing, really, just a couple of things I'm worried about. Things aren't as easy today as they used to be."

That must be it, even if Albrecht didn't know from personal experience how easy it had been for his father before. He asked, "Did someone not pay again?" He knew that lots of people bought things and then let weeks go by before paying. —"Yes, that too. It's just hard."

Excuses, obviously—he was avoiding a direct answer. But Albrecht didn't give up. He kept asking, and he knew how to keep after him until Father finally lost patience.

"What do you care?" he said angrily. "Go upstairs and mind your own business."

Oh, really? What did he care? Quite a lot, obviously, otherwise he wouldn't ask. He was curious and wanted to hear the real reason. "Do you think I don't have eyes or ears? I can tell that something's going on, it's obvious just by looking at you, and Mother's already caught it from you, whatever it is. But whenever anyone asks you, you just say it's nothing, leave me alone, and so on. All right, so if there's no reason, why all this fuss and waste of energy? You're always taking it out on me, so either tell me what's going on or cut the drama—hanging your head, always being in a bad mood, puttering around downstairs at night until it scares us. Pull yourself together. You're not a woman."

A brave speech, by God! The words themselves gave him the courage to keep going. But it would be easy to misunderstand him: he almost seemed bold out of stupidity, foolishly trying to get clear about everything in one go.

Father stood there crushed. His face was white as chalk and he trembled. So accusations and reproaches on top of everything, he deserves that now?

Albrecht: "No one's accusing you of anything, you should just finally say something so I know where I stand."

"I'd like to know that too," Father answered. Now he had the upper hand. "To know where you stand, that's the whole point! But you're too dumb, you don't understand. Go upstairs."

Albrecht said nothing. His father's words made him very angry; he could see that he hadn't accomplished what he wanted, and he would never get an answer out of his father now. He didn't dare to try again—the conversation had gone wrong, miserably wrong. Too bad; it had started off so promising.

When Albrecht picked up the newspaper to take it upstairs,

a letter that had been sitting on top of it fell to the floor. He picked it up and read: "In reference to our letter of the third of this month, may we reiterate that your deadline of sixty days has already been exceeded by thirty days. Requesting your soonest possible resolution. . . . Yours sincerely . . ."

"What's this?" Albrecht asked, looking straight at Father.

No answer.

"Someone wants money from you. How much?"

Pause.

"Go upstairs," Father said suddenly.

Albrecht obeyed, without looking up.

That night Father thought of something, and asked, "Did you pay for your violin lesson today? I forgot to give you the money for it, you should remind me."

"I paid," the boy answered meekly.

"And the money?"

"I took it from my piggy bank." He felt utterly ashamed.

"That's ridiculous," Father said, and he seemed amused by the situation, but a free and easy laugh was more than he could manage. "I'll give you the money tomorrow."

●

Another day: Where were his parents? Albrecht had spent the evening reading and practicing the violin as usual, then got tired and stopped. Where were his parents? After dinner they had stood up and left the table; since then they were nowhere to be seen. Maybe they had gone for a walk, but Albrecht hadn't heard the door. He looked around the apartment. When he stepped into the kitchen, Mother was standing at the stove cooking tomorrow's meal. She had been crying: her eyes were red and she looked miserable. Father was sitting in the corner, on the low kitchen bench, and seemed even shorter than he was. He had his elbows propped up on his knees and his face was covered with his hands, and he crouched there like that, sunk in thoughts. What kind of thoughts? —An unpleasant silence hung in the room.

"What's wrong?" Albrecht asked in surprise. He looked back and forth between his parents; Father's head stayed down and Mother bent farther over the stove. The steam rising up out of the pot enveloped her face and stung her eyes; now she had an excuse for her tears. "What's wrong?" Albrecht said again.

Silence.

He shut the door and leaned against the frame to wait for an answer. Then Mother said straight-out that she couldn't take it anymore, Father had been nagging her for days now, it couldn't go on like this; he was saying such strange things, she couldn't listen anymore.

"What in the world . . . ?" Albrecht asked.

Father raised his head and now you could see how desperate his face looked. His eyes were puffy and bloodshot.

". . . and then he says he'll have to go peddling, that's his word for it," Mother said. She was crying. "A peddler! And he's old now, can he do it? Over fifty, traveling all around the country, in all kinds of weather? But he likes it, he does! He gets a devilish pleasure out of saying how bleak and terrible everything is."

"Yes, but why?" Albrecht asked. Why did Father like doing that, and why didn't he stop when he knew it hurt Mother? What even made him think those things?

It had been another long slow period in the shop. They barely took in enough to cover their expenses, money was tight, and they all were gingerly waiting to see what the next day would bring. There were bad days, as there always are, but now there were too many of them, coming too often; you had to wait too long for a single good day. It took time to get used to this new state of affairs, especially if you had many, many years' worth of memories and comparisons ready at hand, as Herr Seldersen did. Now he was hunkering down on the bench in the corner, depressed, careworn, trapped in his thoughts, unable to get out a single reasonable word. . . . He had to go peddling. The thought had seized him and wouldn't let go . . . he had to go peddling.

When, then? When it couldn't go on, when it was over. Father had put into these words an event that had not yet happened—it was extraordinary, who gave him the right to do that? He himself, no one else. It would happen, he knew it; it was inevitable, there was no room for interpretation, he could no longer shake off the idea. This sent Mother into a frenzy. "Stop it!" she screamed, "you're exaggerating! It's not that bad." —"I'm not exaggerating," was his only response. Silence. They stayed mute, the words roamed the air between them, wounding them anew, again and again, Father in his corner and Mother at the stove, bent over the pot. That was how Albrecht saw them.

The next day, and for a long time afterward, he could not get the image out of his head: he had seen his father crying. It meant more to Albrecht than just a couple of tears—he had ideas of his own about masculinity, about how men are supposed to behave, and what about those ideas now? This was by no means the last of the discoveries he would make in this regard.

·

Fritz was a clown and knew all sorts of tricks that no one else could do. He only had to lift his upper arms slightly and his shoulder blades would jut out so much that they almost poked through his jacket, making a visible hump on his back. He would perform for the rows behind him while sitting motionless on his seat in school or standing up to answer a teacher's question. Or his upper lip: this trick brought him even greater acclaim. He had a little piece of flesh hanging over his upper lip on the left, as though an injury from a soccer ball had healed badly, and he could make anyone in the world laugh by lifting up the overhanging flap and moving it around like a third lip that could move independently while the rest of his mouth kept its usual, normal shape, one lip evenly positioned on top of the other. Fritz had lots of friends and a good reputation among teachers and parents; he was a fun kid, always ready for anything, and a leader too. He was strong, and since he had so many special tricks and abilities he seemed twice as strong. Only his eyes were bad, but that had only recently been revealed, after he had spent a whole year at school sitting next to the window while the blackboard hung dark and dim in the corner. When the year was almost over, he showed up one morning in class with glasses—real black-framed horn-rimmed glasses. At first no one believed they were real: who could tell, maybe he was wearing them as a joke, just to try something new.

There were two other boys in the class who wore glasses. One was Kurt, the oldest, twenty-four years old, who had dropped out of school from a lower grade three years ago and had now come back as a grown man who knew something about life; he had worked hard, and had a good sense of why he was taking this step working toward a proper diploma. He wore glasses as a sign of his age, experience, and superiority. Even the teachers treated him with respect. The other was named Alfred, and he had worn glasses for as long as anyone could remember—was practically born with them, it seemed. He was slightly deformed and pale, wrinkled like an old man even though he was still young. He was always sitting behind a book. And now Fritz too—it was unbelievable, no one could wrap their minds around it.

What on earth are you going to do with your glasses on the field? they asked him. He had a reputation as an excellent player, but with his glasses on he was suddenly a lot less dangerous.

"Keep them on, of course, otherwise I can't see," Fritz said.

Hmm, they would have to just wait and see, maybe he would take them off later after all, when the joke got to be more trouble than it was worth. Meanwhile, they needed to see if the glasses were fake. He took them off and let his friends look through them: objects lurched farther away, got blurry, everything swam together, his friends' eyes hurt and started to tear up, and they took off the glasses in a hurry. No doubt about it, they were real. And he could see with them, he kept them on all morning without his eyes ever hurting. From then on he wore the glasses all the time.

Even at home they made a fuss, his father calling him "Herr Professor" as a joke, for example—Fritz seemed quite proud of that. For him, the glasses meant more than they appeared to on the surface; he had had thoughts and plans for the future, but now they seemed meaningless, impossible. He had wanted to be a forest ranger when he graduated—now, that was a career. He would wear a green uniform and be on close terms with everything that lives and breathes. His house would be deep in the woods, no beaten track to his door, and when someone did come out to visit him they would sit together through the long evening, until their talk slowly fell silent, and then it would be time for Fritz to take his guest on a walk through his territory. All is quiet. Darkness hangs down from the branches like deep sadness. And if the guest flags with fatigue in the midst of this silent majesty—maybe he has come the long way from the city—if he trips over every root and shudders when a bat brushes his face, that would only make Fritz seem bigger and stronger: this is his domain. But those dreams were over. Time passed, Fritz wore glasses, he had grown older and seemed strangely pensive and sedate. Life had begun for him in earnest, in all its immensity. And he thought he had drunk its pain and bitterness down to the dregs.

He spent his time alone, mostly in his room up on the second floor, which you could reach up some stairs from the yard. There he could sit undisturbed. His parents slept in the next room, but the whole apartment was divided in pieces: downstairs, behind the store, was the kitchen, a large room where they ate together. There were tools strewn across the entire apartment, wires, screws, lightbulbs; there was always an apprentice or assistant coming in to fetch whatever he needed for his work. It was not a pleasant place to stay: someone was always passing through, no one ever tidied up, it was never comfortable and homey.

Fritz rarely saw his father, only at mealtimes during the day, and everything was hasty and hurried. His parents usually ate before him. When Herr Fiedler came home, he always asked his wife, "Where's Fritz?"

"I haven't seen him," she answered. "He must be upstairs studying."

"Studying," Herr Fiedler repeated with satisfaction. That was as it should be. Without studying and exams, you couldn't get ahead and move up in the world.

If you saw him you would think he was just a simple craftsman whose hard work and perseverance had brought him a decent life and a good income. But in his younger years, he had been a passionate fighter for liberation and for a just distribution of wealth. He had lost the fire in his belly during six months in jail, but his sacrifice did not seem to have been in vain: he did not need to feel ashamed of what he possessed; he had come by it fair and square through his own hard work, and when he sat down at the table in the inn with his friends at night—honorable citizens every one, who may have ventured a leap or two past the proper bounds once or twice, but who generally gave the eternal verities of society their due—he had every right to calmly raise his voice and venture a word or two of his own. He had had it hard and his son should have it easier—that's why he was sending him to the academic high school.

One day, Fritz's teacher, Dr. Selow, ran into Herr Fiedler on the street. They had already walked past each other when Dr. Selow turned around and caught up to Fritz's father, who stopped and looked at him in amazement.

"Please come see me at school on Friday, Herr Fiedler," Dr. Selow said. "I need to talk to you."

"Of course. It must be something about Fritz? What's the boy done now?"

"We'll discuss it on Friday. Good day." He was in a great hurry.

Herr Fiedler showed up at the principal's office on Friday at the appointed time. Dr. Selow met him there and took him to a small room that was available for discussions like this one.

Dr. Selow was in his early forties; he had served as an officer in the war and he still looked like a soldier.

"I have asked you to come and see me today," Dr. Selow began, "to discuss Fritz." He called him just "Fritz," even though in the classroom and elsewhere he addressed him more formally, with his last name. But with the father he simply said "Fritz," to create a friendlier environment.

Herr Fiedler sat there, with his hat on his thighs so that he couldn't move his legs, and he felt like a schoolboy under questioning. Conversations like this one never went without a certain anxiety, and this was not the first time he had sat there. He had had to walk the road to school rather often already, usually after a letter arrived in a blue envelope with an official seal, so his wife, who opened the mail, was always fully informed too.

"What is it?" he asked. "Is something wrong with his work; is he lazy, not paying attention?"

Dr. Selow shook his head. No, no, it wasn't about his schoolwork, he wanted to say that right up front. It was about Fritz in general, his personal situation.

That was strange, very strange: not specifically about school but in general. . . . Herr Fiedler was very surprised, he had already been through many such conversations but this one seemed different, exceptional, from the beginning. Fritz hadn't done anything, and still Dr. Selow had asked him to come in to talk about his son.

He thought for a long time, then finally said, in a somewhat uncertain voice: "Yes, Dr. Selow, I'm afraid I can't give you very much information. I hardly ever see Fritz at home face-to-face, you see. In the morning he's at school, in the afternoon he's out on the playing field, the rest of the time he sits in his room and studies, what else could he be doing up there? I can't spend too much time worrying about him since I have my own work to do; I travel a lot, but my wife is home all day."

Hmm, hmm. Dr. Selow realized that he wasn't going to get anywhere on that tack. He had to try something else.

"Of course," he said, "of course. I know that you're busy and rarely at home during the day, but still . . . you must have some sense of how he is doing, and I'm sure you discuss him with your wife. . . . Has Fritz been acting unusual lately, or changed his typical habits?" Dr. Selow waited.

"Yes, he's smoking a lot now," Herr Fiedler answered hesitantly. He couldn't think of anything else at the moment. This really was an interrogation. He grew more and more embarrassed and couldn't see how it would end or where it was going. Suddenly he said, and seemed quite demoralized to say it: "You ask me about Fritz, Doctor, and I don't know how to answer, even though I'm his father. But we've never had a relationship where I could say exactly what was going on with him, or vice versa. When I came back from the war, took off my uniform, and took up civilian life again, he crept around me for days and days with big eyes, without saying a word, as though he didn't know who this person was who was moving into the house all of a sudden. I sometimes have the feeling that it's no different today."

Pause.

Then, after thinking for a moment: "You asked me to come and see you, Doctor; there must have been something you had in mind. You must have had a reason for wanting to talk to me, I'm sure of it. Please tell me what is going on."

Dr. Selow shook his head. "Nothing, Herr Fiedler, I assure you, there's nothing at this time. With young people there are so many outbursts and exaggerations, but for adults all you need is a wink, a subtle nod. . . ."

He was a clever man, this Dr. Selow. He knew every twist and turn of the tortuous paths where young people can go astray and eventually lose their way altogether, he knew all about the dangers and temptations they rashly, secretly longed for. He waited and, when the time came, did his best to help, cautiously and deliberately, without pushing too hard, and only at the proper moment.

"And what does this all have to do with my son Fritz?" Herr Fiedler interrupted. He was visibly agitated now and wanted to finally hear what this was all about.

Dr. Selow remained unruffled. He went on, more to himself than to Fritz's father: ". . . but it's also possible to make a mistake, in fact it's all too easy to make mistakes. These boys who grew up while their fathers were out on the front lines, and who then got older and saw everything going under, along with the rest of us—sometimes they don't know how to take it, it's hard even for adults to keep afloat, you know."

Pause.

"Your Fritz is big and strong, almost a grown man. He's been my pupil since his first year here, and I've kept my eye on him all these years. I also know him outside of school, from trips, I have a very clear picture of him, believe me. Nowadays he sits in class so calm and quiet most of the time that I don't want to call on him. He looks like he doesn't know what to do with himself. He's bored and depressed. I often think that there must be something happening to be causing it. That is why I asked you to come in today, Herr Fiedler."

Herr Fiedler was speechless. Everything this Dr. Selow noticed, and now what was the answer he wanted to hear? Now, if Herr Fiedler had cunningly given Dr. Selow a wink and trustingly touched him on the shoulder, the way men usually do when they talk to each other about certain things—if he'd said that there's a woman involved, Dr. Selow, a woman, naturally, what else could it be, you understand, you yourself said he's already a grown man—then that would have been just what Dr. Selow wanted to hear. A woman, naturally, Fritz was in love, Dr. Selow would know just what to do about that, he could have bided his time and then intervened, it wouldn't have been the first time. But Herr Fiedler could not do that kindness for Dr. Selow, and things remained as they were.

Dr. Selow felt how tragic his role was, as a bearer of traditions in an era that had lost its guiding threads, or actually torn them apart on purpose. These traditions had lasted centuries, and had once seemed permanent and enduring, but had now, apparently, lost their validity. He taught what he called eternal truths, but they were illusions, disconnected from the world and from one another, and he taught them with the desperate intentions of someone not fully convinced. During this conversation, he brought up several more things he had noticed about Fritz recently: little observations, thoughts he later took back, but nothing tangible, God forbid! Everything with reservations. Anything he said might be mistaken, after all.

Herr Fiedler breathed more easily; he had been preparing himself for much worse. "Feel free to take him firmly in hand, Doctor," he said, convinced by his own words. "He seems absentminded and dreamy at home a lot too. Don't hold back, he's old enough to learn that he owes everything to his parents and his own hard work."

Dr. Selow said nothing. He didn't know how to proceed.

"We give him anything he wants," Herr Fiedler continued. "Anything, there's no road closed to him. But first he needs to finish school with a diploma; after that he can do whatever he wants, university, anything. We'd like it best if he decided to go into the civil service. And what you're mentioning now," he went on in all frankness, "goes back years, he's a bit lazy, and too comfortable; he gets into trouble at home about his schoolwork; he had to repeat a year, as you know. That can't happen again. If it does I'll take him out of school and put him to work, he knows that. He just needs to pull himself together and make a bit of effort, we all need to make an effort."

Those, more or less, were the words that Herr Fiedler spoke— honest, conventional, straightforward. The meeting was as good as over. All things considered, a somewhat sad proceeding. Herr Fiedler had sat there at first not knowing quite why he had been asked to come in, restlessly fidgeting back and forth in his chair, thinking about all the work he had piling up at home. Then he had got going and all but celebrated his triumph, while

Dr. Selow realized that he had rushed things when he saw Herr Fiedler on the street and decided on impulse to ask him to come in. Fritz's father sat across from him, making, truth be told, a rather sorry impression: he had openly admitted that he didn't know exactly what his son did every day, and, worse yet, how his son was doing in general. He had only guesses. And what he then said was irrelevant, shedding far more light on himself than on his son.

"But it is always a positive thing to meet and talk," Dr. Selow said. He stood up. The meeting was over. He went back to his classroom, he was already late.

Herr Fiedler walked slowly home. The road ran downhill and the next street ran back uphill again; he panted slightly, it was harder and harder for him as he got older. He had had to stand on his own two feet since he was fourteen years old—no one had ever taken as much trouble about him as he had just taken about his son. It wasn't easy, those early years, and now there were threatening signs that pointed toward still more difficult times. But he had provided for his children. His oldest son worked with him in the business and would later take over, although the truth was, he ran everything already. His daughter was married. Only Fritz was left. From the beginning, he had hoped for something better for Fritz, and gave him a good education. Fritz would be able to build a life for himself on a higher foundation.

Herr Fiedler told his wife very little about the conversation he had had, no matter how much she pestered him for details. He himself felt no further misgivings.

•

In the fall came holidays and report cards. Summer had gone into the countryside, warm and beaming—not a season for working and sitting behind books. Fritz's and Albrecht's grades were satisfactory enough: Fritz's were questionable in two subjects, but there was a long time left before final grades next

Easter, there was no reason to get too worried. Even so, he seemed disheartened and demoralized all of a sudden. No one would have expected it from him, least of all Albrecht, who had known Fritz for a long time. This discovery surprised him very much. They got along well: it wasn't a close intimacy of confessions and shared personal secrets—actually there was nothing to share along those lines, whatever might come later— just a healthy friendship in school and playing sports. Their situations and their attitudes about their surroundings were different; the same experiences produced feelings and reflections in them that were as different as the families they came from.

At first Fritz didn't show his face; he stayed out of sight, whereas usually hardly a day went by when he didn't come over, sit in the big rocking chair, and slowly rock back and forth. Then they would drink a coffee with Albrecht's parents. He felt comfortable and happy at Albrecht's apartment, more than at home.

One afternoon, Albrecht met him by chance. Fritz was riding his bike down the street very fast. When he saw Albrecht, he said a quick greeting without slowing down, and at the corner he looked up at the clock tower and started going even faster, even though it was uphill. No question about it, he was in a hurry, maybe he had an appointment somewhere.

The next day, toward evening, Albrecht went to see Fritz. He crossed the small courtyard and climbed up the stairs into Fritz's room; the doors were open. Fritz lay stretched out lengthwise on his bed, fully dressed, smoking and daydreaming. The whole room stank of smoke. Apparently he couldn't think of anything better to do on a day off from school than lie in bed and stare at the ceiling.

"Ugh, the air in here," Albrecht said. He opened the window.

The twilight broke gently into the room. He made himself comfortable on the sofa. Silence.

"No one's seen you around for a long time," he began after

a while. "I thought you must be on a trip. What have you been up to?"

"Nothing," Fritz said. He lay on his bed, lazy and gloomy. Time was trickling away through his fingers.

"And yesterday?"

"I was riding to the Oder, I wanted to go for a swim."

He was speaking the truth. His life went by monotonously, without variety: he lay in bed until noon, since he only got tired and managed to fall asleep late at night. He passed his mornings reading, sleeping, and smoking; then, after lunch was a dead time. When school was in session he would sit upstairs at the table in his room and work, or at least try to work; the hours went by but he just sat there, empty and expressionless, and gazed at the open books in front of him. It was even worse during the holidays, much worse. Then the whole day was free, he could use it however he wanted, but he didn't have any idea what to do. Sleeping, smoking, lazing around—that was all he did, it was a real shame. He had already stopped playing sports. He still ran in school events sometimes, and occasionally won a prize, but he did so without ambition or dedication. As in every other area of his life, a feeble apathy had taken hold of him that no one had seen in him before.

"Dr. Selow left today," Albrecht began. "I saw him going to the train station. He was running, he was in a hurry."

"Yes, he came by here yesterday to say goodbye. I wasn't at home."

Albrecht: "I think he's been having a lot of problems with the director these days."

"Uh-huh."

For the past six months, ever since a new principal had arrived at the school, there had been several incidents, creating a combative atmosphere that wasn't in the institution's best interests. Dr. Selow primarily taught ancient languages, but the school was going through a change that would soon make his position superfluous. Previously, the classical humanist ideal of education had set the tone at the school, but now it was off the program, like a play that no longer brought in the audience and the money. In its place came a direction better suited to practical life, and a new cohort, boys and girls in the same class, was already rising into the middle grades. So there was no place for Dr. Selow anymore and he had asked to be transferred.

"They'll cut his position," Albrecht said, "or who knows?"

"Yes, they'll probably have to."

"It's too bad. I would have liked to keep studying with him for the next year and a half."

"A year and a half, what do you mean?" Fritz asked in amazement.

Albrecht laughed at his friend's stupid question.

"Then we'll be done," he said, "if nothing happens. . . ."

"Hm . . ."

Silence. The sound of footsteps came across the courtyard and up the steps, and Frau Fiedler came in. "Always sitting in the dark," she said, turning on the light. "Whatever you want to think and say in the dark must fear the light of day."

She went to the bedroom next door, and when she came back she stopped for a moment.

"You boys seem to be enjoying yourselves," she said. And at the same time: "You don't look good, Fritz, what's wrong? Don't you think so too, Albrecht?"

She exuded a maternal familiarity.

"All right, Mother," Fritz said; "leave us alone now and turn out the light."

She left. For a moment she stood helplessly in the doorway, looked sadly at the two boys, then slowly climbed back down the steps. Darkness lay across the room again. Fritz sat on the edge of the bed, his hands in his lap and legs dangling in the air. He was agitated—his mother's intrusion had brought him out of his apathy, but only for a moment, then he stretched back out on the bed.

"That's too bad," he said. "I would have liked to see Dr. Selow again."

"You can just go to the station," Albrecht said.

Fritz made an astonished face.

"I never thought of that!" And then: "Ach, getting up and going to the station, that's too much trouble."

"Of course it is, you're too lazy and comfortable here," Albrecht replied sharply.

Pause.

Fritz looked subdued, even defeated. Was there more to this failed farewell than met the eye?

"Yes, you're right," he said after a while. There was a noticeable change in his voice. "I'm not in the mood to do anything anymore, I need a project."

That sounded promising. So he wanted to undertake a project: what did he have in mind?

Silence.

"I've heard that it's always good to take a trip."

"A trip?"

"Yes."

Albrecht didn't know what to say about this answer. So, a trip, not a bad idea, he would like to take one himself. This year was the first time he had had to spend his whole vacation at home, and next year would probably be more of the same. "Where are you thinking you'll go?"

Yes, well, he wasn't entirely sure, so he couldn't say exactly, in fact everything was a bit up in the air with him, but there was one thing he could say for sure, that he wouldn't postpone it for long.

"So, in the next vacation . . ."

"Who knows?"

"You can't leave during the year in any case. . . ."

Fritz said nothing.

"Why not?" he said, after a short pause. "Maybe that's exactly the right time to leave." He didn't make a face—he clearly meant it seriously.

"You're crazy!" Albrecht said. "In the middle of the school

year! I'd like to see how you pull that off. You're making it up, it's another one of your jokes."

No, Fritz wasn't crazy, not at all. On the contrary. Now was just when he wanted to show the world how fully he had his wits about him. He got going, talked faster—it was clear that this idea ran deeper than Albrecht would have believed at first.

"But school," he said, "you can't just—"

"School, school, school!" Fritz snapped at him. "That's all you ever think about!"

Albrecht looked at him in amazement. The idea was new to him.

"Of course it is; school is the only thing we do, for now."

"Hmm. You don't understand," Fritz said after a while. "It's different for me."

Albrecht didn't understand, not at all. Fritz was trying to say he was special? Albrecht thought that was presumptuous and extreme of him, and told him so.

"I've spent more than enough time thinking constantly about school," Fritz answered sadly but definitively. "But now I'm sure of it, I'll never graduate."

Albrecht was totally confused. He hadn't expected that.

"What ever gave you that idea, not graduate? What do you mean? You're not stupid, you've always passed your classes before." He had had to repeat a year, but that wasn't even worth mentioning, that happened all the time. "And your grades are satisfactory."

Then Fritz turned furious. He couldn't take it anymore, he had held it in long enough:

"Satisfactory, that's great," he mocked. "Thanks to lying, cheating, and copying, my grades are satisfactory. Even you have to admit it can't go on like this."

The words hit home. There was no way to gloss it over. Everyone thought they were doing Fritz a favor by helping him, he appreciated their help and everyone thought it was perfectly fine. Over time, habit made the whole situation seem practically sacrosanct. Everyone let him copy their homework or answered for him in class until there was no way to tell anymore what was Fritz's and what was the others' work. Finally, he no longer trusted himself to do anything by himself without someone holding his hand. No one had predicted or intended that as the result, and when it turned out that way there would still have been time for Fritz to pull himself together and throw off everything that had come over him—the indecisiveness, the laziness. But by then Fritz was busy with all sorts of other thoughts directed far into the future.

Albrecht mustered up all the encouragement he could:

"You're exaggerating, really, you're exaggerating. . . . If you just sat down and worked . . . then . . ."

Fritz flew into a rage. "Stop it! That's just the point, it's too late for that, everything's gone too far." He shook his head sadly. "Don't you see," he whispered, as though he were afraid someone might be listening, "you said that just like a teacher, *sit down and work*, all well-meaning and energetic, but that's just it . . . I can't work anymore."

"What do you mean?" Albrecht asked in amazement. "You can't work anymore?"

He looked at his friend. What crazy ideas he had! Not work anymore! Work . . . he repeated the word softly to himself— "work"—and couldn't even understand what it meant. "You think that what we're doing in school is work?"

"No, no." Fritz shook his head. His voice sounded muted. "I'll tell you about that later. . . . It's meaningless work without any connection to anything."

Albrecht thought for a long time.

"What made you think these things?" he eventually asked.

Fritz made a painful effort to explain: "Don't you feel it too? Think about it: we study dead languages, all that vocabulary and tricky grammar, until our heads are about to burst—my father never did that, and he's managed a good life for himself, but that's another story. I keep asking myself: Why bother?

What's it all for? Just to load up my brain and have mountains of dead knowledge at my fingertips? Then, when I come home from school and walk around here, I'm empty-handed, I don't know what to do with myself. School and everything we study there is the past, dead, over and done with, while here there's a totally different, changed life all around me, with its own problems and anxieties, you know?"

Albrecht only nodded. He wondered how his friend had arrived at these ideas; he wouldn't have thought him capable of it.

"I don't see any bridge between the two worlds, no connection at all. They're on opposite sides and I'm caught in the middle. Actually," he went on, "it was Dr. Selow's job to show us the connection, the bridge—don't you think? But he never did. He felt comfortable in the past and never really understood the present, he put it down with little biting comments and insinuations, maybe it's because of the war for him, so that deep down he's as helpless and confused as we are, with only his routine to keep him going. . . . I feel like shock and confusion are all he has."

Albrecht took in his friend's words. They had a lot of truth in them, but just as much exaggeration. Secretly he felt a strange correspondence between what Fritz was saying and the thoughts that came over him more and more often these days when he looked at his own father. But all that, taken together, was still not enough to make him accept his friend's confession in advance, so to speak—he needed more from Fritz than that.

"So that's it?" he asked.

"No," Fritz replied, "it's worse. You asked before if school was really such hard work for me. Look, that was absolutely the first thing I realized—that it wasn't hard work, no effort at all, it doesn't tire me out, I just sit around, get bored, fritter away my time, and that's what makes me tired. Look at me, do you really think sitting on a school bench and exercising nothing but my brain is enough for me?"

He was eighteen years old, he was strong and burning to use his strength, but it just sat there fallow, wasted on little things.

He needed wind in his sails. On the outdoor track he could run so fast that he was already at the finish line when the others were just turning into the straightaway, and then afterward, as they fell over on the grass, half dead, he could walk off whistling a tune. But that's nothing lasting, just a short burst of effort; really, it's nothing but a game.

"What do you want to do instead?" Albrecht asked. He couldn't help it, he just asked it, maybe he'd get some kind of answer. His friend's words seemed so muddled and confused— he must have something specific in mind.

"What do I want to do? Work! Really work, come home at night with my arms and legs tired and fall into bed exhausted and know where the tiredness came from. I want to work in a quarry or dig the soil or something, not just sit around and look on."

Albrecht thought of something, and was glad to have something to say: "Talk to your parents first, or at least to your mother."

Fritz violently shook his head. No, he'd never get anywhere that way. He'd tried once, he'd overcome his shame and hinted at the truth to his mother, as much as he could given how reserved he was. She'd just looked at him like she wasn't sure she had heard him correctly: "Are you crazy? You want to drop out now, with only two years left? The sacrifices we've made for you all these years, the worries—all for nothing?"

She'd called them sacrifices—well, they could afford to sacrifice a few things, it hardly amounted to much, just little things that flattered their vanity.

"What ever made you think of that?" she had asked, and it seemed like she wanted to hear his reasons. So Fritz had tried to explain to her what had driven him to this decision. He wanted to be honest and straightforward, say everything clearly and resolutely. He told her about the malaise he was feeling, how he no longer enjoyed things in his life, and so forth. But the deeper he went into his situation, the more worked up he became and the more he struggled to find the words he needed to explain himself. He beat around the bush, then he realized that his thoughts were all confused; by the end he was all mixed up, everything in the depths of his heart was so tangled and disordered.

His mother thought he was just having a hard time at school, and that she could see through his confused explanations very clearly. They needed to take a hard line with him, she thought to herself. He's confused like a little girl. He had lacked a father's strong hand during those years when the war had emptied the country of fathers and made women be both mother and father to their children.

"You lazy bum!" she said. "You don't have any real work to do, I can see that just as well as you, and I've known it for a long time. Everyone works around here—your father, your brother, me—only you fritter away all your time and get fancy ideas in your head too!"

Fritz felt hope for a moment. "Yes, Mother," he said, "that's probably true."

Mother: "If you know it, why don't you work at school and try to graduate as quickly as you can?"

Then the bell rang in the store. Frau Fiedler was back behind the counter in a flash.

Fritz stayed behind, dejected, completely helpless. His mother had every right to say those things—about sacrifices, his ungratefulness, the cares they had suffered for years for his sake, and more—but not what she'd said at the end, comparing him to his father and brother, and especially not calling him lazy. There she had made a mistake, no doubt about it. She'd never be able to make up for that. She had only reinforced Fritz's way of thinking about things and made his decision easier.

It was about his future, after all, nothing less than that, and he had to come to a decision once and for all, there was no more putting it off. He had enough of an instinct to feel that something was in the air—a kind of need to come to new decisions, a fruitful agitation, anything but relaxing in a safe and comfortable position. He had grown up during the Great War, experiencing it as a child without knowing anything about victory and defeat, life and death. He grew older until he could see, and know, and what he knew was poverty and the collapse of everything all around him. It didn't affect him personally—he had nothing to worry about himself—but the restlessness and confusion lay deep in his blood and slowly ate away at him.

"What else is left for me to do, Albrecht, if you're honest with yourself about it?"

Albrecht thought it over. What should Fritz do? He had started by mentioning a trip he wanted to take soon, in fact right away. Now it was fully clear to Albrecht what this trip meant. He was shocked: desertion, running away, simply making off in the dead of night and leaving everyone else holding the bag. And maybe they deserved it, since they couldn't understand anything about what Fritz was trying to tell them.

Still, the whole thing didn't feel right to Albrecht. Granted, Fritz was having problems, circumstances were more and more against him, life around him was increasingly hard; maybe he was afraid that he'd miss his chance, not get there in time. He had the strength of a grown man and the restlessness of a boy; he wanted to take serious action for once and make something happen, but the first thing he had to do, if he wanted to keep any control of the situation at all, was act against his parents' will.

But surely there were other circumstances at work here—even Fritz had said something earlier about the great deeds that the era was awaiting, the wider world, the courageous undertakings you had to put your whole life behind. Albrecht thought he could see flashes of restlessness, lust for adventure, erratic youth between the lines here. . . . It was suspicious, at any rate.

"Stay here," Albrecht said, in a sudden burst of fear and worry for his friend. "You don't need to let yourself be shot in the head for some South American country, just stay here and finish school, it's better here and at least you'll have a goal. You think everyone isn't as tired of school as you are? I am too."

"Oh, you too," Fritz replied dismissively and at the same time a little enviously. "School doesn't make your head split open, and everything is nice and easy for you at home—"

Albrecht interrupted angrily: "You don't know that, you have no right to say that. Just because I look calm on the outside and don't talk about it, you think . . ."

He couldn't explain himself more clearly. His thoughts didn't follow such a devilishly straight and tidy track like Fritz's. He wasn't about to throw himself into any big decisions at the moment, and probably not later either; he had to stay where he was and stick it out; he felt it himself, he would be needed later.

"Why aren't things going well for you at home?" Albrecht went on. "What do you mean?"

Fritz had an answer for that too. He was ready for anything.

"My father's a good, hardworking man," he said, "no question about it. He's made something of his life. He may have started off as nothing but a workingman, but now he's practically middle-class: satisfied, well-off. But it doesn't matter how you start—don't you think?"

Albrecht thought about it. He wasn't sure where this question was leading.

"Yes," he said, "definitely, your father is now middle-class, if that's how you want to put it, but where are you going with this?"

"Listen," Fritz said, "I've thought this all out very carefully too. Do you know what it's like to have coffee here?"

"No. . . ."

"It's like this," he continued. "There's a big enamel pot that used to be white, which Mother carries into the little room and puts on the table. She puts different cups in different sizes and patterns next to it, the bread is sitting on an oilcloth, next to the pot of drippings and the butter. That's how we have coffee. No tablecloth, nothing more than the barest necessities, no cozy comforts, no plates. Everything is a mess in the room: wires, lamps, lightbulbs, one of the apprentices or assistants coming by every minute, you're never left in peace. We live very cramped at home even though my father owns the whole building."

Albrecht was surprised: "What are you trying to say?"

"It's totally different with your family."

"With my family?" Albrecht repeated in disbelief.

"That's right, your father comes upstairs at the same time every day, you sit at a cloth-covered table, the cups are on saucers with another plate for the bread, you have two rooms where you can sit undisturbed, everything is comfortable, neat and tidy."

Albrecht stared at him. Fritz was saying these obvious things as though he had made some kind of big discovery.

"My point is," Fritz said, "no good middle-class family lives the way we do."

Albrecht looked up and laughed a little. "That's nonsense! You're all mixed up! I could make the same comparison just as well between my family and Herr Dalke's across the street, they have a lot nicer things and a lot more impressive meals. But I never think about that, I'm satisfied with what I have, and my parents are too. What should I criticize them for? Everyone does whatever they're used to and whatever they can afford to do in their position."

"That's not what I'm saying," Fritz answered, annoyed. He had clearly had enough of trying to give explanations and express how he felt.

"And do you think workingmen have what you have?" Albrecht asked.

Fritz shook his head.

"No, no," he answered quickly, "what I said about being neat and tidy—I don't want to make that comparison, that's dumb, I'm sure it depends on the individual case. I'm only trying to say that in our house we live like people who haven't found any stability—everything is still undefined and up in the air. We could afford proper silverware and a comfortable place to live, we have enough money, that's not what we're missing, but it never crosses my parents' minds to make their life match their outward success like that, to present a well-rounded picture to the world. Earlier, when my father didn't have anything, he was a radical and out in the open about it too. Now, when he's achieved something, he seems to have forgotten his past. He's middle-class, conciliatory, politically moderate. And there's a lot that goes along with that: he just doesn't know it, or at least doesn't seem to. Maybe he's surprised himself with his rise, his success. But he doesn't know where he's going. I'd rather he knew exactly where he stood, then I would too. . . . Anyway, now you can go and tell them that I'm planning to run away."

Albrecht, after a long while: "So that's what you think of me." He stood up. "Goodbye."

Silence.

"My ship is leaving in six weeks, at ten a.m., from Genoa to Spain."

Pause. Albrecht slowly walked back into the room.

"Spain?" he asked in disbelief. So Fritz actually had a concrete plan, more than he had let on at the start of their conversation. Spain—he couldn't wrap his mind around it.

"Why do you need to go to Spain?" he asked, afraid. How did he arrive at that idea? Was he hoping he'd find some kind of job there?

Fritz stood facing him, standing up straight; if before he looked beaten and helpless, now he was confident—his whole powerful body quivered with confidence. He had a plan, he knew what he wanted, no power on earth would be able to stop him. Albrecht could feel the confidence and strength coursing through his friend's body. It was depressing. This was his friend, but nothing Albrecht could say would make any difference. Fritz was trembling with excitement. What was Albrecht supposed to say? He said nothing. He felt his friend's decisiveness and knew that nothing he said or did would make Fritz waver; his plan had put down roots too deep inside him. There was no point in even trying. Albrecht felt small and abandoned.

"But why?" he whispered again.

"I want to get as far away from my parents as I can," Fritz said in a calm voice. "Otherwise they'll bring me right back, I know they will, and I don't want that to happen."

"I see." Albrecht thought hard. Was that the only reason? Didn't Fritz realize what he was doing, did he really want to burn all his bridges? Had he thought about what it would be like to be suddenly all alone in a foreign country, whose language he didn't know, a complete stranger no one knew? That was an adventure all right, Albrecht was sure of that. Should he try to talk his friend out of it? There was no point—he would just decide on a different country. So, off to Spain then, if that's what he wanted. But Albrecht could not pretend to be happy about it.

There was much more to discuss, of course. For one thing, where was he going to get the money from? His plan certainly required money.

"I've been saving up for a long time," Fritz said.

"Saving?"

"Yes."

Now Albrecht knew just how much six months of the most disciplined saving could add up to.

"That's enough for the boat and no more," he said. "How will you manage on that?"

He could travel around the world with all the money he had.

Albrecht stared at him in disbelief. Fritz gave a mischievous laugh, however out of place it might seem at that point. Finally he explained: "The money I get from my parents would never be enough, I knew that from the start. So I had to figure out how I could cover the costs. Look, it's no problem around here in this chaos. No one notices if you go to the cash register and take out a little money. My father knows absolutely nothing about it, it's Mother who takes care of all the money. She keeps the day's earnings in a drawer under the counter and takes out whatever she needs during the day. One time I found an envelope full of money under her bed. I'm just doing what she does, nothing more."

Albrecht was shocked. Fritz always had a lot of money—he was often generous and liked to spend—and Albrecht had never thought about how he came by the money. He didn't have much himself, not even an allowance; his father paid for everything and added an extra couple of marks for the piggy bank, especially at the end of the month when he balanced the books. Albrecht would never have dreamed of taking money from the till on his own. His father always knew exactly how much was there at any moment and demanded a detailed report of every single mark that the family spent—any tiny amount Albrecht took would have been quickly discovered. Money was at the center of their lives, not that they worshipped it and danced around it, but its well-ordered movements in and out of the house were what guaranteed a secure and dignified existence. To work and to make money: these two concepts were the foundation on which life was built. Was it possible that there was another way to live?

.

Friday. The factories handed out wages on Thursdays, but only on Friday did the women come in to shop, pay their debts, and make new ones. Like a sack that you don't finish mending in one place before it needs mending somewhere else. The Seldersens stood in the store and waited.

It had been three weeks already since Frau Köppen had come in. She still had debts on her tab from the previous year. But there she was with her son, coming out of Wiesel's store with big packages. Suits for her boys, no doubt; one of them is about to be confirmed next Easter.

"If I see her on the street I'm going to have a word with her," Mother said. "I've wanted to for a while. And old Frau Lorenz and her daughter-in-law—when they need something on credit they come to us, and then they spend their money somewhere else."

Father defended them: "Her husband's sick, her child's in the hospital! It's too hard."

Shopkeepers always have a precise picture of their customers' family situations.

The first customers showed up around five and walked up to the counter with resounding footsteps. Mother was sitting there.

"I have money for you, ten marks."

"That's good. Out alone in the city today? What's your mother doing, is she here too?"

She didn't expect an answer most of the time, and when one came she rarely paid attention to it. The amount would be crossed off the sheet of paper that recorded the total tab and the figure would be noted down in the books. Every client had their own account that they could look at whenever they wanted. Three long thick lines meant it was paid off. Then they started over on a new page.

"I need a Sunday suit."

"Yes, we have nice suits. Come back next Thursday."

The customer stood rudely in the doorway, not budging. He actually needed the suit that day, but he didn't say so.

"It won't be too much?" he asked.

"No, no, we'll work something out, just come by on Thursday."

The suits were hanging in the corner on the racks; he could see them there in their long rows and he looked at them greedily. So, next Thursday. He'd much rather get it today, but dammit, anyone could see that he didn't have any money in his pockets today.

People came in who slaved away from early till late seven days a week and still never managed to get ahead. They walked in and excused themselves; they don't have much on them at the moment, but next time they'll definitely have more, they have to pay for the furniture at the carpenter's, the potatoes—it never rains but it pours. What they say sounds memorized. It was as though they had only a few naked words at their disposal. Mother, at the counter, tried to calm the woman—she praised her for coming in and telling them where things stood, gave her credit, and walked her to the door. The woman offered more and more apologies while Mother was more and more generous; finally, the woman left the store, saying: "Thank you, thank you so much."

Frau Seldersen, still in the doorway, turned around with a look on her face as though asking: Okay, now what? Father stood in the background, his head tilted to one side, as though he wanted to rest it on his own shoulder, he was so tired. His fingers fidgeted with the stays in his shirt collar.

"She'll pay," he said, "obviously, but we need the money today. It's hard for people, they're really struggling."

Silence.

The dark fabrics made the shop look gloomy. The white lightbulbs come on overhead, and a woman walks in with a long story to tell. They all have a lot to say, not always lies, but hardships make a person hard and blunt. This one has some money with her: not enough to clear her account. When that's taken care of, she hesitates a moment, then says, as carelessly as she can—it's clearly a piece of artful diplomacy on her part—that she still needs a lot of things, can she buy more items and put them on her tab?

Yes, they'll give her more, up to a point. She is one of the worst, who has bought a lot and not paid much yet. A big family. She lists off what she needs: sheets, stockings, fabric for clothes, and much more.

Frau Seldersen throws the stockings back in the box and says: "Sorry, cash only." Her tab is too big, she needs to pay off at least half first. Then she can buy more.

The woman starts to groan, and launches into her story again from the top. They believe everything she says but it's just not possible, not with the best will in the world; at some point enough is enough. She leaves the store sadly, turns around one more time, and promises to come back soon with money.

Albrecht, who has followed the whole conversation, goes over to his parents and asks: "Why didn't you give that woman anything? She only owes twenty marks, there are a lot of people with much bigger totals in the book."

Father says nothing. Mother: "We can't sell our goods if we only see the money a year and a half later. If that's how we wanted to do business we might as well shut our doors tomorrow, Father could go peddling, and we"—she corrects herself—"and you, what would become of you?"

"Ah, I see," the boy says, "it's because of us, right? Yes, I understand now, it's because of us."

He leaves the store.

·

Then many things started to take a much more serious turn for Seldersen's shop. It started with what was at first just an isolated event, a letter, but soon turned into a long chain of them. The mailman brought it one day and Father had never seen a document like that before, he felt terribly anxious and didn't know how to pull himself together. He wrote back evasively, and it took a lot of effort before he could write back at all, something with a good balance, not too subservient and not too aggressive: there had been a minor slowdown but he hoped to remedy everything shortly; they should not withhold the trust that they had so amply shown him over the years. The letter did its job. He was an old man and in all the years he had been in business no one had ever had any problems with him, he was in a position to request a little consideration and forbearance, and he got it. They stopped pressuring him. He sent the company part of his outstanding debt as quickly as he could and the situation seemed to be resolved. However, letters with similar contents soon started arriving one after the other from other firms; the same slowdown had rippled all down the line. Some of the letters were written in a sharper tone, with clear warnings, even though it was often only ten days after the due date; they threatened straight-out—they wanted their money. Not that the senders had any particular fear of losing their money in this case; the letters were all written in general terms, they could equally well have been sent to other debtors. It's just that they were in an embarrassing situation and they needed their money urgently themselves. Whenever the mailman came—first once a day, then every time the mail was delivered—he had another such letter with him. Father lived in constant fear of the moment the mailman would walk into the store.

"Well, what do you have for me today?" he asked lightly, taking the letters. He didn't even need to look at the sender's name—he usually knew in advance who the letter was from. He had fallen badly behind in his payments and owed money everywhere. Then he read what the letter said, and fear crept over him every time, even though by that point, after all the frequent repetitions, he should have been used to it. There was nothing else for him to do but sit down and write endless letters like the first one, asking for them to continue to extend their trust, pleading for consideration. . . . He was soon quite masterful in composing these letters. He presented himself humbly, bowed deeply, it truly pained him greatly. And he tried, as much as he could, to conceal his circumstances from everyone.

One Sunday morning, Albrecht woke up early. Still half asleep, he heard voices from the kitchen, muffled, but fiercely and audibly arguing with each other. He could clearly hear his father's voice telling his mother: "You just need to pull yourself together! You can't let yourself go with these desperate moods. The boy doesn't need to know what's happening, he has enough to think about with school. I'm holding things in too—if I wanted to show you everything that happens every day . . . !" He kept a lot to himself. "But I keep the boy out of it."

Much later, Albrecht could still remember these words. He stored them up, even though he didn't know what to do with them besides classify them with what he already knew. His father had worries on his mind and didn't want him to know about them. Fine, he would wait and see how serious they were. Maybe they were exaggerated, blown out of proportion, and they would collapse on their own before long; or maybe there was a lot of truth in them after all.

.

School had long since started again and now there was some kind of conflict between Fritz and his teachers every couple of days. Dr. Selow had been replaced with a younger teacher, a student teacher who was still in school himself. There were changes and reschedulings in the lesson plan all the time now.

Fritz sat there and made it clear to everyone that he no longer thought he belonged there. He was bored, he slept in class, and there were other things too. Sometimes he completely forgot that he was still in school; when something seemed ridiculous to him he just went ahead and laughed out loud, while the rest of the students at least put a good face on their bad behavior. Once, when the principal was holding forth in class yet again about great men—he liked to talk on that topic, and his voice would tremble every time, tears would come into his eyes—and he said, "When the storm-trooper squadrons of great men come—" he broke off in the middle of a sentence and screamed:

"Fiedler, why are you laughing?"

He shook with rage and ran over to Fritz's desk.

"Why are you laughing?" he screamed again. Fritz slowly rose and stood tall next to the principal, looked at the blackboard without moving, and said nothing.

"I have had enough of your impudence," the principal said, barely keeping control of himself. Who knew what he was thinking about Fritz, and what bad thoughts he thought Fritz was capable of? Fritz calmly sat back down and the class went on.

These incidents came often and Fritz eventually got tired of them. He stayed home, pretending to be sick, and maybe he was sick—his forehead was hot and his lips were always dry, he drank like a veteran drunkard. A few days later he was back in school, but he no longer showed the same nonchalance as before. He had clearly thought things over and decided to make an effort not to stand out so much.

Genoa didn't work out, as it turned out. He had made a mistake and the ship left four hours earlier than he had thought; he couldn't take the next ship, because he would lose the three days' head start he was counting on. He was sure he needed three days if his plans were to go undiscovered. So now he needed a new plan. He didn't have any other options at hand. Albrecht almost had the impression that Fritz was not in as much of a hurry as he had been—he had been saying he wanted to head out without delay and now he was suddenly talking about waiting, preparing more carefully.

And so the autumn passed, the first storms came, the forest floor was damp and soft from the rains so that you could no longer lie down in the grass. The two friends walked their old familiar paths almost every evening; only there did Fritz feel safe and free. He lost his outward shyness and reticence and talked about his escape, his plans, and what he thought the immediate future held for him.

"It won't be rosy for me," he said. "I'm sure of that."

Albrecht nodded.

"But if I can only get out of here, I'll accept everything else without any complaints."

He really was serious: he had thought his plan out all the way through and no fear could hold him back anymore. The fact that he had seemed so patient to Albrecht, almost as though he had changed his mind, was only a sign of how he had worked everything out. Albrecht, full of amazement, looked into his friend's calm face; it showed no hint of tension or excitement.

"When do you want to leave now?" he asked.

Fritz: "I'm not exactly sure yet."

He wasn't exactly sure—that meant he didn't want to say, he was clearly still afraid something might come up.

"I'm telling my parents that I'm going to visit Kern, the forest ranger, in F., and that I'll stay there hunting for a few days."

"But hunting season is over now," Albrecht said.

"Right, I'd almost forgotten!" It would have been an unbelievably stupid thing to say; it could have ruined everything. "Okay, I'll forget about the hunting and just be going to visit him. He invited me to come see him a long time ago, my parents know that."

They walked on and eventually reached the city.

"Here's where you live," Fritz suddenly said. He stopped on the corner, in the middle of the conversation, not even answering the last thing Albrecht had said. "Good night."

They said goodbye and Fritz set off to walk the short distance home. After Albrecht had already unlocked the front door to the house, he ran back to the corner and looked down the street. His friend was walking calmly along the edge of the embankment, with his shuffling gait, his upper body bent forward. It was quiet on the street; you could hear every footstep. Even though Fritz was just going home, it almost looked like he was turning off into a little street on the left. Albrecht waited. Just before he got home, Fritz turned sharply off to the right, opened the doors—the sound echoed down the street—and slammed them shut. Albrecht turned away and went inside. The night watchman was standing on the corner, his dog lying next to him on the ground.

.

Only Frau Seldersen had any complaint about the evening walks: she accused Albrecht of not caring about his father, letting him go out alone every evening like that. She herself was too tired to go for a walk with him after dinner; Father tried to walk slowly, but after only a couple of minutes he was back to his regular fast pace and she was panting alongside him. They never matched. So, unwillingly, she let him take his walks alone.

Albrecht promised to do what she wanted. The next evening, when Father said that he wanted to take a little walk, Albrecht said he'd go too. Father was surprised, and said no, he could just as well go by himself, that way he could at least walk at his own pace.

"If you want," Albrecht said without further argument.

Herr Seldersen left the room to put on his coat.

"Go with him," Mother ordered.

"But he wants to go by himself!"

"Go anyway. He doesn't want to admit it, but he's glad you want to go with him."

The front door shut.

"He's left already, hurry up."

The boy stood up reluctantly. He had planned to spend a pleasant evening at home, reading and practicing music. He made a fuss about putting his coat on, then left and caught up to his father with a few quick steps:

"I'll walk with you for a little while," he said, as though the idea had just come to him.

"You don't have to, I'm fine on my own." But actually he was glad Albrecht had joined him, even if he knew Mother was behind it. They walked through the streets in silence. Herr Seldersen held his hat in his hand so that he didn't constantly have to doff it when people said hello to him. Everyone knew him, and greeted him, even in the dark. They left the city and turned onto the promenade. Father had his hands behind his back and was looking down at the ground, and he let out a soft groan at every step, as though carrying a heavy weight that left him short of breath. The sound came from deep inside his body, from far away, rose up, evaporated, and turned into a soft whine.

"What are you groaning about?" Albrecht eventually asked. "Please, I can't listen to it anymore."

That sounded a little harsh, although he hadn't meant it that way. He gently put his arm around his father's shoulders, which was easy to do, Albrecht was already so much taller. They calmly walked on, and Father cleared his throat. After a while he slowed his pace and suddenly stopped, nodding his head.

"Hmm, hmm." But not another word. He started walking again. Then, after another couple of steps: "Hmm, hmm." And so on, for a long time, as though he were giving answers to all the many questions he was thinking about during their walk, questions demanding answers. "Hmm, hmm . . ."

Albrecht waited.

"It really is too hard," Father suddenly said. "If only I can hold out long enough for you to finish school."

Pause.

"Hmm, hmm . . ."

So that was the great worry he was carrying around with him all the time. It was the first time he had spoken so openly about it.

"Do you really think it can't go on?" Albrecht asked gently, but he hadn't fully thought through what his father was saying.

"No, no, it can't last much longer," Father replied.

Silence.

"Hmm, hmm . . ."

Could it really be possible? That something slowly and laboriously built up through years of work, enduring such a long time, might collapse overnight, as though a puff of wind were enough to knock it down?

"And that you have to watch it happen—you, Mother, and Anneliese. That I can't keep these troubles from touching you. . . . But there's no way, I've tried and there's no way."

These last words threw Albrecht into confusion. He wanted to console his father and stuttered out a few set phrases, whatever came to mind: that others were going through the same thing— of course that wasn't any consolation; or that it wasn't Father's fault if the money just dried up. "You don't need to worry about me, it's good for me to see how things really are from the start, for us and in general."

They walked on in silence.

Herr Seldersen had long since made his peace with the state of society and the dim outlook for the future, as far as he was concerned personally. Being content with what you have, living your life as the times require, simply and without making great demands—that was important too, and honorable, just as bringing your little ship safely into port is under healthier, more straightforward conditions. But it wasn't as simple as all that: there were many other considerations. He wasn't alone in the world—he had responsibilities, a wife and children. And he was a man, the father, the breadwinner, and his security was based on his own hard work. Everything was closely connected with everything else; when one little stone came loose somewhere, the whole structure would collapse.

The path led off to the forest and passed an outdoor restaurant at the edge of the woods. They stopped in and sat down under a trellis; two other customers were sitting far away on the other side. Father ordered something to drink. There were lightbulbs hidden in the hanging flowerpots dangling from the arcade, casting a dim light over the tables. Albrecht and his father leaned back in their hard garden chairs. Ahh, it felt good to just sit there and relax.

Father looked rather lost, like a small child sitting on a chair for the first time, his legs dangling in the air, arms stretched out pressing against the tabletop, as though feeling the aftershocks of a great strain inside him.

So this is my father, Albrecht thought. He sat across from him and could not stop looking at him, surreptitiously, again and again—his face, his hands, his whole tired body. He's worked hard his whole life and now this is the end result. All right, then. He apologized to me just now for not being able to make our lives better, and what did I say back? Something or another, but there are no words for it. He hasn't shaved; it makes him look worse, and much older. I think he's even crying, to himself, you can't hear it. I heard him cry once before, it sounded like an animal crying, not a big outburst. It makes you think all the bitterness is just sinking deeper into him.

Suddenly Albrecht was overwhelmed with great pity for his

father, sitting across from him—old, lost, hopeless. If before he had thought that there was a certain amount of exaggeration and self-aggrandizement hidden behind his father's gestures and actions, and if he secretly persisted in certain opinions of his own, now he was converted, now he believed. He didn't know much about his father, except that he did his work faithfully and with real love; he didn't know much about his father's early life. Father never said much about the past on his own, even though he couldn't have had anything to hide. He had served in the war, four years, and received the Iron Cross in recognition, but he never wore it; it lay in the cupboard, wrapped in silk, and when Mother was cleaning out the drawers she would always come across it. She would take it out, look at it for a long time, then carefully put it back in its place. And that's how it was with everything: something had happened, once, in an instant, and then it was buried, dismissed, probably not forgotten but simply withheld—it lay in a corner, and you came across it only when you were rummaging around for some reason. Albrecht suddenly saw his father's life spread out before him, even without knowing any dates or details or external events; he saw its line, its arc, curving from the beginning to now, which was in any case not its end. Later he would remember this moment very precisely, the moment when he and his father were sitting together and he came to understand him. He remembered it as a moment when he had gained enormously in experience, taken a giant step far beyond his own age.

"When did you leave school?"

Father had to stop and think. "At fourteen," he said.

Albrecht was surprised. "You were younger than I am now!" He laughed, and Father nodded and grimaced slightly.

"When I was as old as you are now, I was already an apprentice, almost done with my training."

Pause. The thought came to Albrecht that he was now seventeen years old. He felt a little ashamed.

"Why did you leave school so young?" he asked.

"We were a big family, and I couldn't keep up; even in elementary school I never had time for homework because I always had to watch my little sisters, and then my father took me out of school."

"But your father had lived in England a long time, he knew what was important."

"He was an educated man."

"And the large family?"

"He supported us; my mother didn't make it easy for him. Later he told me a lot about it, but he never complained. He was always satisfied with his life."

The conversation went on, with Albrecht asking and his father answering, until finally he didn't have to ask any more questions and Father just told the story himself. A simple life: work, a little success, and more work. As an apprentice he polished young men's boots to make some money for food, since the meals in his cheap pension were inedible. He became a traveling salesman and rode around the country, and people were always happy to see him. He was friendly, obliging, and clever, did well, and saved three hundred thalers. "Just think, three hundred thalers, how much money that was back then." He opened a store.

Pause.

And all of a sudden his father was so downcast again, bent under the weight of his sorrow. His hands would fly off if he didn't quickly clutch them together. It didn't help him anymore that he was the older man, the father—here he was the weaker of the two, and God knows where his manhood had disappeared to.

Albrecht felt his father's great sorrow and the burden he had carried in silence up to that point. He clasped his father's fists in his hands and whispered to him the same thing he had said before—that it wasn't his fault, that lots of other people were in his same situation.

"No, it partly is my fault." He spoke the words slowly and with difficulty, as though they carried with them an incalculable admission.

"How?" Albrecht asked. He trembled a little in expectation. Was he onto something?

Father, in a serious voice: "Back in the years when inflation was astronomical, and after that too, I should have understood what was happening better . . . but who could know?"

Then Albrecht firmly pressed his father's hands and calmly said: "You couldn't have known. Leave it to the experts; you couldn't have known."

Father nodded, satisfied. "No, it wouldn't have helped anyway."

Silence.

"How could this all have happened so suddenly?" Albrecht asked.

Father shrugged and said, looking thoughtful: "Suddenly? No, it's been happening for a while, you just haven't noticed."

"I noticed," Albrecht said; how old he felt in that moment.

Father, after a while: "Everything hangs together, it all stretches further and further back and reaches all the way up to the top." He couldn't find any better explanation than that.

Albrecht pensively shook his head.

"No one has money, only very few people still have work, and so it goes on, it'll never change, there will never be enough. . . . Look," his father continued, "if a worker has no money, he needs to buy his clothes on credit, because he needs them, he can't walk around naked. But then I don't have enough money, and I can't pay my suppliers, and they had to buy the goods somewhere too. So the slowdown keeps going, all the way up, to the factories that make the products and the banks that give them credit. Whoever has the strongest lungs wins—whoever can hold out the longest. Usually that's the one who has capital behind him. Today only someone with capital behind him can survive, everyone else is going to go under."

"Is that really what you think?" his son asked.

Herr Seldersen nodded. "It is," he said.

"Do you think Herr Dalke really hurt you?" Albrecht asked next. He himself didn't know what had made him think of Herr Dalke, who owned the big store up on the corner across the street. Father said nothing. He knew Herr Dalke personally, they even spent time together outside of business, even though they were competitors.

"His calculations are nothing like mine, he has a lot at his disposal," he eventually said. "He's been on top of things ever since he finished the building and added another floor. . . . We can't compare ourselves with him."

Herr Seldersen avoided directly answering the question of whether Dalke had harmed him. He let himself ask it only in silence, to himself, or maybe the question had never crossed his mind before; he didn't like reflecting on such things, he had his pride too, after all. The fact that he was in such a tight position now was his own fault only in the most minimal way—he had never in his whole life been presumptuous. But Herr Dalke, now that was a totally different case. He lived, or rather he ran his business, on essentially another level, you couldn't compare the two. Herr Dalke had money behind him, capital, and that made for a totally different picture.

It was late by then and they walked home, saying little. Later, when Father was lying in bed, the boy gently came up to him and kissed him on the forehead. In return, as usual, his father kissed him twice: once on the cheek and once on the forehead. Albrecht was about to straighten up when the arm around his neck pulled him lightly downward and he felt a light kiss on his mouth. "Sleep well, my boy."

Albrecht went back to his room and got ready for bed, scrubbing himself with a cold washcloth.

·

"Nelken's coming tomorrow," Herr Seldersen told his wife one day after opening a letter. "I just heard when he's getting in. We'll have him over for dinner tomorrow."

Mother wanted to say something but Father didn't let her open her mouth; he knew what she wanted to say.

"There's no way around it," he said. "Every time he comes he's our guest, this time would be the first exception. We can't do that."

Frau Seldersen mentioned the expense of having him over, trying to change Father's mind that way. But Father had already had the same thoughts. "That's the way it is," he said finally, to end the discussion. "We can't make him suspicious. We have to stick it out as long as we can." Mother obeyed.

Nelken arrived the next day—a tall, impressive-looking man, a director in a large firm with which Herr Seldersen had had a close relationship since he started his business. Herr Nelken usually brought three large suitcases with him, which the porter of the hotel he was staying in had to haul around to his clients' businesses in a wheelbarrow. A kind of friendship existed between him and Herr Seldersen. Herr Nelken didn't pay visits to everyone, heaven forbid; he traveled to see only his elite clientele, so to speak, including Herr Seldersen. It was a great honor, and he knew enough to value it and try his best not to lose it. Herr Nelken would come for dinner, bringing flowers and chocolate, then there would be conversation after dinner, a little card game, and he would set off again.

This time he came with only one heavy suitcase and two light ones. A sign of the times, he told Herr Seldersen. They spent a moment reminiscing about the past and then got down to work. Herr Seldersen had drawn up a list of what he needed beforehand; Herr Nelken pulled out one after another of the countless samples from his suitcase and presented them. Then he wrote out the orders in his notepad.

"No," Herr Seldersen interrupted him, "there's time. Don't write it down, I can always order anything else I need later; you always have it in stock."

"Of course," Herr Nelken assured him. And he knew exactly why Herr Seldersen was being cautious with his orders. He ran

into the same fearful caution everywhere, and he let Herr Seldersen know it.

Everyone was waiting and seeing, trying to spend as little up
front as possible. Herr Nelken got around a lot and had plenty
of stories he could tell.

The stock in his suitcases was far from depleted; he brought
out more and more new items, but Herr Seldersen stood firm.

"No, we can't take those anymore, they're much too expensive. What are you thinking? No one has any money." He told
Herr Nelken about the fire that had robbed two hundred people
of their daily bread. Whatever the reason, it quickly led to further
cutbacks, he said; other factories were announcing layoffs every
week; the construction business was in a slump, the bricks
heaped up high in the warehouses with no orders coming in.

They were already finished by early afternoon—it used to
take two days to place all the orders.

"We're expecting you for dinner tonight, Herr Nelken,"
Father said. "It's a sacred tradition." He laughed.

Herr Nelken looked at the time.

"Actually, I can still make the train to E.," he reflected. "It
leaves in an hour." He looked questioningly at Herr Seldersen.

"If you want, if it's important to you to finish your trip."

"It would gain me half a day, and I might even get away without unpacking there, then I'd save a whole day." He thought
about it while Herr Seldersen stood there in silence.

After a while: "I'm not trying to press you to stay, Herr
Nelken, if it would save you a whole day's costs. . . . After all, it's
your business, the expenses come out of your own pocket. But
we'd be glad to have you over tonight, for a simple meal—you
know it's no trouble, we have to eat too."

Herr Nelken eventually decided to take the afternoon train
after all. He said goodbye to Herr Seldersen, told him he should
definitely come by whenever he came to Berlin and needed
something. Herr Seldersen had one other question: about the
payment terms, how many days he could have.

"Same as always, Herr Seldersen, naturally," Nelken answered in surprise.

"All right, forty days. That's a little short, you know, everyone else is giving me sixty."

Herr Nelken thought for a moment, then said: "Hmm, I see. I don't know if we can manage that, in our firm."

"You can manage it better than anyone!" Herr Seldersen said. Who knows what he meant.

Herr Nelken laughed: "What do you mean? We have our own bills to pay too, we'd have to change the contracts with our factories; it's not as simple as you think. And then there's the union. . . ."

"Of course." Father nodded. "Of course."

"Well, never mind all that, we've known each other long enough, I'm sure we can work something out."

"What about the letters?" Herr Seldersen blurted out.

"The letters? What letters?"

"Well," Herr Seldersen said in a joking tone, trying to make light of the situation as much as he could, "you've sent me a couple of letters recently, account statements. . . ."

Nelken understood what he meant. "Hmm, hmm . . ." Then he said: "I don't have anything to do with that."

Herr Seldersen looked at him suspiciously. Nothing to do with the letters? Who else if not him? He was the boss, wasn't he?

"Our branch office sends them out without showing them to us; they're responsible for handling such matters on their own. You're not the only one, you can be sure of that. And why would you be? It's the same everywhere these days."

"Yes, yes," Herr Seldersen repeated a few times, "little reminders." But wasn't it more than that? Should he tell Herr Nelken about the anxiety, and the other feelings that came over him every time he saw the mailman come into his store these days?

Herr Nelken shook his hand. "Don't worry, such a longtime customer, like you . . ."

Father thanked him for the comforting words, and in fact he looked visibly relieved—someone believed him, he was still worthy of credit. What more could he want? But Herr Nelken's claim not to know anything about the letters was beyond him— he simply didn't believe it. Was there anything that happened in his own business that he didn't do because he wanted to and then carefully keep track of? And here was Herr Nelken, claiming that in his firm . . . No, he didn't believe it. He knew all about the few customers that Herr Nelken honored with his visits. There was no deception about that. He was trying to make Herr Seldersen feel better, nothing more—he didn't want to embarrass him, that was why he denied knowing about these letters, no question. A longtime customer like you, he'd just said. Then Herr Nelken left.

Mother and Father ate alone that night, all the food Mother had bought especially for Herr Nelken's visit. But they ate without taking any special pleasure in it—in truth, they almost had to force themselves to swallow it. Neither of them could stop thinking that now they had spent the money for no reason. They couldn't get the thought out of their heads; it was as though they had committed a sin.

•

That winter, times were tough and expectations were low for a lot of people in the city. The factories operated with a small workforce; they were promising new hires in the spring, but in the meantime construction jobs were on hold for the season. A depressed, defeated mood held sway everywhere. The boys who had left school at Eastertime lazed around in the streets without any work to do; only a few of their fathers were making a living either. But everyone wanted to live, and needed money to buy food and warm clothes—it was getting colder and colder.

So Christmas approached. In the end it *was* a holiday, and people celebrated it, even if they weren't really in the mood. Not even in the war years had spirits been so low. But then came New Year's, and people spent New Year's Eve having fun and making noise. Exuberance and confidence filled the city—cannons were fired off, people toasted one another and sang songs, only a few kept their clear-eyed gaze on the year to come. But after all, it was good to have hope.

In the middle of all the commotion, Fritz Fiedler suddenly appeared on the street in front of the Seldersens' home. He shouted, waved up, and Albrecht's parents invited him in. Before they could blink, Fritz had clambered up the outside wall, swung himself over the balustrade, and was standing in the room. After a warm welcome and best wishes for the new year, Fritz was given a full glass, drank it down, and Herr Seldersen added: "To your graduation!" He had a long way to go before graduation—next year would have been a better time to toast it—but what else are you supposed to wish for a schoolboy?

"Why?" Fritz cried. His eyes shone; he couldn't understand why Herr Seldersen was saying that now. There was still time, thank God. But thanks in advance!

He had already had a bit to drink at home and was in high spirits. He grabbed Albrecht by the arm and pulled him aside. "Come here a minute," he whispered. "I have to tell you something." Then he told Albrecht in a quiet voice that he intended to use the last three days of vacation to put his plan into effect.

"Your plan?" Albrecht asked. He hadn't had anything to drink that night, but still didn't exactly have all his wits about him at the moment.

"You know." Fritz got impatient and started fidgeting.

Of course Albrecht remembered. He was completely focused again.

"Shh, not so loud," Fritz said. "Don't give anything away. Look, I'm only acting, I think they think I'm drunk." He was suddenly deadly serious: "Next week," he said. "I'd love to know where I'll be by then."

"Where?" Albrecht asked. He wanted to know right then.

"I don't know," Fritz answered. "I'll come by again before-hand, but now let's go back to the others."

Albrecht nodded in silence, and they rejoined his parents.

He had been in a troubled mood all night. He didn't drink, didn't cheer and make noise, nothing except toast his parents and a few friends they had over when the clocks struck midnight. He watched his parents kiss with tears in their eyes, saw how Mother patted Father encouragingly on the shoulder and how Father kept quiet, off to the side, as usual. He only gradually warmed up and showed that he was capable of more than just hanging his head all the time. How had he been before, before the war, before the current hard times? Fun-loving? Strong and confident? Yes, yes. Did he even remember it himself? Then, later, when Fritz came over and told Albrecht about his upcoming departure, it brought him even more forcefully back to the present. He recalled the conversations, the walks, all the things they had done together—and now Fritz was heading out into the world, in a week he would be who knows where. A week! Albrecht shook his head. No, he had never really believed that Fritz would actually leave. He had thought in all seriousness that the whole thing was just a daydream, a thought experiment— and now Fritz was off.

Fritz came to see the Seldersens several times in the next couple of days. The two friends were together until late at night, but then again, they often were; it would have attracted attention if they had acted any differently. On the last night, they parted as though they would be seeing each other again the next day—no lingering goodbye, no words of farewell, just a simple handshake. "See you later, take care." Then Fritz headed out into the world.

The next morning, Fritz got up at the last possible minute—he had to hurry or else he would miss his train. His mother and brother were standing in the store and he ran through it, hurriedly pulling on his coat.

"Gotta run," he said, "I'll be back Thursday, I've already packed my books, they're in the knapsack. 'Bye."

"Be careful," his mother called after him.

His suitcase was waiting at the station—he had taken it there the night before, secretly, full of anticipation. Then the train pulled in and Fritz found a compartment where he could sit by himself. He had his school cap on his head; his heavy suitcase was in the net up above. He would have to get out at the next stop if he wanted to visit Kern the forest ranger. The train stopped. Fritz looked out at the platform. A few young people boarded his train car. Then the train moved on. Fritz leaned far out the window—fields, meadows, forest, a river, and in the distance a church spire rising up from a bright red cluster of roofs. He watched it for a long time as it grew smaller and smaller. Now it was no longer his. None of it had anything to do with him anymore. In Berlin, he threw his school cap into a dark corner of the station.

That afternoon, Albrecht dropped by the Fiedlers' yard and whistled and called until finally Frau Fiedler appeared at the window and said: "Fritz is visiting Kern, the forest ranger. Didn't he tell you?"

"Ah, right," Albrecht answered. "He did mention it once. When will he be back?"

"Thursday."

Albrecht was suddenly in a hurry and quickly said goodbye.

Classes started on Thursday and Fritz Fiedler's place was empty. Every teacher asked where he was when their class started. His mother spent the day at home and when school let out she waited to see Kern's son.

"No, he wasn't at school either," he said.

"So he's still at your house?" Frau Fiedler asked.

"Our house?" The boy was genuinely surprised. "He was never at our house."

Then she understood. She ran home without saying another word and went up to her son's room. The bed, unslept-in, the same as the day before; the knapsack, on the table, with the books neatly stashed inside it; everything tidily in its place. You could tell that no one had been there for a few days. She opened the closets—and they were empty. She looked under the bed and the suitcase was gone. She couldn't stop crying and her short fat body was shaken with gasps of breath and she screamed out loud in pain. She tore the sheets off the bed, rummaged through all the closets and drawers, and found books, notebooks, shoes, but not what she was looking for. The picture on the wall—a class photo from the previous year—was gone. She kept looking and could find nothing personal left—he had burned it all. In the middle of her search she stopped; now she realized why she hadn't seen him do the trick with his lip for a while: he was letting it heal. One less distinguished feature. He had prepared his escape down to the last detail.

That afternoon she visited the Seldersens. They had just sat down for coffee when Frau Fiedler arrived, her face puffy and streaked with tears. The Seldersens couldn't tell what was wrong at first, and Albrecht acted innocent too. Then they were shocked and upset. Father paced restlessly back and forth, fidgeting with his keys, while Mother sat at the table and joined Fritz's mother in crying.

"We liked him so much too," she said, as though he were already dead. Albrecht sat there and had to listen to everything.

Didn't he know anything?

No, he was just as shocked as they were.

But they had spent so much time together, especially recently.

That's exactly why it's so shocking. Fritz hadn't said a thing, it must have been part of his plan. He asked the stupid question: How did she know? Fritz went to see Kern on Monday, she'd told him so herself. Did he run away from there? He hadn't thought anything was wrong when Fritz wasn't in school that day.

Then, finally, wringing her handkerchief, Fritz's mother told them the whole story that Albrecht already knew. . . . Not one photo, not one memento—he had burned it all beforehand. He'd been acting so strange recently, she said, she had asked him over and over again what was wrong but he never gave her a straight answer. And he hadn't even trusted his best friend.

When Frau Fiedler got up to go, she took Albrecht in her arms and kissed him.

"The only thing that makes me feel better is that he has a little money with him, but will it be enough?"

"Yes, don't worry about that," Albrecht said suddenly. "He has money, he dropped hints to me once, he told me he could travel around the world with the money he'd saved."

He came up with this little story quickly, to make Frau Fiedler feel better. She gave him her heartfelt thanks and left.

Albrecht and his parents stayed where they were, sitting around the cleared table, each with his or her own thoughts. Finally, Herr Seldersen stood up: he had to go back down to the store. He turned around in the doorway, thought for a second, and then said:

"He always had too much money at his fingertips. If he knew how hard it is to earn money, he would have thought better about all this."

Albrecht leapt up; he couldn't take this accusation calmly, but how could he answer? He didn't have much time to think. In the end, he said nothing. He just stood there, young and in turmoil. What did his father know about inner struggles?

·

Time passed and everyone got used to Fritz not being there. At first everyone was talking about it, but gradually people's interest petered out. There were new things happening, which were more important and required more attention. A shopkeeper had shot himself in the neighboring town, out of poverty, despair, shame, God knows what. His misery was at an end, although in fact he hadn't been doing nearly as badly as all that, he could have stuck it out a little longer, but he didn't want to wait. He shot himself.

"It's a hell of a time we're living in," Herr Seldersen said. He spit into the fire, rubbed his hands together above the iron stove in the middle of his store, and said: "At least it's nice and warm in here."

He didn't have much money in the register from that day, but it didn't matter. He had recently started going through wild mood swings: he would come upstairs to the apartment in high spirits, looking satisfied even after a day with terrible sales, and say, "Now I'm upstairs, I don't have to care about anything. Here at least I'll have my peace and quiet." But even upstairs, he couldn't escape everything.

"We have it good, don't we?" he would start up again. "A warm room, enough food for a good meal, who else can say that these days?"

It gave him visible pleasure when his thoughts ran along these lines; clearly it made him feel better. Mother said nothing except, "Yes, of course you're right." But secretly she still believed that they both deserved something more than a warm room and enough to eat. She kept her thoughts to herself, though. Why should she bring on another of his moods of despair? She was happy when Father suggested, on his own, that they take a little walk. They sat in a bar with a crowd of other people from the city, but alone at their own table, or else they went to the movies, though not without first considering the step from every angle. In the end, they did need to distract themselves a little, think different thoughts for an hour or two; it helped them when they came back to their everyday life. Then there were times when they both felt happy, for no particular reason. Father called her "my dear wife," and hugged her and kissed her as he hadn't for a long time. Mother pushed him away, no doubt a little ashamed. In her confusion, the words escaped her: "But we don't have any reason to."— "But Trudy," Father answered, his face in a grimace, "you're not mad, are you? I can't do anything about that, my dear Trudy."

His face was completely serious and he leaned against the door, tears in his eyes. It was true. He couldn't do anything about it. It wasn't his fault.

Every day could be the day it overtook him; any minute could be decisive. All their attention was on it, the way a dying man can't stop thinking about his funeral. One day it comes at last. First, the shame. Herr Seldersen was ashamed of himself, ashamed before his wife and children and everyone else, at finding himself in this situation. What else could he do? He had done everything that lay in his power. Still, he felt ashamed. Not that anyone had reproached him—what was the shame in having fallen victim to the same fate that so many others shared? What wouldn't he have tried to do to save himself and make it through? But he realized more and more clearly over time that it wasn't up to him, nothing was, he was simply being driven along unstoppably toward—terrible thought—the end. Then came the despair. The least little thing would plunge him into a despair that was worse than the end would be. What was it going to be, actually, this end that was so painful to anticipate? Bankruptcy, losing the business, a livelihood that had lasted a lifetime finished. And not the final line under a calculation that had worked out, everything balanced with nothing left over— the way it should be at his age—but rather a road leading into endless mystery, with no resting place, no prospect of relief. It wasn't a neat and tidy end that goes with a new beginning on a higher level, it was the path of someone condemned to live, or blessed with life if you prefer, but old in his moment in time, even while time itself is perpetually renewed. When they sat motionless at the table, man and wife, staring into space, their silence was more eloquent than a loud, desperate scream. It wasn't even an accusation, because who could possibly be hauled before the judge as a defendant? It was just a realization of how things are, and a faint undertone of marveling at all the realignments and changes taking place. They had thought it would be different, both of them had—that they would at least find a little peace in their old age. But it didn't work out the way they had expected.

·

Even an old workhorse stays alive, dragging its cart slowly down the road. Even lame, he moves forward. It wasn't much different with Herr Seldersen and his shop. He limped along for a good long while with his payments; he received warning letters and wrote back, sending a small sum of money every now and then so he would be left in peace for a little while—not long, but long enough to catch his breath. Was this condition worthy of a man who had run a good, upstanding business his whole life, to the very end? How long could he stand it? The very air around him, wherever he turned, was stuffy and stifling, like damp, worn-out laundry—everything stuck to him, clung to him, pulled at his hands, his body, and sullied him. He had a constant feeling of needing to wash himself—no, it couldn't go on like this, he mustered up his courage and decided to finally put his affairs in order. But how? On his own, or if not, then with whose help?

He went over to City Hall one day and asked to speak with the manager of the municipal savings bank. He was seen right away, skipping the line, and they gave him a courteous greeting, the way anyone greets a customer they want to keep happy. Herr Seldersen had been with this bank ever since he moved to the city; he knew the current manager from back when he was a simple teller, and later an account manager. His own account was there, along with his wife's and children's savings accounts—no great sums anymore, everyone was cautious about putting much money in savings after the hyperinflation. Basically, everything went through the bank. Herr Seldersen deposited the money he took in during the course of the week, and withdrew it again later to pay his bills. Eventually, when the income was not enough to pay his bills, he had to borrow. He did so carefully, since he wasn't used to it; he had never had to turn to this last resort before, but then . . . yes, he got used to it, even if he never felt entirely comfortable with it. The amount the bank granted him was kept within reasonable limits, appropriate to Seldersen's reputation and standing, which was all the collateral he needed.

This time, when Herr Seldersen asked to speak with the manager, he had come intending to exceed this fixed amount. Secretly, he was by no means happy about what he was about to ask for, but he found the courage to ask, heaven knows where.

The manager didn't know offhand how high the line of credit was that Herr Seldersen had been extended, which was excusable, of course; he had to keep so many things in his head at once, why should he know this particular figure by heart? He quickly fetched the file and flipped through it. When he compared the line of credit with what Father was asking for now, he hesitated a moment, and said only: "That's a bit of a very high number, Herr Seldersen." He looked at him. Herr Seldersen explained why he needed that amount—he wanted to transact certain business and it would be best to have the whole sum available at once. It was a great burden for the time being, certainly, he admitted that, but then it would be a great advantage, you couldn't deny that either.

The manager thought about it for a while.

He said, with genteel restraint, that he was personally responsible for such substantial loans, so he had to be twice as careful about checking every step. What about the collateral? No businessman would think to grant such a high line of credit without first making sure that there was some collateral as security for the money, it would be crazy to do otherwise, and irresponsible, especially in his position, since he was managing the savings, the property, of the city itself and its citizens, so to speak.

"In your case, Herr Seldersen, I've known you long enough that I can safely say I have no concerns. But since I am responsible to the city, I do have to jump through the hoops and make sure we have a sufficient security for you as well, especially since you are asking for quite a substantial sum."

"Security?"

"Yes, yes."

Herr Seldersen had listened carefully and knew exactly what

the manager meant by security—naturally, the bank needed to protect its investment, he agreed with that. But what kind of collateral was he supposed to give?

He asked, in a rather heavy-handed and blunt way, what they wanted as collateral.

Well, that could certainly be discussed, something with an appropriate value but at the same time that wouldn't be too much of a burden, maybe the furnishings in the store—the chairs, the shelves, the tables, all taken together. He should go home and draw up a list of everything at his leisure.

"Hmm, I'll have to think carefully about that." Herr Seldersen's eagerness collapsed at once; all of a sudden he wasn't in such a hurry for the money. The manager emphasized again how willing he was to help, and then Herr Seldersen left.

He took a whole day to get used to the idea: putting up the furnishings of his store as collateral! And who knew if it would stop there? He looked around; maybe he'd have to add other items, from the apartment—the manager hadn't asked for that— already the thought came over him that his own apartment was nothing more than a furnished rental, he felt that nothing in it was really his.

Finally, that night, he told his wife about the conversation. To his amazement, Frau Seldersen didn't overreact at all, and did not seem the least bit surprised or demoralized.

"If you get the money," she said, "then it's good."

Father stared at her—what could be making her so bold and reckless? But think it over, he wanted to object; he could offer several different reasons against his plan. In the end, though, he reflected, she was right, of course she was, the main thing was to get the money and wipe out a large part of his debts at once. Then the endless warning letters would finally stop coming. As for whether he would ever be in a position to redeem the collateral—he couldn't think about that now. To pledge these things as collateral was only the beginning, it meant that they no longer belonged to him. They were lost. He drew up an inventory and went back to City Hall the next day. It turned out that the bank did indeed require a few more items before they could offer him the full loan: the piano from the apartment and the balances of the two small savings accounts.

It was all the same to Herr Seldersen. He signed those over as well, without thinking too long and hard about it, just a flourish of the pen.

Frau Seldersen, though, had a different opinion this time. "I wouldn't have done that," she said. "Not the piano. I wouldn't have crossed the line into the apartment."

"Why not?" he asked.

"That's different," she replied. "In the apartment? No!"

She was certainly splitting hairs here.

This time, Herr Seldersen showed himself to be the more bold and reckless of the two. Only you couldn't quite tell if this boldness was real and serious, or just put on for show.

In any case, he had the money in hand and he spent it in a few days: paying off his main debts and making good headway. Now he could count on getting deliveries of spring items. He immediately wrote to ask for them. Two crates arrived that week, and several smaller packages too—the mail truck had to make a special trip just for him. The shelves were fully stocked and there was peace and calm in the house again, for a while.

·

Ever since Fritz had disappeared, Frau Fiedler rarely showed her face on the streets and came to visit the Seldersens even less. When she did come by, she sat for a long time, talking, remembering, crying, complaining. There was no word from Fritz, no letter, not a single sign of life. Was he even still alive? No, no, she was about to stop believing it. Albrecht's parents stayed quiet, asking no questions.

"If only we had let him do what he wanted and drop out of school," she started up again. "He asked me often enough. Maybe everything would have been different." She had realized several things by that time, when it was too late, but she was still plagued by questions and doubts; she was honestly suffering terribly, but she couldn't undo what had happened. "What was his problem with school, anyway? Why didn't he want to study anymore? He could have started out on whatever he wanted to do a little later, we wouldn't have stood in his way." She didn't understand, she said, sobbing softly. It was as though she had given up hope.

"It's like that with young men everywhere today," Herr Seldersen said. He was sitting bent over his books and doing calculations while he followed the conversation; now too he spoke without looking up. "This cold shoulder everywhere, what are they supposed to do? They've grown up, they've seen everything, you can read all about it in the papers, and what are their prospects? Think about it. When we were that age we could have faith in the future." He fell silent.

His thoughts had run away with him again. In any case, that was all well and good, but it didn't help Frau Fiedler understand why this had happened to Fritz in particular. She shook her head in silence and then said goodbye.

As long as he has enough money, that was what she was most worried about; he just doesn't know how to handle money . . . if he's even still alive . . . no, no, she almost doesn't think she will ever see him again in her life.

One day, a letter came for Albrecht from Austria. The postmark said Mariazell, and he recognized the handwriting at once.

"So here I am in a little village near Mariazell," Fritz had written, "after five days zigzagging through Germany. First I went to Hamburg to take a ship abroad, but no luck, there were no steamers departing just then, plus I didn't have all my papers. I looked around, and on the evening of the fourth day I heard my description over the radio. I took the train south that same night, from one city to the other, always on the run, until I got here. I'm working on a farm, there's a lot to do here even though it's winter, and I have what I wanted: work, honest tiredness. Someday I'll buy a farm for myself. How are my parents doing, have they accepted my leaving? I feel bad for them, if only I could help them. —There's deep snow here, I've bought snowshoes and I go snowshoeing whenever I have time. It's great. Write back soon."

Albrecht felt a great sense of relief. Fritz was living on a farm, happily working hard, and he hadn't forgotten his parents.

When Albrecht walked down the street that afternoon, Frau Fiedler was standing at her window. She had grown very serious and when she saw him she gave him a melancholy greeting. Albrecht went into the store to see her and said:

"Hello, Frau Fiedler. You look so serious."

He faltered and felt annoyed at his own clumsiness; Frau Fiedler said nothing. Then she asked him about all sorts of things, including school, and he eagerly answered.

"You are not as honest with me as you used to be," she said all of a sudden. She shook her head sadly.

Albrecht was confused: "What do you mean?" he said, almost inaudibly. "I just wanted to see how you're doing, and ask if you've heard from Fritz."

"No, still no news. We've done everything we could to find out where he is, but there's no sign of him. If only I knew where he was, if he's still alive. . . ."

She put her head down on the counter and started crying softly. Herr Fiedler came into the store holding a piece of pipe and his tool bag.

"Still no news from our Fritz," he said, going straight back out the door. He had aged, he no longer enjoyed going out at night; he seemed not to understand life anymore, the life that had sprung up around him, what was happening every day. He often sat in the kitchen for hours, unable even to slice his bread.

"Frau Fiedler," Albrecht said after a while, "I got a letter today. From Fritz."

Her head jerked up.

"He's in Mariazell, in Austria. He's doing well and he told me to tell you he says hello."

"Thank you," she said without moving, and her face remained stiff. Then she ran out of the store, into the back room. Albrecht followed her and found her bent over the table, crying more violently than he had ever heard anyone cry. It was as though she were crying out all her misery and worry from the depths of her soul. She was shattered, her body shook. Between her sobs, he heard:

"I didn't deserve that from him, no, not that."

He stood next to her and looked helplessly down at her. He felt a very strong desire to stroke her arm, as though that would help calm her down, or even to take her into his boy's arms. If only he had had the courage! But he didn't know what to do, and suddenly he felt afraid. He could no longer keep still, his hands were wet with sweat, and he could feel his pounding pulse in his neck. He fled, running out of the room. Out on the street, he ran and ran without turning around, but he couldn't get rid of his fear, he had the feeling that it was sinking deeper and deeper into him, taking more and more possession of him. It's not fear, he said, half out loud, but then what is it? He didn't know. He got home late that day.

·

At the end of the month, Albrecht's sister came home for the holidays. She had been away almost a year now, and had changed—time changes everything, it never lets up. A year ago, when she'd left home, she had been a young girl, with daydreams, eating candy. Now she was standing on her own two feet in life and things had changed. She worked as hard as a man and had become a full-fledged woman as well. It took very little time before she understood how things were going at home, but still, she wanted to be sure.

"What's wrong with Father and Mother?" she asked Albrecht with an innocent look on her face, as though simply asking for information. "They both look terrible, haven't you noticed?"

"When you're with them all the time you don't notice," he answered. The truth was, he never would have noticed on his own; he silently vowed to pay closer attention in the future. "I think Father is worried about things," he continued, "but you can't get anything out of him."

"You think?" she shot back in a nasty voice. "You live here with them and you say you *think*? Don't you know?"

"Of course I do," he said heatedly. He couldn't reveal the extent of his ignorance. "I know that he's worried—but so's everyone these days."

Anneliese wasn't satisfied as easily as that. "But surely you see what's going on around you, or do you spend all your time dreaming?"

No, he's not dreaming, what makes her think that? He may not always be perfectly alert and focused, he admitted that. But all their parents ever did anymore was worry, it had slowly taken over their lives. The life they would lead in their old age depended on what was happening now; it was no wonder they thought about it so much, every hour of every day, but Albrecht was a lot less affected by it, he thought about it only now and then and was busy with other things the rest of the time. Was he really supposed to spend his young life brooding? And Father himself always tried to protect him from their troubles, didn't he? He knew what was happening, he knew a lot, but did he need to spend every hour of the day thinking about it?

"But don't you talk about the situation at the table or anything?"

"No, never. It's all just hints and suggestions. I think they're ashamed."

"Ashamed? Hmm, yes, you might be right about that," Anneliese said. She even marveled at her brother for a moment. How had he come to that idea?

Not long afterward, when she put the question to her father

to learn once and for all how things really stood, he turned nasty, downright abusive. As always, he answered that it was his business, he didn't want anyone else to interfere, she was probably worried about herself, about getting married, and who knows what else, which he quickly and vigorously dismissed. All nonsense!

Anneliese just laughed—thinking about herself and getting married? Now that was a bit much. "You don't need to worry about that," she said, "and by the way, I'm leaving tomorrow if that's the way it is here. I feel sorry for the boy, I can't stand it myself."

"Go ahead," Father answered. He stayed pigheaded, with a tense, grim look on his face, but totally confused, you felt sorry for him.

Anneliese put her arms around his shoulders very affectionately and said in a soft, calm voice: "But I really would like to know. . . . Maybe I can help, you get to know a lot of people when you live in the big city, or don't you think so?"

Herr Seldersen nodded. "But what do you want to know? Nothing's changed, I just have to make sure that I can pay the interest on time, on top of the current bills."

"Interest, what kind of interest?"

"I borrowed some money from the bank a few weeks ago, so that I could buy inventory."

"They just gave it to you?"

"No, of course not. I had to put up the furnishings of the store as collateral."

Pause.

He had forgotten about the savings accounts and the piano. He didn't mention them.

"That was the right thing to do," Anneliese said after thinking about it for a moment, "if it meant you got a little breathing room."

"Breathing room, yes, of course," Father said quickly, "for a little while. But the debt remains, you can't deny that, and now there are interest payments too!"

Of course the debt was still there; it was anchored in place, so to speak, and the relief that they felt at first was soon revealed as perhaps nothing more than self-deception.

"And now?" Anneliese asked.

"Now nothing," Father answered. "Wait and see, who knows what'll happen?"

That sounded dismal. Anneliese thought some more.

"Maybe it wasn't the right thing to do after all, to take the money so quickly. You should have thought it through more carefully, maybe there were other options. But when you always act alone and never tell anyone anything, you never have a complete view of the situation!"

"Hmm, hmm, you may be right," Father said, abashed. He was not as young as he used to be, that's true, but what else could he do? Oh, she could talk, but what did she know?

No answer. Then, after a while:

"You should have tried to come to some kind of agreement with your creditors and pay off all the debts at once."

Herr Seldersen didn't understand. "Give up the store and file for bankruptcy? I couldn't do that," he said in disbelief. "Then what?"

"No, that's not what I mean. You could continue the business: not even the newspapers would find out, everything would be arranged privately. You agree to a fixed sum with your creditors that you then pay off at once and the rest of the debt is canceled."

Pause.

"Yes, yes," Father said. He did not want to admit straight-out that he hadn't thought of that possibility. In truth, he had only a vague sense that such agreements were even possible, outside of court.

"It wouldn't be exactly pleasant," he began, "to go to people I've been ordering goods from for more than twenty years with a suggestion like that. . . . And anyway, to be able to offer a fixed sum like that, I'd have to have the money ready, and where would I get it? Tell me that! I'm not in a position to come up with even that much. You can't forget, we don't have capital backing us, we don't have reserves, that's the cause of the whole catastrophe."

"Catastrophe! You're always exaggerating like that," she replied sullenly. She was sick to death of hearing her father use such expressions. He always did, taking visible pleasure in anything that minimized and devalued himself and his situation. His eyes turned red and he was short of breath. In truth, you had to pity him, standing there so small and beaten down, no longer wanting to appear the way he really was.

"Really, you haven't saved or put aside anything you can use now? That's impossible!"

"It's true." Father nodded his head. Nothing saved, nothing put aside—he had to admit it, it was incredible. Anneliese fell silent. The situation was hopeless, if you really thought about it; there wasn't the slightest chance it would work out. Did he realize that himself? Was he constantly carrying this certainty around with him? She could not think of anything more to say—now she felt shattered herself. The more time she spent at home, the more she longed for the day when she would leave. No, she couldn't live in this gloomy environment for long without being infected herself with the discouragement and dejection filling everything. She secretly wondered how Albrecht could stand it: he was still young, after all, and had a right to expect and hope for certain things. Either he didn't understand what was happening and just daydreamed his way through life, or else he was coming to terms with everything only slowly, with a while yet before he was done.

The days passed quickly and Anneliese went back to Berlin.

•

Early that spring, the workers at the nearby brick factories went on strike, demanding higher wages. About four hundred men refused to continue working under the old conditions. It was a delicate situation: many new hires had been made at the start of the year and they actually had every reason to be happy that they had been given work again, but prices were higher; life was more expensive, while the wages stayed the same as before.

It was the first time in a long while that something concrete and serious was in the air. The events of that year didn't stop outside the city gates—their city too was tangled up with the fate of the country as a whole, and had to bear its part of the burden. But everything happened less abruptly and definitively here than events seemed to elsewhere. Even a firm resistance lost something of its power here, and the distinction between it and what it was opposing seemed muddier somehow; a kind of easygoing slackness affected everything, even the most dramatic undertakings. The people looked around less questioningly, they thought things through a bit more slowly, even sluggishly, if simply and directly. It took some time before any new experience took hold in them, and then—well, maybe everything had been going well enough for them before, so that they had no reason to complain. They did their work, earned their keep, found their pleasures and diversions, and had the forest and rivers, the endless vistas over the fields, and the spring breeze. Was there anything else one could want? Still, as things got worse and worse over the years, here too, the change came over them to a greater extent. Where had their peace and laughing contentment disappeared to? What was going on now had nothing in common with the meaning and spirit of the landscape of that place—something else had forced its way in, something that had not grown from this soil and that threatened disruption and unrest.

The strike lasted for three weeks, then the money ran out and the workers had to give in. Their representatives entered into negotiations and an agreement was reached. Only three hundred men were rehired; the rest were let go. The three hundred who could keep working did so under worse conditions than before the strike. That was how every attempt the workers made to improve their situation ended.

But meanwhile, business was at a standstill except for the grocery stores, and they had to go deep into debt too. Trade stalled, sales plummeted, bills that came due could not be paid. Each turn of events pulled the others along with it, in a long chain of misfortunes following one upon the other.

Then the factories started operating again, but the bitterness remained. Four city policemen and four rural officers were permanently stationed there—in times of unrest, the gendarmes of the neighboring villages were called in. Tensions between the population of the city and the rural police ran especially high.

Again and again something was secretly brewing among the workers, but it never broke out into the open in earnest. One day, when notices were put up in one factory calling for a new strike until the hundred laid-off workers were hired back, management fired fifty men on the spot who seemed especially unruly and dangerous. That afternoon there were rallies on the market square. Groups of five and ten workers filled the streets and sidewalks, stopping traffic. But they just stood around, without starting anything serious. They lacked a unifying leadership and decisive will, they looked over to where the police were standing; clearly they weren't sure what to do in this situation. What would happen? There was an uneasy tension in the air, but neither side could make a decisive first move. The police didn't dare to take action, since they were obviously in the minority and wanted to wait for reinforcements. And aside from that, there was no reason to act yet. They made do with patrolling the streets and sending home curious children who were standing around watching. When they weren't obeyed right away, they often reinforced their warnings by grabbing the little scamps and bringing them back to their homes. But nothing happened, other than a lot of talking and shouting. And it was the same the next day. The reinforcements from the neighboring villages were sent back, no longer needed. It seemed as though the excitement was gradually subsiding and the calm of the spring was returning to the city.

Then came news of another outburst. The district capital, with more than thirty thousand inhabitants and major ironworks, lay a half hour's train ride away. The unrest there broke out much more seriously than in Albrecht's hometown, with street fighting, casualties, and many injured. The uproar spread out to the surrounding countryside. One day the rumor went around that rioters were coming in a convoy of trucks—but it was only a rumor.

Again all the streets near the market square were filled with people looking around, anxious and agitated. The shops closed and shopkeepers rolled the grates down over their windows. This time it was serious. You could feel an enormous sense of decisiveness in the air, although for the moment a strange hesitation held everyone under its spell. The police sat in the guardroom and waited; one of them stepped outside now and then, looked up and down the street, and disappeared again. Finally, all the way down at the end of the street, there was a glittering and flashing in the sunlight that seemed bigger than anything that had come before. It was blinding. Twenty armed rural police had arrived on bicycles, with sabers affixed to their handlebars and guns strapped to their backs, chinstraps holding their shakos in place. They came riding slowly up the street, an impressive troop, and disappeared with their bicycles into City Hall without paying any attention to the threatening looks and shouts on all sides. The crowd in front of City Hall—old men, married men, a few women, isolated young people—started moving; slowly they started pushing forward toward City Hall from all the streets nearby. The guardroom door slowly opened and policemen came out, calm and full of dignity: twenty-five of them, led by their major. He demanded in a loud voice that the demonstrators disperse, clear the streets and the square. The first rows of the masses pushing forward didn't change direction, and although a few, less courageous ones in the middle tried to stop where they were, the crowd shoved forward and carried them with it. The policemen formed a chain, but the crowd broke through it and the individual policemen stood hemmed in by the demonstrators. They shouted at the crowd to come to their senses—did they want it to end in bloodshed? The men looked furiously, silently, down at the ground; a few women and young men shouted out loud curses. They pushed ahead. What did they have in mind? They reached for the saber that the major had drawn.

Then he pulled out his revolver and beat a circle clear around him, and every other policeman did the same. Already the front rows were pulling back and the women started screaming, running, and the young people turned pale when they saw the black mouths of the guns in front of them. The men in the front rows were not rowdies or daredevils; they had come through artillery fire safely, and burning villages, and undermined trenches, and gas attacks, they had stayed alive and now they were standing in their homeland looking down the barrel of a gun pointed right at them.

The rows of protesters loosened and the policemen forced their way into them, pushing the protesters apart with their polished sabers. No shots were fired and it stayed calm that night. The next morning, the first time anyone tried to repeat the events of the previous day, several men were arrested, handcuffed, and led through the streets to prison flanked by three policemen with bayonets drawn.

•

Fritz Fiedler came back home of his own free will. He had come to an agreement with his parents that they wouldn't force him to do anything anymore. When Herr Fiedler had heard where Fritz was staying, he wanted to go straight there, but his wife held him back. So he waited patiently, let three more weeks go by, only wrote a single letter, and finally, one day, set out. A kid like that, he murmured quietly to himself several times. . . . And what was he doing down there? Working for a farmer! It was a mystery to Herr Fiedler. But he went with the firm intention of convincing Fritz to come back—amicably and without any pressure. He wanted to bring him back in person. Fritz was not especially glad to see his father show up there one day. "What a beautiful place you've found!" Herr Fiedler said admiringly, and it was a nice place to stay for a few days, he thought. Fritz, meanwhile, kept working for the farmer; there was a lot to do, and at night he fell into bed exhausted and happy. His father occasionally asked him how long he really planned to stick it out there. "As long as they'll have me," Fritz answered without a second thought. "Or until I find something better," he added after a moment.

Then Herr Fiedler thought the time had come to tell Fritz everything he and his wife had figured out during their weeks of painful brooding. They had realized that Fritz was serious about his decision to drop out of school. They had accepted it. Now he should just come back and look around for a new career in peace, one he was suited for and that offered good prospects for the future. They wouldn't push him into anything—it was all going to be left up to Fritz, Herr Fiedler promised. But he should come home.

They left together after a week and spent a few days in Munich, in perfect harmony with each other, before returning home. Fritz was suntanned and in excellent shape, without a gloomy, melancholy mood in sight. He joked around and made everyone forget what he had just put them through. His mother hugged him tight and this time he calmly let her do it. Before, this tenderness would have felt like a burden to him, and he would have tried to get away as fast as he could.

On his third day back, he saw Albrecht. They sat across from each other, both a bit awkward (Albrecht more so than Fritz), and had trouble starting a normal conversation.

"So, you're back," Albrecht said. It seemed so strange to him that he had to keep reminding himself, over and over.

"Yes," Fritz said, "now I'm back. I guess you didn't think I'd come back?"

Albrecht, hesitantly: "Yes, I'm surprised."

"My parents convinced me."

"And that's all right with you?"

"Yes, or did you think . . . ? I proved to them that I'm serious about not going back to school." He was finally free of that terrible burden, thank God.

Albrecht said nothing. He was a little ashamed; Fritz had read his mind, at least partly. Maybe Albrecht thought he could see behind his friend's words a longing for adventure, maybe a wish for clarity and real life—maybe both. I'm serious, he had just said, and his voice had sounded strong and confident, infallible. He was speaking the truth.

"So, what now?" Albrecht asked.

Fritz stayed silent. He couldn't say anything specific, he had various plans, his parents and brother-in-law were looking into a few things for him, he couldn't say for sure at the moment.

After a few days, he had come to a decision. He left for Hamburg and became an apprentice in an export business. He was happy.

"In an office?" Albrecht asked in amazement.

"Yes," Fritz answered, a little sadly, "there's no other way, you just have to accept it. But on the other hand, it's Hamburg, by the sea"—that made up for a lot, for him. "And the company has big offices overseas," he said, and already his imagination had gained the upper hand. Overseas . . . even the word was seductive, suggesting that there was still a lot to discover: the wider world, other peoples, foreign languages, hidden wonders, with a beautiful fog of foreignness and danger half concealing it all. "I'll stay here in Germany at first, of course," he went on, "to learn the business; it's not so simple, you have to stand your ground there too. But later, I'll transfer."

"Where?"

Fritz laughed. "Overseas, of course."

He said goodbye and started his job on the first of the following month.

Albrecht went back to school in a new class—it was his final year. He did his duty, kept his head down, and gradually grew completely isolated from the other students. He had never had friends besides Fritz, and now Fritz was gone. Albrecht was left alone with his books and his violin. In fact, books became more and more important in Albrecht's life. That was partly for another reason: Albrecht had met a man who exerted a great influence on him and effected a big change in his young life. For a long time, this man would be his guide and his friend. Albrecht saw him for the first time at an evening lecture of the Literary Society, a group he had long made it a habit to attend.

Their town had a literary society for a few years. It led its own modest existence in a somewhat different category from the numerous societies and clubs that filled the city—sports clubs, political clubs—the main differences being that it never had a booth in the market square on holidays and festivals, and never marched in parades as the other groups did. For it had no flag. What in the world was it supposed to have as its symbol on a flag? The abstract, sexless mark of Literature?

Albrecht Seldersen often attended their events, which took place in a park outside the city in the summer, and in an unpleasant meeting room in evenings in the winter. He went whenever there seemed to be something he might profit from. Even his schoolmates' teasing couldn't stop him—which was strange in itself. What could he have been looking for there? The answer was that, with time, he had discovered that sometimes a thought he vaguely sensed in himself (merely a breath of air, a soft sound) could, when he sensed it in someone else, a poet, be transformed into a fixed, clear harmony, ringing out loud and clear and purifying and strengthening his soul in a strange way. Whenever this happened, he felt it as good for him, like the refreshing bath he would take after a game at the gym or an event at the track, which drove all the fatigue from his limbs and cleansed his body.

He would sit inconspicuously, near the foot of a long table, for they drank coffee at their events, or else he would drag his chair into the corner, put another chair in front of his chair as a kind of barrier, rest his arm on its back, and watch. The coffee cups clinked. Old women—little old spinsters, who had belonged to the uppermost circles before the war but who now, economically shipwrecked by the new social conditions and lacking all influence in society, spent friendly hours with one another there—listened to lectures, nodded in approval, and raised their cups to their lips. The masculine element was not very well represented, numerically speaking, but what men they were! A retired major was in charge: an upright man always on the lookout for new attractions to rope into his club. He gave the majority of lectures himself, when he couldn't find anyone else, which overtaxed him even though he was still extremely spry for his age—in winter he used to wash himself with the snow from his balcony, and he did gymnastics in the nude with like-minded cohorts in a field that had been set aside for the purpose. The local bookseller was also in the club: once a wild and temperamental man, he was now, with the strength of his second youth, wrestling with his genius and forcing it to produce little short stories that even made their way into the mid-level family magazines.

The out-of-work actor—left behind after the summer theater had closed for the year to proclaim poems and dramatic scenes in grand theatrical style before the art-loving citizenry—had moved on to another town, but the major kept his eyes peeled and then, at the start of the new year, a young judge appeared, a recent graduate sent to the city by his supervisors right after his exams and entrusted with a commissionership. He was from the Rhineland, on the western edge of Germany, and he carried himself freely and easily, a tendency that often butted up against the more rigid Prussian formality of life here. But here was where he found himself now, and unless he wanted to strike up a conversation with himself alone in his room or out on a walk in the woods, he would have to have recourse to the people interested in the intellectual life here. The major welcomed him with open arms and invited him to give a talk; reluctantly, he agreed.

The events were advertised for days beforehand with flyers hung in the windows of a bakery and the bookstore. And sooner or later everyone who up until then had led a secret life, communing with the intellectual currents of the world within their own four walls, found their way to the society.

That year, the lectures took place in an empty guest room of a hotel, reached by crossing a courtyard, climbing a dark flight of stairs, walking down a narrow hall, and taking the second door on the left. There were all sorts of things going on in the hotel: a hiking club danced folk dances in a club room downstairs, with someone hammering away on an out-of-tune piano whose grating sounds made their way upstairs; in the next room, the maids were giggling with the waiters above the restaurant, while a choir practiced in another of the back rooms.

The lecture room filled up. The chairs were set out close together, with only a narrow aisle in the middle left free. The major welcomed all the newcomers with a beaming face, shook their hands personally, and thanked them for coming out to join them. So many people!

Entrance was free; a charge imposed at the beginning of the year gave you free admittance—and a little steamboat ride in the summer too.

Ten minutes after the time he was set to start, the lecturer appeared with his landlord's wife and the daughters of one of the local district court judges. He was a head taller than everyone there except the major. He quickly glanced around and saw almost no one but old people: women, not many men, two teachers, and one student in short pants and a brown corduroy jacket, blond, with wide, surprised eyes: Albrecht Seldersen. The young lecturer nodded across the room to him, even though they had never met. There's an ally, he thought, and when he sat down at the table in the front of the room, he again gave Albrecht a friendly look. Then he started his lecture.

He spoke in an excited voice, enthusiastically, with sweeping gestures, and slowly but surely achieved the miracle of sparking to life in this cold room, in front of so many people with whom he had nothing in common. All the faces around him grew blurry and melted away into the shape of the schoolboy's face all the way at the back, which was staring fixedly at him. He bent forward slightly, to be a little bit closer to that face, and spoke to the student as though the two of them were alone in the room: "But Tonio Kröger keeps his distance. All he knows how to do is play a little violin, write a little poetry, and indulge to the fullest in a mood, with all of its longing and all of its suffering. Do you understand why I am talking to you? You are sitting there in short pants, with an open collar, surrounded by old people, and you think you have it in you to fight to the death until your last breath. But against what? Against whatever is crude and loud and vulgar. You play your violin in a dark room while pacing around the table. The next day, you win a pentathlon. You fight whenever someone insults you, and then sit here in the evening and listen in amazement to what I am telling you. That is how it should be. Because what matters is the life of the mind, and our love for the spirit, which is what makes us able to act in the world. What else could bring me to give a lecture in your frigid little backwater, in this inhospitable guest room, in front of people who still have the taste of their dinners in their mouths?"

After the lecture, Albrecht waited by the door. Then the speaker emerged, with two women talking animatedly with each other. Albrecht turned around, intending to go home, when the lecturer held out his hand to him:

"Good evening. Did you enjoy the talk?"

Albrecht bowed deeply, not wanting anyone to see the blush on his cheeks.

The next day, when they saw each other on the street, they said hello as though they had been close friends for a long time.

"My name is Albrecht Seldersen," he said.

"A pleasure to meet you." The young man already knew his

name, of course. "You must come and visit me. When are you free?"

"I'm in school," Albrecht answered.

"Yes, of course. Would you like to come by tomorrow evening? Not too late, please." He gave Albrecht his address. Albrecht accepted the invitation.

When he opened the garden gate the next day, Dr. Köster was already standing at the window upstairs and he called down a greeting. He welcomed Albrecht warmly upstairs and Albrecht immediately felt right at home. He looked around the room. There was a large shelf full of books against the wall and colorful piles of sheet music and more books covering the grand piano.

"Have you already eaten?" Dr. Köster asked. Albrecht said he had.

"I thought," Köster went on, "that we would stay here for a while first, then perhaps go for a little walk up the street or into the park. How does that sound?"

"Great," Albrecht answered quickly, "I'd like that very much. There are lovely walks you can take around here, sometimes for hours without seeing a soul. That's about all that we have here, to tell you the truth. But you haven't been here long, have you?"

Dr. Köster laughed. "I hope to get to know everything in the area soon. Would you be my guide?"

Albrecht looked at him in silence. Then he only nodded.

They talked for a good long while. Albrecht waited nervously for each new question and tried hard to answer it well. Once, when there was a slight pause in the conversation, Dr. Köster jumped up, sat down at the piano, and sang and played a short song, one which you heard everywhere in those days.

Albrecht stayed sitting in his chair. His short pants had ridden up slightly on his muscular legs and his knees were bare. His socks were rolled down.

Dr. Köster stood up from the piano.

"What do you think, Albrecht? Do you like it? I heard it somewhere recently and forgot it, but it just came back to me."

They talked more. Albrecht let the other man do most of the talking; he liked listening to him. Köster was originally from a small town too, his father was a medical doctor like his grandfather before him and his grandfather's father as well. But he himself had broken the chain. His studies had taken him to numerous cities and now he was working here, at the district court; he was a respected official, but this evening he was acting in a private capacity. Most of his spare time was spent on a major project that would surely keep him busy for several years—he indicated only very generally what it was, and Albrecht didn't ask any questions. Earlier, in high school and during his first semesters at university, Dr. Köster had been an avid hiker. He still wore his hiking club's pin on the lapel of his waistcoat.

The evening went on and it seemed to Albrecht, more and more, that his own life was being laid out before him, by a stranger who nonetheless knew his life and many other things too. It was downright uncanny a lot of the time, and unspeakably thrilling. Albrecht felt like he was on his mark, waiting for the pistol shot to start the race, and here was someone he could ask: What's it all really like? . . . But he didn't think any more about that. He loved the culture, the well-proportioned order and civility emanating from the older man. Whenever Köster read or sang him something and he lay on the sofa to listen, he was filled with a deep sense of satisfaction. It was a wonderful sight he was presented with. Albrecht felt drawn to him with both youthful admiration and a warm camaraderie. He anxiously tried to think of something he could do to prove himself to Köster in return, some way not to come to him empty-handed. But there was nothing Köster wanted from him. When he left, Albrecht said that Dr. Köster should come over and visit his parents. They would surely also be glad to meet him. Dr. Köster accepted.

Some time went by before he kept his promise. Albrecht meanwhile saw him on the street a few times, always in the company of women; he greeted him from afar as respectfully as he could, not daring to speak a word to him. But one day he appeared at Albrecht's door, laughing, merry, and carefree. He sat right down at the piano and played, sang, and helped Albrecht past the first awkward minutes. Frau Seldersen walked in and Albrecht introduced them. She invited Dr. Köster to stay for dinner, and he immediately accepted. Mother set the round table in the front room for them, the room with the bookshelf and the writing desk. When she brought out the tray, her hands were shaking a little. Albrecht noticed. Herr Seldersen showed his face too, shook hands with Dr. Köster, and said a few words: he was happy to meet him, and hoped Albrecht wasn't too stupid. Dr. Köster laughed and looked at Albrecht, who was leaning forward over the table, embarrassed and angry at his father's words, forgetting to chew even though his mouth was full. Herr Seldersen vanished again, and they were alone once more.

"What was that about?" Albrecht asked.

"Don't actually be stupid and prove him right," came Köster's rejoinder. "Or did you want him to walk in and compliment you?"

Albrecht shook his head. They ate.

Then he realized that he hadn't yet told Dr. Köster anything about his friend Fritz. What would he think of Fritz's situation?

Dr. Köster listened to the whole story, his face growing serious and distant. Finally he said:

"And how old is your friend?"

"Nineteen."

"Well, in that case he must know what he's doing." It sounded like an accusation.

Silence.

"I must say, such things have no appeal for me," Dr. Köster admitted. "I don't see the point, or the inner justification, for taking such far-reaching decisions and drastic action, the way you say your friend has done. I understand it, but I don't believe in it. I tell you, Albrecht, there's nothing I hate more. And a word of advice for you too: don't let yourself become an activist or join the struggle or God knows what else. I have always been careful not to do that, and I think you could use the same counsel. You did hear what I just said in my lecture, didn't you?"

Albrecht said nothing. He couldn't deny what Köster had said, even if he also felt that some aspects of it were still unclear. He had only a dim sense of what was visible through Köster's words, but he knew he did not want to spend any more time in its company.

Dr. Köster stood up and walked over to the bookshelf. He opened the glass door.

"Read, Albrecht, that's much more sensible, and it helps more. You own books, that's good. Have you read them all?"

Albrecht stood next to him. "Yes."

"I'd be glad to loan you more books, if you want. You'll take good care of them. Books are your friends."

Albrecht said he would be very glad to read anything Köster chose for him, and promised to take good care of them.

And Dr. Köster kept his promise. He loaned Albrecht books, and those books entered Albrecht's life, coming to occupy an important place there. Before long, they became central to how Albrecht thought about his life.

One of the books Dr. Köster loaned him had a captivating, melancholy sweetness that Albrecht had never come across before. He read it countless times until he almost had it memorized, and every time revealed something new. There was the world, brightly colored, frightening, and full of inexplicable events, and here, off to one side—a great distance off—was Tonio Kröger: no conquering hero, no man of adventure or bearer of glad tidings, but someone who reined himself in tight no matter what he was doing, someone who knew too much, who sensed a thousand things in the smallest revelation, a scrupulous observer of everything, to the point of losing himself and spoiling every pleasure he might have had. He was an odd man out, redundant in life. Even as a young man, he seemed destined to perceive every revelation of life in a melancholy and painful way, and to relive it inside himself. He suffered when he loved, and kept apart while other people simply took as their due whatever life had to offer—and yet he had the understanding and the pain, the knowledge and the renunciation. Without realizing it, Albrecht lost himself in the book's enchanting voice; no longer thinking, he felt, or dreamed, the wavering borderline where life and death, health and sickness, gently met. Grand, strange, wonderful thoughts came to him, and he had no idea himself how they had arisen, but for the time being astonishment and uncertainty outweighed everything else. This fateful book was decisive for Albrecht. He felt understood, acknowledged; he felt that the book could see right through him and that it sketched out in advance the possibilities and potential of his own life. He stuck to the once-hidden path it laid out—he even felt that whenever he risked diverging from it was just when he needed to make every effort to find his way back to it again.

•

The fall season at the store was a disaster, not that anyone had gone into it with great hopes, but in fact the sales were worse than even their worst fears. The previous year was the closest thing they could find to the pitiful results now. It was awful: the wares sat on the shelves, and only rarely did a possible buyer walk through the door. The few people who really did need things, because they had large families or because they had gotten by without anything new the year before, couldn't pay for anywhere near all they wanted, and Herr Seldersen had no choice but to give it to them on credit and write up the amount in his book. What else could he do? If he didn't offer credit, another store would. There were still a few people who regularly spent money in the shop, but they couldn't make up for all the rest.

It's also the case, of course, that people without much to spare don't necessarily need new clothes for the fall season, as opposed

to continuing to wear whatever they wore through the summer—
the air is not quite as warm as it was, true, but it's not yet freezing cold as in winter, it's actually a rather pleasant balance
between the two. If you go around in summer, in the hot sun,
with a shirt and pants, then you can pull on a jacket or another
pair of underwear now that it's colder; you don't need to buy
new clothes, you can hold off until winter comes.

So Herr Seldersen consoled himself: winter was coming,
surely business would pick up then. But not to put too fine a point
on it, winter was no great shakes either. Even during the afternoon, when his store was technically open, Herr Seldersen had
time to walk up and down the street and check in on the competition to see how they were doing. He did this secretly, in a roundabout way—with a letter in his hand, as though he were going to
the post office, for example. His walk to the post office took him
past various stores and so he had opportunity enough to observe,
confirm, and go away reassured—his competition wasn't doing
any better than he was. He often dropped in on Herr Wiesel and
stood talking with him for a long time, trading stories about
how badly business was going. They always found another angle
from which to approach what they really wanted to talk about.
Then a customer came in, or sometimes several at once, and Herr
Seldersen quickly said goodbye and walked home. His wife met
him at the door, where she was leaning in the doorway and
watching for customers. She didn't hide the fact that there were
no customers there at the moment.

"Come inside," Father said. He didn't like it when she stood
in the doorway, telling the whole world: Look, no one's here.
"Come inside," he urged her again.

Mother didn't want to, and didn't understand what Father was
after. "Leave me alone," she said, "I'm just standing here keeping
an eye out. You think it doesn't concern me too?"

This woman, Herr Seldersen thought, shaking his head. He
went inside and hid in a dark corner. Every now and then, Mother
came in and announced that Frau Zorn had just come out of Herr

Wiesel's holding a large package, even though she still had a huge tab here at the Seldersens' shop. Then she took up her post again, until she had more news to report. Herr Seldersen eventually lost patience and sent her upstairs. There were a lot of disagreements between the two of them in those days.

Suddenly, the last two days before the holidays, there were such crowds at the Seldersens' that they barely found time to eat. Three of them worked in the store—Father, Mother, and a shopgirl—with Albrecht at the cash register. They needed his help, there was no way around it. At night his parents collapsed into bed, but their happy knowledge that they were still in the game far outweighed their exhaustion.

"Believe me," Mother said to Father and Albrecht, "believe me, whenever someone gets work, everyone gets work, and whenever one person is waiting downstairs, everyone else is too, believe me. The same bread is baked for everyone."

Herr Seldersen only nodded. These past two days had ended up being almost too much for him. He was beside himself with happiness. Finally, he said:

"Yes, yes, but what's the use? It all depends on who can stick it out longer."

His old suspicions and mistrust were back—all the hopelessness he felt was in these words. It was better for him to keep quiet, after all; then at least he wouldn't destroy everyone else's hopes.

The following weeks were quiet, merciless. It was harder to bear everything now that winter had come. The city was as if deserted; no one dared set foot outside in the cold.

Fritz came home again over New Year's. He took a few days' vacation and spent it with his parents. He looked good; apparently Hamburg was agreeing with him. He walked proudly through the streets of town and his parents didn't try to conceal their satisfaction. Yes, he lived in Hamburg now, he had his career, it was going well, he had a lot to tell Albrecht. Especially about the city—there was so much to see there, it was full of beautiful secret spots. Down by the harbor, in the pedestrian area, in St. Pauli, and then the surrounding suburbs, the river, the sea! He couldn't get enough of the sights, and even now he hadn't seen everything. Albrecht listened eagerly, looked admiringly at Fritz . . . he had seen all that. "And your work? How's work going?" he asked. After all, the reason he had gone to Hamburg was to apprentice in an export firm, and here he was, reminiscing and telling him about the city all this time, about how much he liked everything—but not a word about his job.

"How are the prospects?" he asked again.

Then Fritz grew rather awkward, and had to think for a while before he knew how to answer. "Well, you know, it doesn't go as fast as all that, I still have to study and learn the ropes, then we'll see. . . ."

Fritz's answer made Albrecht stop and think. Was Fritz unhappy there? If not, what would make him express himself so carefully? "It must not be the way you imagined it would be," he said cautiously.

Fritz nodded. "Yes, it's harder than you'd think, suddenly all sorts of problems turn up that you'd never thought of, incredible complications, you wouldn't believe it . . . yes, well, we did lose the war."

"Lose the war . . ." Albrecht repeated. So that was the cause of the problems and complications Fritz was describing, visibly dejected. That's what his friend had learned up in Hamburg?

"How's the foreign trade?" he asked.

Fritz, bashfully: "I told you already. What do you know, anyway?"

"What do I know?" Albrecht was taken aback. He didn't claim to know anything; he was only thinking about all the things Fritz had told him about foreign trade when he was about to start his apprenticeship: in his innocent happiness he had talked about exotic peoples, foreign languages, ships crossing the ocean, it was exciting, there were discoveries to be made, and now . . . "Foreign trade is going badly," Fritz said. "Imports, exports, tariffs, sales, foreign competition—everyone's plotting against us. . . ."

Albrecht listened eagerly to what Fritz was telling him, and he could see that it was hard for his friend to state these truths. It must have been even harder for him to face them straight on and see them without self-deception, to admit to himself that that was the way things were—he had seen it with his own eyes. And there was more. Fritz told his friend about the companies he had gotten to know in Hamburg, the ones that had already thrown in the towel, that had been left lying dead on the side of the road. His own firm? Nothing to be afraid of there, thank God, it would definitely stick it out and get through the tough times. That's what he hoped.

So even they are having trouble? Fritz didn't deny it. His face grew serious and thoughtful, as though he were personally responsible.

"How much longer is your apprenticeship?" Albrecht asked.

"Two years."

Fritz left to go back to Hamburg the day after New Year's.

Best of luck! Albrecht thought. He hoped for the best for his friend.

.

It was an eventful winter. In January, the co-owner of a major firm in Berlin with business connections throughout the country shot himself. It was a significant event, surprising more than anything else, and depressing—it revealed with merciless clarity where things were heading and what the uncertainty and troubles, growing more and more serious everywhere, had in store. The next day, all the papers had stories and specific accounts of everything that had led up to the suicide, down to every detail.

Herr Seldersen read the article in his paper over and over again, shaking his head every time; he just couldn't come to terms with it, it surpassed his understanding. An immense sadness came over him.

"What do you think about that, Herr Wiesel?" he asked. "What do you say to that? They've been in business eighty years! Who would have thought?"

Herr Wiesel shook his head. He wouldn't have believed it himself. Of course everyone knew that the times were taking their toll there too; it wasn't like the old days anymore, not at all. New businesses had come on the scene—fresher, more dynamic, with fewer burdens; there seemed to be a new way of doing business; even the market had completely changed in the course of only a few years. Payments came in late, faithful customers and purchasers they had had for years suddenly disappeared, it was one thing after another. They had the big banks behind them, no question about that, who were always ready to jump in and help; the situation hadn't yet worked its way down into private, personal poverty on their part. But troubles were piling up. The company's name had once been a byword, a fixed star in the business sky, and now it was gone, along with the honor and respect it once commanded. And so one of the directors, fifty-six years old, had decided to end his own life.

"Shot himself . . ." Herr Wiesel whispered. The death itself seemed much more important to him than the circumstances that had caused it.

"And the consequences, beware of the consequences, Herr Seldersen. An event like this always ripples out a long way." He did not want to say anything further.

He was right. It was like if Europe had suddenly disappeared off the map.

Only now did it become clear how deeply even the smallest everyday occurrences were interconnected—how fatefully everything was bound to everything else, in mysterious but indissoluble chains.

Herr Seldersen had ordered clothes from this company for all the many years he had been in business. It was a great honor for him, and one he felt proud of: not everyone was accepted as one of the firm's clients, and whoever was had a secure place in the eyes of the world. And now this, and the consequences it brought in its train: as Herr Wiesel had already hinted, Herr Seldersen was to be affected too. It didn't take long. He received a letter requesting him to immediately pay all sums due to the firm. The company was shutting down; several other firms, the main creditors, had agreed to take over the company and conduct business under a different name. But before they made the change, all outstanding debts had to be cleared.

What was Herr Seldersen supposed to do? Until that point, he had paid his debts by dividing whatever money he had at his disposal at any given time into numerous parts, sending a small sum to each of his creditors, enough to satisfy them for a short time, at least. He had worked out a whole system, which had kept him above water so far. It was a miserable, limping survival, truth be told, but it kept him out of trouble, and as long as no one unexpectedly threw a wrench in the works there was no reason he couldn't keep it going. But now he suddenly had to pay a sum that would have been enough to keep six other creditors happy for months.

Was this the end? Had it come so fast, surprised him so suddenly, after creeping closer and closer for so long? Was there no way out? Father wrote to his brother, a lawyer in M., who had a lucrative practice and was doing well. They had been a large family, with many brothers and sisters, and life had scattered them far and wide—years went by between occasions when they saw each other in person, during which letters with boring family news kept their slim family connections going. They all had enough to worry about on their own; everyone had his or her own job with its own obligations. Father wrote to him: "Dear Brother," but already there, right at the start, he could not go on. After a surprise attack with a stranglehold slowly tightening around his neck, he was supposed to sit down and calmly write a letter? He had never been a letter writer. He sat huddled over the writing desk in his store all day long, and then, when he went up to the apartment that evening, he locked the door to the room, pulled a chair up to the desk there, dipped his pen in the ink, touched it to the paper . . . and wrote not one single sylla- ble. The ink dried out and covered the nib with a thick black crust. He'd never be able to write with a nib like that. He pulled it from the pen, looked at the ink stains on his hands, went out to wash them, and started over. Then the thoughts that had long lived hidden in his head, unbeknownst to him, burst forth in all their sad, stunted misery. He had never in his life had to turn to anyone, much less had to write a letter like this, but now it had to be. He wrote: "My dear brother, I have no choice but to write to you like this today, it's my only option. You know I've worked hard all my life and never thought of anything but that. Do you want to hear more? You are too involved in life yourself not to know how hard it is today for anyone who has a business as I do and has kept it going through all these years without ever over- stepping his bounds. I have not been spared either. We had good times, but now they seem to be over. It can't go on. It's not my fault."

And the words of his own father, long since dead, came back to him. He wrote them to his brother: "As our dearly departed father is my witness. He had ten mouths to feed, and Mother didn't make it easy for him, but he often told me—I was still young, in my first year of training—he said: I didn't inherit riches and will not pass them on to my children, but what I earn I earn honestly and through my own hard work, that is the only luxury I can afford."

He ended by writing very openly and directly about the situ- ation he was in. His creditors were after him, it had always worked out until now, but not anymore. What was he supposed to do? Close the store and start something new, change careers at his age, fifty-six years old? Resign himself to fate and fold his tired hands in his lap? No, he didn't feel old. But something had to happen. He wanted to keep trying. But for that he needed one thing: money, money to meet his obligations in one stroke and start with a clean slate.

.

No storms came from the east over the river, and then suddenly the clouds were bunched in an eerie black ball in the sky and the rain would not stop pouring down. By the third day, the farmer was worriedly shaking his head: the prospects for this year's harvest didn't look good; if this endless rain didn't stop falling, everything would rot in the fields. After four days, the sky was a bright blue. The sun shone down and soon drew all the moisture from the soil, until the farmer was shaking his head again: if it didn't rain soon, he said, all the grain would scorch and dry up in the fields. He was always dissatisfied with something, but he never left his plot of soil. . . .

.

In the long run, there was no way to keep what was happening a secret. Frau Seldersen was the first to find out, then the children. Father was most upset about Albrecht knowing—just when the boy needed to devote all his thoughts to school, here was this unfortunate situation. But there was no way around it, the time had come to reach a decision, something drastic and far-reaching had to happen at last. They had anxiously seen this moment coming for a long time now; it almost felt like a relief to be able to take some kind of action again, make something happen and come to closure. There is nothing worse than having to sit around waiting, unable to do anything, like someone who no longer has any power to shape the course of his own life—out to pasture, with nothing to do but be patient, endure, and stay calm.

"If I had money to work with," Herr Seldersen said, "I could start over again from the beginning." It was like he was taking a vow.

The words sounded strange enough in his mouth, since they

were being spoken by an old man, one who actually should have been thinking about the end, rather than about starting over from the beginning. Anneliese and Mother openly expressed their faith in him; only Albrecht kept quiet. It took him a while to get used to the idea that his father, over fifty years old, was talking about making a fresh start.

"If you had the money, then are you sure you'd be able to take care of everything, not just now but in the future too?"

"You can always hope," Father answered, much less confident than before, "you can always keeping hoping, otherwise it would just be too sad."

Pause.

Albrecht: "I think that as long as you live, that's true."

"As long as you live?"

"Yes, or do you think . . . you can't leave anything untried."

Herr Seldersen suspected that Albrecht had had something specific in mind with these words, but he wasn't quite sure whether he had said them intentionally or thoughtlessly. But at the moment, he was inclined to give a lot of credit to conscious intentions, and so he felt a certain respect for his son. Up until that point, Albrecht had seemed to be facing the events around him without much insight or feeling, as though he lacked the necessary seriousness and maturity to come to terms with them. Father was worried about the boy's future, and with reason; he often talked it over with Anneliese, and then there were the worries about choosing a profession. What would happen? How would it all work out? He could see no good answer. Albrecht seemed not to think about it as much. He just waited and did not seem anxious or in a hurry to come to his decisions.

Every night he sat at the desk in the small room in front, with a pile of books, notebooks, and sheets of paper covered with writing in front of him. His eyes hurt, his head throbbed with a dull ache; he laid his head down on the desktop to rest for a moment. The warmth of the overheated room and his own body got to him and he jumped up, opened the window, leaned out, and breathed in the cold air of the winter night with relief. The streets were empty, the trees bent under the white weight of the snow. The stars glittered in the sky, every constellation so close you could almost touch it. Down by the front door was the landlord's maid, who had not been working there long. Albrecht could recognize her by her curly blond hair, framing her head like a fur hat. She dressed like a lady; when she was done with her work, she went downstairs and waited in front of the house. Everyone who passed by looked at her long and hard—maybe she liked that. A man, still a boy really, walked up to her and Albrecht recognized him: the carpenter's apprentice from across the street. He was tall, strong, with long limbs. What were they saying to each other? Albrecht listened.

"Hi, why are you so late today?" She had been waiting for a long time.

"I couldn't come sooner," he answered curtly.

Albrecht could hear every word— the air was clear and cold, with no wind to carry away the sound. A simple greeting. Silence. They stood facing each other. Why didn't they take each other's hands, warm each other up?

"What's wrong?" the girl asked at last. Her voice sounded surprised but calm.

"I have to talk to you, Johanna." The words came out slowly, as though he were still wondering whether he should say them at all. He leaned against the wall. After a while:

"I went to the doctor today. I couldn't take it anymore, the master had already noticed, he was asking me what was wrong."

Silence.

"Why didn't you tell me you were sick?"

"I'm not sick anymore," the girl answered. "I'm better now."

Again, the firm, clear ring in her voice, making the boy feel uncertain.

"But why didn't you tell me you had been? I could have maybe been more careful."

She laughed quietly, not mockingly: "You really were wild,"

she said, and suddenly she was very shy and timid. "You couldn't wait, it was just the first time and you . . ."

She fell silent.

"But you didn't say anything; just one word would have been enough."

"I really thought I was better, and then . . . I wasn't only thinking of you."

"Not only of me? What do you mean?"

Silence.

"Why won't you answer? Fine, I'll report you, Johanna." Now his voice has grown firm and clear, he is so sure of himself, he is standing in front of her, right up next to her. She still says nothing. Then she takes her key, unhurriedly opens the door, and bolts it from the inside. The young man steps to the door and grabs the iron grate of the window.

"Johanna," he calls out quietly, "Johanna!"

Albrecht heard her slowly, then faster and faster, going upstairs to her attic room. The young man went home through the snow. Albrecht shut the window. He was done working for the day.

.

When his brother wrote back that he was prepared to help out with the necessary sum of money, under certain conditions, Herr Seldersen wrote to his creditors: he intended to pay off his debt at once, in return for their willingness to write off a certain percentage of it; they would discuss the particulars in more detail if they agreed, but he was looking forward to restructuring and rebuilding his business in accordance with modern principles as quickly as possible. This was the common form that settlements out of court generally took. Many days went by before the answers started arriving, one after the other. Some creditors agreed at once, others only with reservations. But his main supplier was the most stubborn of all: they had a lot of money at stake and a lot to lose, so they kept finding new reasons to try to get a special deal. Herr Seldersen had done business with them since he'd opened his store—it was the company where Herr Nelken worked. Herr Seldersen had visited the old boss in his office many times, spent hours talking to him. Finally, the situation grew serious enough to make him go to Berlin again to discuss matters in person. He put on his blue suit, shaved carefully, and in general took every pain to make the best possible impression. He went with the best intentions, and now he was sitting there like someone who was only allowed in up the back stairs.

"How many proposals like yours do you think we receive these days, Herr Seldersen? The answer is three or four a day, sometimes more. We've taken great losses, and always from businesses such as yours, which have been around for many years. People leave home without a penny in their pockets nowadays."

Herr Seldersen nodded. Certainly, the general poverty had not just affected a single business, not just him, they were all in it together.

"And as for your case, I have to tell you we are very surprised. You have continued to place orders with us, our salesmen have been paying you visits even recently." He paused for a moment and looked at Herr Seldersen.

Was he accusing him of something?

Father thought and then said: "Of course, you keep trying everything you can to the bitter end, you don't leave out any possible chance no matter how few you have." Really, he didn't deserve reproaches, he wasn't trying to trick anyone or take unfair advantage of his desperate situation to pull one over on his creditors. Let others try tricks like that, if they're lying flat on the ground and still have the strength to try to outwit their attackers and go down to their deaths with the knowledge of their final triumph—not him, he had other ideas. He just wanted some peace for once, at last. Peace! No more terrifying ups and downs all the time, mixed with despair about a future that seems twice as deadly since you can't see it coming. He didn't have the courage for it anymore, or the strength. Did his situation really make the other man think he was in a strong position?

"Yes, yes, of course, you're trying to do what you can, but the percentage is too low for us, we would lose too much money."

Father replied that he had been doing business for twenty-five years . . . and then everything else he had said so many times already, and more, things he had thought about only in silence. It all came to him now and he said it out loud, without shame. But it didn't touch him anymore. He was old, and the older he got, the shakier the ground felt under his feet. He had had to live to see that, and, he said with mild astonishment as he stood there, he was still alive. It was true, they had always given him the best possible terms in their dealings, but now they were forced to act in their own best interests without any leniency and without taking account of personal relationships.

.

It was a hard struggle, a test of Herr Seldersen's nerves and patience. The other man wanted to think it over some more: there were numerous factors to consider; he had to consult with the other directors, Herr Nelken too. That reassured Herr Seldersen; he was sure Nelken would agree. He tried to set up a meeting with Herr Nelken in person, but there was never an opportunity, they always said he was not in at the moment, or, if Seldersen ever caught sight of him from a distance, Nelken always ran busily off somewhere else. Herr Seldersen could not help but think that Nelken was avoiding him, which deeply depressed him. He lost all hope.

It stretched out more than six weeks—all the letters back and forth, the long and tedious negotiations. The snow was slowly starting to melt away when Herr Seldersen had everything worked out. He paid the agreed-upon percentage of his debts, from the money he got from the bank with his brother's guarantee. They charged interest, of course, or did Herr Seldersen think he could just get the money loaned outright, on faith? Naturally, he had to pay interest, but it was an extra burden, no question about it, a heavy burden. At first it didn't matter much, Herr Seldersen thought he could take it on; only later did he realize how much worrying and difficulty this interest alone would cause him. His debts were paid off, the creditors were satisfied, Herr Seldersen's shelves were fully stocked and apparently the goods were all paid for. It seemed that a new day had dawned.

.

Albrecht passed his final exams in the spring. It wasn't an especially good performance: how could he concentrate? He stood in front of the teachers who had known him all these years, or thought they knew him, and he answered their questions thinking all the while about how he could best help his father finally be happy and dignified again, both now and in the future. Yes, happiness and dignity—that was what was going through his head, everything else was lies, just endless, vicious lies. He had nothing but contempt for his teachers, a proud contempt for the fact that they were testing his maturity and fitness to receive a diploma while knowing nothing about his most burning, desperate cares and worries.

Albrecht went to Berlin and enrolled in university. What else could he do? Become a shopkeeper? God spare him from that, his father had said, often and with feeling, to anyone who asked him. And the others had agreed—no, no, not a shopkeeper, there was no future in that, you would end up with nothing. But they couldn't think of anything better to suggest in its place. When you really looked at the state of things, there was practically nothing that you could say in good conscience had a promising future, everything was slowly, unstoppably going downhill, if it hadn't hit bottom already. Father, who already had troubles enough, now had that to worry about too—apparently he would be spared nothing. School was the last hope; at least there you were busy doing something that had a certain aura to people on the outside. You could try to arrange things so that it wouldn't be too expensive, you could make a little money on the side, and it would last a good long time, several years, during which at least you would not have to face any final decision and you didn't have to be afraid of ending up out on the street after classes were over. You could wait and see—that was it, wait and see how things turned out.

One day, among all the advice and well-intentioned suggestions coming in, a distant relative offered to send a small sum of money for Albrecht every month. Finally, something solid you could build on: a promise—or more, an unexpected windfall. So Albrecht went to university, to wait and see. He went to Berlin.

It was hard for his parents when he left them; he was not going far, but now they had an empty nest.

"We're getting old," Mother said. She forced herself to laugh, as though she were joking, but it was bitterly serious for her. Father said nothing: he was old, and had had to face his age in his own way. He thought that when you're old you should keep quiet, because an older person does not belong in his times anymore.

Albrecht stood on the street and said goodbye to all of his friends.

"You're off to Berlin?" they asked. Albrecht nodded.

"That's the life! Not like here, this old backwater. Oh, if only I could get out too! So you're going to university?" They wished him good luck. Yes, he'd really have a great time. They knew what it meant to be a student.

He left; he walked through the streets of his hometown, and the buildings he knew so well stood on either side of the road and bade him farewell. Albrecht was moved. I'm leaving now, he whispered, I have to go out and see the world a bit, but I'll be back soon. The stone structures nodded gravely at him and said nothing. Albrecht took the road up the mountain and shouted down into the forest for the last time. The echo came back loud and clear. He strained to listen, and then joy came over him. He threw stones into the air, at the birds that had already found their way back, drawn by the warm air of the season. Hooray, he was leaving, and he would return.

Albrecht said goodbye to his friend Dr. Köster too, the young scholar who spent his days in his room writing his big book. They had grown to be close friends in the time they had known each other, and now Albrecht was leaving him here alone. It was a difficult goodbye for Albrecht—he had so much to thank him for, so infinitely much. Dr. Köster warned him not to forget his books and reminded him of everything they had often discussed together. He gave him countless pieces of advice, with words and images he found for Albrecht from his own early years, which seemed suddenly to have come back to life for him. Albrecht had some sense of what it meant to be a university student, he had seen a glimpse and knew—but only the half of it. Albrecht took in everything Dr. Köster said, and as he said goodbye, he thought that now he would have the chance to try out what had only been empty knowledge until then, and experience it in real life. Maybe it would open up many new things to him that he hadn't known; yes, maybe he would gain a new and completely different kind of knowledge.

Before he left town, one more thing happened: Fritz came back from Hamburg. He had announced his return on a postcard one day and then there he was, to great consternation. He had spent almost a year in Hamburg, everyone had hoped he had found his footing there, but it was all for nothing; cast to the winds, Fritz just came back home and no power on earth could keep him away. And the reason? What could have made him suddenly decide to come home?

"It all happened so fast," Herr Fiedler said, adding: "Couldn't you keep up anymore?"

"No," Fritz replied, "they couldn't keep me on anymore."

But why? Had he done something wrong? He had been apprenticed there more than a year.

The reason was simple: the company had gone bankrupt; Fritz was out on the street. He had done everything, long hours at the office on a stool, bent over his desk in a cramped, stuffy room, for more than a year—now he was out on the street. He was upset and angry, you could tell by looking at him that something bad had happened.

"What else can I do?" he said, by way of apologizing to his parents for being a burden on them. What had happened to his company wasn't his fault, of course, but it had affected him too, and hit him as hard as though he had suffered a great loss himself. All in all, this one year in Hamburg had taken a lot out of him: he was still healthy and strong, more manly than before, with eyes shining behind the lenses of his glasses, but he no longer had the boundless energy and proud confidence he'd once had. He had seen a lot in Hamburg, more than he could describe. He had talked with sailors from every country, stood on the docks while the ships set out and came back, attentively followed the course of events in Hamburg and around the world. In the business he was in, he could see for himself exactly how everything was going: the offices abroad, once flourishing, proud possessions, and now . . . He quickly realized that he had no prospects for taking over a department in the immediate future; on the contrary, they were slowly letting employees go, and it was unclear if they would even keep on the trainees once they had finished their apprenticeships.

Albrecht felt sorry for his friend. "You had bad luck, damn back luck."

Fritz shrugged. "Never mind that." Yes, it definitely affected him, it was his personal misfortune, but deep down he had foreseen this happening a long time ago; the situation didn't surprise him anymore, it was so universal and widespread you couldn't really call it a matter of individual luck. Everything was slowly falling apart—old trading firms that had once been powerful and respected were closing their offices, long lines of their ships were in the port bobbing in the water, left abandoned to every storm, it was like a graveyard. It had been a long time since they had taken on any cargo and traveled to other parts of the globe. The sailors drifted around the city or had moved on, they went on the dole or tried their luck somewhere else. Everything was slowly coming apart, Fritz had seen it with his own eyes.

"And how have things been going with you?" Fritz asked.

Oh, Albrecht had a lot he could say on that subject; he had been through a lot that year, but he didn't come out with it. It was strange, he couldn't bring himself to talk about it; he kept thinking that Fritz could now be in the same position as him if he hadn't dropped out. Everything had seemed different back then. Albrecht didn't hide that for a while he had thought Fritz had made the right decision, and that his future was very promising—his friend had tried to make a real start, and it had worked for more than a year—but now he was out on the street, without anything to do, the year was a dead loss. Just out on the street. He could manage, he wasn't going to go hungry, his parents were still doing well—his father had in fact retired and his older brother Erich, who had in truth been running the business for a while, was now officially in charge. And now here was Fritz, who quickly realized that he was not needed at home. They never told him so—no, they showed nothing but understanding for his situation—but he was too independent to try to crawl back here and start over. What he needed was something he could cling to: some kind of major task that would keep him in its grip for a long time, an idea that would hold his attention for the long haul and not plunge him back into isolation. Albrecht was familiar with all those feelings, even if they weren't so clear and specific with him. A great task: that was what mattered.

"So, you're going to university?" Fritz said.

"Yes," Albrecht said. He felt slightly ashamed, though he didn't know why himself.

Pause.

Fritz just sat there and put his hands on his knees.

"What made you decide to do that?" he then asked.

"Oh . . ." Albrecht considered how he could answer.

"I mean," Fritz interrupted, "are you happy about it?"

Happy? Why shouldn't he be? To be honest, there was nothing else that he wanted to do; he just wanted to explore around a little, be left in peace. The presence of his friend didn't seem to lift his spirits; he felt no particular ambition, it was as though he were calmly just letting things happen.

"What else should I do?" he said in a calm voice.

Yes, well, there you have it. What else should he do? Fritz said nothing.

"And what will you do next?" Albrecht asked.

Fritz looked at the ground, as though trying to pick up what to think from down there.

"I'll try to find a place to stay somewhere." No, he wouldn't be beaten as easily as that, his brother-in-law and parents would help him, maybe he would learn to drive a car first, but he wasn't quite sure yet, something would work out.

.

Albrecht quickly got used to his new life. Everything was relatively easy and simple. He had rented a room on a quiet side street in a formerly elegant neighborhood in the southern part of the city, with a large chestnut tree in front of his window, whose green and mighty branches covered almost the whole high opposite wall of the courtyard. The apartment's owner, an older lady, spent her days outside the house, managing a salon. There was a maid to do all of the housework, from the time when the parents of the spinster who lived there were still alive; she had stayed on and was old, taciturn, and worn-out. At first, when Albrecht moved in, she was grumpy and suspicious; later, she took great care of him.

In the early days, Anneliese checked up on him; their father had asked her to, reminding her of the days when she had arrived in the big city all by herself for the first time. The boy is so helpless, he had said, he looks so confused, who knows how he'll manage—but still, he has to set out on his own sometime. Anneliese promised to look after him; they ate meals together in the afternoon. She knew her way around everywhere and didn't hesitate to share what she knew.

"You have to be especially careful crossing the street: always look both ways, you can't fall asleep or daydream like you used to at home."

Albrecht, surprised: "Fall asleep? Daydream?"

"Yes, that's right, but here you have to keep your wits about you, there won't always be someone running along next to you to look out for you."

"I don't need anyone to do that!" Albrecht replied angrily. He had had enough, she was going a bit far with her advice and supervision. She was acting like he went around in a daze all day and never paid any attention to what was happening around him. But she wasn't done yet.

"Another thing," she added, and you could tell from her voice how important she thought this next piece of advice was: "These days, crowds gather on the street sometimes and occasionally it turns into a serious situation. Just keep walking, don't get involved, it's always the innocent bystanders who get the real beatings."

Albrecht promised to follow this advice. He had a vague sense of what his sister was talking about; he had read about these gatherings in the newspapers often enough; at home too, he remembered, there were sometimes rallies and protests marching through the city. Shut the window, his father had always ordered. It always ended harmlessly enough, though. But here, in the big city?

It didn't take long before Albrecht got a foretaste of what his sister had been darkly, vaguely hinting at. One night a couple of days later, he was strolling carelessly down the street, with no particular goal in mind. It was bright out, with advertisements lit up everywhere, marquees jutting out into the streets, display windows clamoring brightly in every color. There were a lot of people out, but that was nothing unusual, you always saw lots of people on the streets, day and night. Among the crowd were policemen patrolling in twos and threes. At one point, when Albrecht stopped to read the bold letters of a newspaper headline, a policeman came up and told him to keep moving. His helmet was strapped on tight; a truncheon dangled threateningly at his side. The crowds of people on the sidewalks grew more and more dense, carrying everyone along with them in the same direction—it wasn't a well-defined procession, but they were definitely all together, there were even people overflowing the sidewalks onto the streets. The electric streetcars and buses made a huge racket with their constant bells and signals; they could barely move and they were packed with people. Everyone was in a hurry. Albrecht found himself among them and he followed their pace, you could almost think he was one of them. Posters covered the utility poles; the ground was littered with newspapers and flyers; suddenly someone distributing flyers pressed a whole stack of them into his hand. Not now, Albrecht thought, and he let them drop to the ground, keeping only a few to read at home. At first he wanted to get out of there. But he was curious too, curious about where everyone was heading. The police were standing on the streets, close together, and they divided the people streaming past them into different groups without moving from their posts. The rows of people separated and then rejoined one another behind the policemen, split apart again, separated, and rejoined one another, until they got to the front lawn of a large restaurant. Everyone went inside. They stepped over the barrier chain, holding little red tickets high above their heads so that the men would let them through without making them wait. A meeting was taking place inside. Albrecht stood indecisively with the others in front of the counter, with a long line of people in front of him. Various considerations ran through his head. When he got to the front and they asked him for money—not much, but more than he had imagined paying—he quickly took back the money he had held out. "No thanks," he said, "that's too much for me, I can't pay that." The girl behind the counter gave a little laugh and he took a step back; the man behind him had already counted out his money and he put the exact amount on the counter and took his ticket, without a pause.

There he stood, having made a fool of himself in front of everyone. He had lied, an outright lie; he could have said that he was a student, he only had to show them his ID card and he could have gotten a cheaper ticket. For whatever reason, he felt ashamed at that moment, ashamed of relying on his student status. He no longer had any interest in going into the hall and joining the assembly, and he started to walk away, a little ashamed. Leaning against the rail next to the cashier was a man of medium height, whose job was to stand there and make sure everything went smoothly, with no delays during the rush. He had been watching Albrecht the whole time—how he had indecisively joined the line and then suddenly jumped out of line. He laughed a big, wide laugh with his whole face, walked up to Albrecht, and casually offered him a free ticket. There it was in his hand: a free ticket. Albrecht was confused, but took it; it made him visibly uncomfortable to be faced with another decision. The man calmly stood next to him and waited to see what he would do. "No," Albrecht said—he suddenly felt the decision fully formed within him. "Thanks very much, but I can't go, I just realized at the last minute, when I got to the front, that I have something else planned tonight. When I walked by and saw so many people going in, I forgot about it and got in line. No, thank you, otherwise I would have bought my ticket in advance."

Fine, a polite refusal. The man grinned and returned to his post, watching the line. Albrecht was left alone. Bought it in advance, he had said—and he had felt very uneasy when this nonsense came out of his mouth: if he hadn't happened by he would never have known there was a meeting here tonight, so how could he have bought a ticket in advance? He left the restaurant and hurried home. He turned off into his street, and only when he saw how calm and empty it was did he realize how noisy and crowded the main streets had been. The children who played their games in the street, who made the only noise there was on this street, had long since gone to bed; the grown-ups were leaning out of their windows and looking up at the sky, or down at the street; whenever anyone walked by, they gazed up at the opposite wall, where the residents were leaning out of their windows just as contentedly, taking in the events of daily life. It was all so immutable, so constantly repeated, it would never change. The only place Albrecht felt comfortable was here, in the lonely calm of his street. He walked a few steps back and forth on the street and thought about his situation. He had been in the city awhile by this time, had thoroughly explored it, his days were full. He had school in the morning, then the rest of the day belonged to him. He gave lessons to earn the money he needed. Actually, he had imagined everything would be much more dramatic and extreme; the truth disappointed him a little. He had thought that he would have to seize life with both hands from the very beginning—he didn't want to be left with nothing in the days to come. He silently nurtured great hopes, dreams, and promises to himself. But here he was, wandering around lonely and empty-handed the whole time; everything was totally different from what he'd expected, he hadn't achieved a single thing. And gradually, as he wandered around, the realization came to him that nothing would be different in the future either. He had to resign himself to a long period of waiting: first he had to gain knowledge of the world, he always needed to know a lot about something first and only then tackle it, take action, and accomplish something. For now, there was nothing to do but look on, alertly, in silence, and note it down inside himself, so to speak. He thought back to his small hometown, the forests and all the places where he felt safe and secure, even when he was alone. Why in the world was he here? How had he ended up here, where he wasn't happy, and where life was starting to unfold in a powerful but at the same time almost indecent way? No, this was not for him, he would never be able to stay here long. But had he already forgotten how, such a short time ago, he had looked forward to coming here, adrift in the most exuberant daydreams? What had happened? What had made him change, where did this confusion come from? Hadn't he always felt *Easy, easy, no need to rush things*? And then something else too: Who in the history of the world had ever understood when they were young, really understood, that they too would someday grow old?

In any case, he soon changed his mind. Barely a week later, there was another large assembly in the same hall, and this time Albrecht saw the announcements in advance and bought a ticket. What he experienced that night was a magnificent march and a rousing speaker; the crowd listened attentively and were carried away by the speech, and showed their approval with cheers and applause throughout. He witnessed it all with a combination of personal detachment and objective recognition of the event's success. He saw and heard it all as though he were sitting in a theater, losing himself in the colorful artistic element, with a kind of self-satisfied pleasure, without denying to himself the humiliating recognition that underneath it all he shouldn't be there, he was a stranger somewhere he didn't belong.

After a while, when he went back home for the first time in several weeks, surprising news was awaiting him. It bowled him over at first: Fritz Fiedler was going to America! He had made his decision and was leaving in just three weeks.

Ever since Fritz had had his great disappointment in Hamburg and had come home with his belief in himself shaken, full of doubts he had never known before, he had been drifting around constantly, looking for something to do. His parents and brother-in-law tried to help him and remained hopeful that at some point they would manage to find Fritz an apprenticeship.

It wasn't easy, and Fritz himself never had any great illusions. He tirelessly looked around, went to offices, interviewed, followed recommendations, but it was no use: he couldn't surmount the obstacles standing in his way. He did not have a diploma in hand, a lack he now felt only too often, knowing that it was his own fault. Aside from that, he had been an apprentice without completing the apprenticeship either; it may not have been his fault, but still, the year was lost, he had to start over again. That was the only way anyone would be willing to take him on. Fritz would eventually have agreed to this condition, and accepted everything, if he hadn't felt a final doubt: Who could guarantee that his second apprenticeship wouldn't end up just like the first, with him out on the street before it was over? He woke up out of his lethargy, clenched his fists, and rebelled—his voice rang out loud and demanding, he didn't understand why there were so many hurdles he had to overcome.

If he had had to, he would have found something somewhere: a job in a small business, behind a counter, in cramped, narrow rooms, working and at the same time apprenticing in the business. But that wasn't what he wanted and he refused to do it. He prowled around the house, full of anger and unused strength—he would do it, he would prevail and not give up. He had to finally find some work to do, he could feel it more and more strongly the longer he spent at home. Everyone had things they needed to do—Father, Mother, Erich—only Fritz was stuck idly looking on. He had tried to make connections but had not succeeded. Time was not on his side, without his being fully aware of what a dangerous enemy he was facing. In the long run, Fritz couldn't keep up his brave defense; his resistance weakened, he grew tired, and he entered a phase like the one he had already lived through before he ran away: weeks of dull, sluggish inertia. It was no use. Here in Germany he couldn't get anywhere, there were no more options for him. And once he realized that, he had already come to his big decision. He would leave the country, for America, for somewhere. Good, if there were prospects anywhere on earth then it would be in America, he thought. Off to America! Everywhere else was a disaster. He told his parents, and then the real battle began. Why couldn't he stay here with them? They hadn't bothered him about anything, hadn't criticized him, not even the tiniest hint. But no one could dissuade him, he would do what he wanted, and if it was like before and he had to . . . His parents knew not to take any chances with Fritz in this regard, so they reluctantly gave their approval, they did not want to lose him. This way there was always the prospect of seeing him again, and besides, they would be able to stay in contact with him while he was abroad. Fritz plucked up his courage and eagerly made his preparations, he didn't want to lose a single day! Now he had a goal, a purpose, and new hope! His thoughts were already across the ocean. He said his farewells. Goodbye! Off to another country. He laughed: Who could be expected to keep riding a workhorse that was about to collapse? Not him, he was off to America. His mother took him to the ship.

·

Albrecht stayed in the big city, it gripped him and held him tight no matter how hard he struggled. He scurried around, and whenever he left the street where he lived and set foot on the main street, he always found himself caught up in the middle of rushing chaos. He soon picked up the habits of the city dwellers: running behind the streetcars, hurrying everywhere, eating while standing up, learning how to use his elbows in the middle of crowds of people. He grew rude and heartless and lost his sense of humor too, if indeed he had ever had one. Deep down, everything about the way people talked and lived their lives was exactly the way it was at home. The only difference here was that each individual was not the center of the world—he was submerged in the crowd and forced to confront much more directly people who were different from him. But he liked to think that back home, in his small town, there was more real life—that love, hate, friendship, and every other human relationship, no matter how banal and ordinary, was more relaxed and free, less stiff and constrained.

Before long he knew his way around the big streets as well as he did around the forests of his hometown, and the same out in the suburbs too, where the villas of the rich stood amid magnificent gardens. He strolled along the boulevards and looked at the expensive goods in the shops, saw the beautiful people carelessly dressed in their tasteful clothes as they sat in cafés and laughed and joked and bored one another. He eavesdropped on their conversations, got to know their cares and sorrows, and saw them again in concerts, theaters, everywhere, making mountains out of molehills and heedlessly ignoring what really mattered. He got to know his way around the parts of the city where the workers lived, where poverty crawled out of their rooms onto the streets, visible in even the smallest children. The poverty and misery dug its claws into him too, although only in the way that a painting or piece of music could grip him and move him. And then there were also the many people who lived their lives hidden away, heads down, buried under their problems, trapped in a hopeless battle with circumstances—the laborers and small shopkeepers, employers and employees, everyone who had a job that ground them down. They didn't create the social conditions, but they fell victim to those conditions. How they bore up under it all, with an ancient, angry pride twisted into outright lies. They lived here in large numbers, and they cried out too, presenting their suffering and asking for help. But their voices were not powerful enough—and, more important, not free of shame. Deep down they were ashamed of their plight, and always with an eye on the bliss that was denied to them. They had not yet understood that a change was taking place, proclaiming itself precisely through them. Where would it lead? They hadn't the slightest idea and only continued to torment themselves; whenever anything confronted one of them, he would laugh a humble laugh and act hopeful, then maybe go and shoot himself the next day, or stick his head in the oven. That's how it was in the big city. Meanwhile, Albrecht lived his life as a student and earned a little money with the work that presented itself. He was lucky; he had a good position, many people would have envied him for it: he tutored, and when he stayed late he was given dinner too. That helped. But he didn't like it, and he didn't want anyone to see through him and realize how things really stood with him. He submitted applications for financial aid, filed for welfare, and found it all not a little painful.

He was still indecisive—he still didn't realize that one day he too would have to come to certain decisions. He saw a lot, did his work, but refused to draw any conclusions from what he saw around him. It wasn't cowardice or fear that held him back; he could have covered up those feelings with words and disguised them. Maybe it was that he was too caught up in his own situation to see the rest of the world clearly, that as he became more and more deeply immersed in his own sphere, his work and his struggle were two giant walls that overshadowed everything else and gave him only limited access to experience. He didn't talk to other people very much; he was strangely preoccupied with his own thoughts. He was fully satisfied when he could analyze everything and break it down into its causes and contexts. Once that was done and everything was ordered and proven, neat and tidy, he was done with it and something new attracted his curiosity. Let other people worry about solving the problems and doing something constructive.

•

They had cut down the woods up on the hills outside the city and made a path, with a bench. The view stretched all the way to the meadows and the remaining forests on the main high road. Even chopping down the woods didn't bring in enough money for the city to make all the social welfare payments it needed to. The city borrowed money, built roads, improved streets and sewers; for a few months everything was taken care of, but then it had difficulty paying the interest on the loans, and the burden was heavier than before.

Herr Seldersen was untroubled, though. He had a stock of goods on his shelves, bought and paid for, and that was all it took. The mailman came twice a day, but his arrival was no longer cause for alarm and despair the way it had been. He and Mother went to bed at night, slept well, woke up in the middle of the night and drank a sip of water, and drifted back off into a peaceful slumber until it was light out. Then they got up, didn't have to worry about what the day might bring, and got to work calmly and dispassionately. Herr Seldersen sat in the shop, or stood in the doorway and looked out at the street—always the same picture. People came into his store, bought things, put sums on their accounts, told stories of their troubles, asked for special consideration; nobody had gotten any richer. Life took its course, monotonous and unvarying, with only occasional great events that overshadowed everything. Then they could feel a tense excitement in the air, even there in their small town, until that too turned out to be nothing.

One day not long afterward, Herr Wiesel dropped in.

"I've been standing in my store for three days and barely made anything," he said, visibly agitated. "Just think of the expense! And all to get a few pennies for the till." He had never experienced anything like it.

Herr Seldersen understood his agitation only too well. "It happens sometimes," he said; "why get so worked up about it?"

Herr Wiesel was an old businessman, his business on Eisenstrasse always did well, his stock was all paid for: why shouldn't he have to feel the tough times for a change too?

"I've never had anything like that happen to me," he repeated several times.

"It all depends what you're made of," Father said.

"I don't understand," Herr Wiesel shot back. "What you're made of? What does that mean?"

"I only mean that some people can survive it, standing in their shop for a long time making hardly anything; others can't. That's the difference."

"No one can survive these days," Herr Wiesel insisted. "That's what I say."

Herr Seldersen disagreed. This one will shut in six months, that one will stick it out for three years, it's a big difference. A lot can change, and improve, in that time.

Herr Wiesel couldn't deny that. "But we're all heading in the same direction, I don't think any of us have three years."

"And what about six months?" Father asked seriously.

Herr Wiesel said nothing. "You made a mistake, Herr Seldersen," he began gently. This was actually the real reason he had dropped by: he wanted to discuss things out in the open. "You made a big mistake when you settled your debts last year."

"You know about that?!" Father exclaimed.

"Of course I know; you thought no one would know?"

In truth, Herr Seldersen hadn't believed it would stay a secret, although he would have preferred it if it had. As was typical for him, he hadn't talked about it with anyone. But it couldn't stay secret forever; it eventually got around that Seldersen's shop wasn't doing so well. People shook their heads, they didn't want to believe it, and every time they walked past the shop they craned their necks to peer in but only saw the same thing they had seen there for years: Seldersen sitting behind the counter, making sales or doing some other kind of work, saying a friendly greeting to everyone who passed by and looked in. He looked old, that was true, but who among us doesn't bear the traces of time? He also looked a bit troubled and anxious; that fit with the rumors.

"What do you mean, made a mistake?" Father asked earnestly. "There was nothing else I could do. Should I have shut down?"

No, no, he didn't mean that, everyone was having trouble, the difficulties just had to be overcome, that's what made you a businessman, especially in tough times.

"So what was I supposed to do?" Herr Seldersen asked helplessly. He hadn't been able to think of anything; he thought he had explored every option. What did Herr Wiesel mean?

"Why did you do everything in secret, without talking it over first with me or someone else? We would have been happy to give you advice. But no one can come to you with help if you don't ask."

Herr Seldersen groaned at the accusation.

"If I were you," Herr Wiesel said thoughtfully, "I wouldn't have offered my creditors a settlement."

"No settlement? Then what?"

"They got their money back from you."

"Only half," Father replied. He told him the percentage.

"That's much too high—it's ridiculous, your creditors got a good deal there. You had to borrow the money, and now you're paying interest on it on top of everything."

"That's true, but what else could I . . . ?"

Then Herr Wiesel said: In Father's place he would have filed for bankruptcy. That's right, bankruptcy.

Herr Seldersen was stunned. "And then?"

"Then your creditors could decide whether they'd be happy with the percentage that came out, maybe a third of what you owed them, or else I'd come to an arrangement with them offering five percent more."

Father leaned against the counter, thunderstruck.

"You would have pulled it off, believe me, you would have pulled it off."

Father, after a while: "Who could think of doing something like that?" He couldn't betray his creditors like that, they were already losing enough money on him.

"Well, if that's how you feel," Herr Wiesel said. "Weren't you a good customer all the years you've been running this store? Didn't they get their money when times were good?"

"Yes, but . . ."

"In cases like this you have to look out for yourself, not for anyone else."

"That's right. And I did that for once, it wasn't pleasant, it was very unpleasant—when you've been somewhere twenty-five years, my wife, the children, all of it together, you understand, Herr Wiesel, I didn't want the situation to play out before everyone's eyes, and then . . . then I would have lost everyone's trust, and credit, that's the most important thing."

"Trust, right, but what about now?" Herr Wiesel said. "Aren't you having the same problem now?"

Yes, Father admitted, he certainly was facing problems. People were suspicious of him, they gave him credit but it wasn't enough, the shelves were still empty. At the beginning, he went around to his longtime suppliers and asked them not to leave him in the lurch, since he had just found his footing again and was trying to make a fresh start. It was hard enough to have to ask, but what else could he do? Eventually he was given a little credit, but they demanded that he pay even the slightest amount promptly. So he went looking for new contacts, where he could come across as being in better shape and get better credit. He spent a long time looking around, put in big orders, but in the end he gave in to his doubts and canceled half of what he had ordered.

Pause.

While they were standing there together, the cartload of timber came by. Every day, at the same time, between twelve and one, a horse-drawn cart passed through the street loaded with thick, heavy tree trunks that had been cut from the woods above town. The cart came down the high road, and since it was downhill all the way to the bottom, the driver always had to keep the brakes applied; the horses proceeded in a leisurely trot, no longer needing to pull a heavy load. The street had a sharp curve in front of the shop, where the driver would dismount, throw the reins onto the horses' steaming bodies, and run ahead to see if a car was coming in the other direction. Then they took the big curve—it was not always easy to make it, especially when there were long logs loaded on the cart. There was no room on the street for any other vehicles during the maneuver: the timber wagon took up all the space.

Herr Seldersen and Herr Wiesel were happy to watch the show—it was nice to look on at the driver's skillful performance. Not many loads of wood came past anymore. The forest, the beautiful forest, was getting more and more sparse.

"But it would have been better for you." Herr Wiesel came back to where they had started the conversation. "Now you have to pay the interest too."

"Yes, but don't you think that things are ever going to get better?"

Herr Wiesel shrugged. "Do you think they will?" he asked back.

Father said nothing. Did he really think they would?

"You know how many people are unemployed in America and England," Herr Wiesel went on. "Think about it: America and England, and they're the ones who won the war, you know?" And then, in a secretive, lowered voice, Herr Wiesel told Herr Seldersen the rumor that was going around: a huge company, with offices all over Germany, was in trouble—bad trouble, its stock price as low as it could go; the stockholders had to take loss after loss; the banks who stood behind the firm had to keep jumping in because they couldn't just let the company go under.

What a disaster, and it's taking everyone down with it. Even the bank's reserves will run out at some point.

Father said he had heard about it, and at first he couldn't believe it, but by now it was public knowledge.

"Yes," Herr Wiesel said, "this'll be a fun winter." Then he said goodbye, repeating his advice not to do things in such secrecy and isolation. They were all on the same side, they would all stick together and help one another out, definitely. And if Herr Seldersen ever needed any items, for instance if a customer asked for something he didn't happen to have in stock, he shouldn't hesitate to send around to Herr Wiesel. He'd be glad to help out if he had the item himself. He'd pass it along at cost, Seldersen could mark it up however he wanted.

"And then we'll split the profit," Father said.

No, no, Herr Wiesel wouldn't hear of it. If Herr Seldersen made the sale, he'd keep the profit.

Herr Seldersen was touched. Let me shake your hand, Herr Wiesel; now that's a true friend, always up front and ready to help. People could say whatever they wanted about him, how he acquired his money. . . . He didn't even want to split the profit! Your hand, Herr Wiesel!

.

Some nine months had gone by. Then, one Saturday when Albrecht was supposed to get the week's money for his tutoring as usual, his student told him that his mother had forgotten to give him the money. Forgotten—all right, everyone forgets sometimes. Albrecht didn't say a word; he wanted to be patient. They gave him a small sum at the beginning of the following week: a quarter of what he was owed. The week went by and his student had to keep putting him off to the following day even though it obviously made him uncomfortable. Albrecht kept waiting.

Finally, at one point he couldn't keep it to himself: "But you know this is what I live on!"

Of course the student knew, but why talk to him? "Talk to my mother," he said. Albrecht rarely saw her. He stayed in his job, sacrificed his time, was given dinner whenever he stayed late, but only received his money piece by piece. He couldn't understand why they weren't paying him—they had two cars, a large radio; they lacked none of the outward trappings of success and respectability. They did not have much time for their children—the parents were always busy, invited out, staying late in the city, or receiving visitors themselves. When Albrecht saw them, he didn't dare talk to them. Finally, though, his student's father brought the conversation around to the topic himself.

"Be patient," he said carelessly, "I'm having difficulties at the moment." As though that were all it was.

Albrecht bowed and said that he lived on this money; he had enough for the moment, he had saved up a little, but within a week at the most he needed to know what the situation was.

"I'll see what I can do," the man answered calmly. "It's beyond my control." He meant his own difficulties; next to those, Albrecht's concerns certainly seemed minor, but in any case he couldn't alleviate them, he didn't have any money to give him. He had suffered major losses, there had been a couple of very bad days on the stock market; he had a big apartment and two cars but didn't own anything else anymore, he had long since mortgaged or signed over everything—now he couldn't even pay his son's tutor.

Albrecht realized that his job here was drawing to a close. He would have to find some other way to make money that would be more certain. He was tired of giving lessons anyway. He'd been doing it for nine months—not a terrible experience by any means, he was honest enough to admit that it was bearable, even almost pleasant, for a few months. And even if he often enough felt embarrassed and self-critical when he took his meals there, that was probably mostly due to his own sensitivity, his way of observing any situation from every angle and clearly labeling to himself the position he occupied in it. So he started looking around: he had options; he could apply to work at the post office, beat rugs, wash cars, all sorts of things. In the end, he fell back on something he had been doing for years just for pleasure, never thinking that it would one day take on a whole new meaning: his music. He had played the violin for years, with ardent enthusiasm and average ability, but that was enough for him, although even here he sometimes tried to achieve a bit more with it. He had spent fewer and fewer such hours of deepest happiness and complete devotion since moving to the big city. But in looking for a new job, he thought back to those times, and more: he remembered a conversation he'd had recently with a schoolmate. He had often seen him carrying around a long black case, which he guessed held an instrument, a saxophone or something along those lines. His guess was confirmed before long—the student played music and managed to make a living at it: a relatively good one too, better than a lot of people. On the other hand, he always looked tired and pale and short of sleep.

Albrecht asked his advice straight-out. He was in a band almost entirely made up of students, he said, and he invited Albrecht to a rehearsal and told him to bring his violin. When Albrecht arrived, they gave him a friendly greeting and told him to join right in, but Albrecht asked politely if he could just listen the first time; he knew that the music they played there was different and new for him, and he wanted to get familiar with its rhythm, its soul. They said that was fine and he sat down in a corner and listened eagerly. Oh, what he discovered that day! The musicians were mostly young—students, focused on the task at hand but having a good time. Only the trombone player, the last to arrive, had a miserable-looking face, and apparently had trouble holding his instrument and keeping up with the rest. His sad face! The others praised him: he hadn't been playing the trombone for long, they had convinced him, lured him, practically made him take it up, since that was the instrument they were missing and they couldn't find anyone who could play it. There were at least two people playing every other instrument, all except the trombone. So this member of the group was patiently learning the trombone, to help out—trying hard until his lips swelled red and puffy, so that anyone who saw him on the street wondered what had happened to him. He kept at it, though, and his pimply, swollen face twisted in pain every time he played. Hence the miserable expression. Only later did Albrecht find out the underlying reason for his sadness: the trombonist was in his second-to-last semester already and would soon have to figure out what to do next. . . . And he learned the trombone, since he needed the money and hoped that he would have a marketable skill at the end. He earned money, all right, but wasn't able to concentrate on what was important: his studies. Although he needed to work and prepare for his exams, he spent his time practicing instead—since he had to practice constantly or he wouldn't earn anything. He played his music and made ends meet, for himself plus the forty marks he sent home to his mother every month. Was that actually being a student? No, and his sad face as he blew the trombone was the best possible indication of that fact.

The other musicians were happier, better suited to their respective instruments and in high spirits. The pianists—there were two grand pianos in the room—were locked in a bitter struggle over who could play the most notes; the musician making the most noise was, without question, the drummer, sitting upright on his stool and pounding the bass drum, playing drumrolls, tinkling the chimes, and smashing the cymbals, with lots of inimitable tricks and effects thrown in. And he kept the beat too; the band's fate was in his hands. Standing in front, like a dancer, the conductor did his part: seducing the saxophones, subduing the brass, encouraging the banjos, jumping up in the air unexpectedly at a certain point and landing with a powerful stomp on the floor. All the while, everyone in the orchestra was keeping time by loudly tapping his right foot, so that the people renting the apartment downstairs sent their maid up to tell them the chandelier was about to fall out of the ceiling. Albrecht thought the rehearsal was a lot of fun and looked forward to many pleasurable hours in his new side job.

Then he met Hermann. Hermann was a nineteen-year-old music student, and he told Albrecht about the first time he had played a dance number for his piano teacher. The old man felt it to be his duty, felt obliged by his conscience, to write to Hermann's father and threateningly demand that he put a stop to this damaging behavior. Hermann was simply throwing away the musical education that he, the teacher, had taken such pains to inculcate in him. Hermann started a band with Albrecht and three other students and they played together every Sunday, year-round, in a restaurant out on the edge of the city: dances in a dark, smoky hall. Before long he was engaged to play everywhere—at balls, weddings, parties, public dances, for sport clubs and dancing clubs and savings clubs—in smoke-filled rooms with curtained windows and dim light or bright, well-lit halls. He went everywhere. He sat on his chair and played while other people danced and had fun. Early the next morning, they all went home tired, but with different kinds of tiredness: the other people because they had spent a happy, enjoyable night, and Albrecht and his bandmates because they had worked—it *was* a job—and earned some money. Sometimes, in the middle of playing, when he looked at the people on the dance floor, he had a sudden, desperate urge to get up and dance and enjoy himself with them. But that wasn't his role. He stayed put and played: that's what he was getting paid for, after all. The others could dance and have fun. It always lasted all night and then he would fall into bed exhausted the next morning.

He played in cafés, monthlong engagements or longer; sometimes he traveled out of town for a few days; and all the while he was still a student, which meant in his case that what he actually wanted to do was study.

He met lots of young people who were earning their money like he was. When they got together, the first thing they brought up was always exams: everyone asked about them, and Albrecht very quickly realized why. They were hanging over everyone's heads, they were merciless, coming closer and closer every day. The fact was, the students all wanted to pass their exams, even if they meanwhile had to play the trombone or the saxophone or what have you and neglect their studies. But what did that even mean: their studies? What were their prospects afterward? So they played music and lived on the money they made and supported their parents too. Weeks and months went by; Albrecht's health suffered, but he was making money, he was a student—who knew what tomorrow would bring? He sometimes convinced himself that he had already found a career. He knew a lot of people who dropped out of school, including the trombonist he had noticed that first day because of his sad face. They were left behind, they decided on their own not to take their exams. Maybe it was for the best. But no one knew what would happen next.

•

At the end of every month, Frau Seldersen sat down with the books where all the customers' debts were recorded and copied out long statements to send to the people who were overdue on their payments. But that wasn't enough—what was much more important, she felt, were the accompanying notes she wrote. They had big bills to pay too, she admitted openly, and then she sharply and ruthlessly warned the customers to pay up—or warned them less drastically, she knew her audience. The shopgirl brought the letters around to the customers' apartments.

A few days passed before the customers started appearing in the shop. They had received a warning, that was fine, they understood, but it wasn't on purpose, they weren't staying away intentionally. They brought some money with them—not much—and gave roundabout apologies for not having more in hand; they promised to come back soon and were allowed to leave on good terms. They wanted to be able to get clothes there the next time they came back.

But not all the people she wrote letters to came in, not by a long shot. A significant number never appeared. They lived outside of town, or in the housing developments or the tenements, and didn't give a damn about any warnings. Why should they make the big trek into town just to stand helplessly in the store, since they didn't have any money to bring? It was better just to stay away.

Frau Seldersen accused Father of being much too nice, just

giving anyone who walked in credit without checking up on them more closely. . . . Checking up on them! He laughed. Did she want him to conduct an investigation on them, when he already knew what the results would be anyway? And if he didn't give them anything, they would just go somewhere else and get what they needed. Period.

"But you go too far, it's too much, and then later you're too accommodating too. You need to be firmer with them."

Father laughed again. "What, I should repossess their things?" he asked lightly.

"Yes," Mother answered in a decisive voice.

"Are you serious? They don't have anything to repossess; I might as well save myself the expense."

But Frau Seldersen didn't let up and eventually convinced him to try it, at least once, to see what happened.

So Herr Seldersen wrote to the bailiff and sent him the addresses of many of his customers, with exact tallies of their debts, just to see what happened. After a while, he got a letter back, saying that there was no point, absolutely none, the bailiff had made sure. Only in one case had he discovered anything to impound: a sewing machine. And he asked for further instructions. A sewing machine!

The woman who owned it came into the store and without beating around the bush started in with what she had to say. She was not angry or upset, not in the least, on the contrary she exuded an eerie calm that made Herr Seldersen uneasy, almost afraid.

"So, my sewing machine," she said with a little smile. "That old thing." She told him how she had inherited it, how it sat in her kitchen and when she was done with her work—she was a cleaning lady, and delivered newspapers, but it still wasn't enough, she had a lot of mouths to feed, including her husband's— she would sit down and sew clothes for her own children, and for the neighbors' and friends' children. Sometimes she stayed up all night, but it brought in a little extra money.

"If you take my sewing machine," she went on, quite slowly,

and almost as though it didn't matter to her at all, "you'll have less of a chance of getting your money from me than before, you'll be taking away my income." Didn't he see that? What good would an old sewing machine do him, anyway? The couple of marks, at most, that he could sell it for . . . ?

"And my money? Your debts?" Herr Seldersen asked. "What about that?"

"You'll get your money," the woman promised, "when it's your turn."

"My turn," he repeated.

Surely he didn't think that he was the only one who gave her credit? A person needed more to live on than what Herr Seldersen gave her!

Hmm. True.

But he did not want to give in so easily—he had decided to act merciless and ruthless, for once, the way everyone treated him. It was the principle of it: people needed to realize that he was no longer willing to be put off by their promises and assurances.

But the woman kept fighting for her sewing machine too. When she saw that he wasn't giving in, she said, as calmly as before (but Herr Seldersen had a good ear, he could pick up on subtleties): "Go ahead and take it. I'll make sure everyone hears about it."

Then nothing. She waited. What would Herr Seldersen do?

What could he do? Did he really want the woman to tell everyone she knew that he was impounding things from people's apartments now? And who would she tell? Seldersen knew exactly who she'd tell: these friends of hers were his customers. No, he couldn't seriously consider it, and what would he do with an old sewing machine? He wrote to the bailiff that same day, telling him not to repossess it, and sighed with relief.

Then he stood in his store, with his wife restlessly pacing back and forth. She had listened to the whole conversation and she couldn't think of anything else he could have done either.

"I'm not going to take things out of anyone's apartment," he said solemnly.

Frau Seldersen said nothing.

"They're my customers," he went on. He was proud to have them.

Frau Seldersen again said nothing. She had been figuring out all too much recently about who came into their store and who didn't. Frau Lanz, from town, the wife of a high official, a good customer for years, and Frau Uhlfink, who owned a small farm down by the river—they didn't come in anymore, they shopped at Herr Dalke's, and a lot of others like them. Frau Seldersen could list them all. They had various reasons for staying away; each was involved in different circumstances and intertwined in different ways with the general course of events that the Seldersens were bound up with too. It was a sign, though. And the customers who took their place were in bad shape. One sewing machine among the lot as collateral, and you couldn't even claim it! Those were their customers now.

.

Albrecht continued to follow his path, although he only vaguely knew what it was and could not foresee where it might be leading him. It was a lonely, painful path, but he kept the pain inside him as he followed it—it didn't seem right for him to expect a harmonious whole when he hadn't fully committed himself either. He kept himself under control—he found it disgusting the way so many other people let themselves go. He allowed himself no half measures, especially since he was forced in the course of his daily life into so many makeshift arrangements. He often found himself sitting on the edge of his bed in his bare room and wondering what it would be like if he was living farther south, in a university town, like so many people his age, wrapped up in tender memories of his small hometown, in groups of people he would be connected to with a firm, solid bond of friendship. But there was no point thinking about it—he had to stay here, where he could earn some money; he had to spend his nights flogging himself for other people's pleasure. He had to stick to his post, stick it out . . . even if his studies went to hell in the process. He loved precision in everything he did—for him it was linked to an inexpressible idea of health and strength. And yet he could not attain it, since he was forced to live a chaotic and stressful life, his concentration scattered among thousands of things at the same time. What he still remembered from school, what he admired and strove to attain in himself, was the classical ideal: a healthy mind in a healthy body, the beauty of strength, the dignity of virtue. His longing for this ideal drove him to harden his body with running and sports, make it strong and hardy. That was as much a part of his life as playing the violin and reading books.

But then came weeks when all sorts of more urgent things made him neglect his body altogether, not letting him recover. The stench of smoky, stuffy dance rooms was lodged in his clothes, and he felt when he wore them like he was in prison, miserable and abandoned. Then he would open the drawer and take out his diploma, with the athletic prizes he had won printed on it, and his eyes would rest on it for a long time, and he would think back with melancholy longing on the years when he had been able to spend time on such things, when he had not had any idea of what it meant to be forced to act and live in the real world.

He didn't rebel, didn't kick and scream, or even raise his voice—that wasn't his way. He preferred to keep quiet, observe, endure, rather than adding his own confusion and dissatisfaction to that of everyone around him. Even as a boy in school, he had internalized the notion—maybe originally born from exaggerated and presumptuous ideas about himself—that he was here on this earth to create order, to alleviate unease, to bring clarity to people's chaotic, desperate lives. Yes, he even went so far as to decide—and he later had to laugh at himself for it—that it was his destiny to play for others' dances but never to take part in such pleasures and dance for himself.

And how did he feel about the age he was living in, and the events taking place all around him, which he could see in more and more different forms, ever more clearly? He didn't walk around with his eyes closed, and his gaze was very analytical too: he saw right through external events to their causes, their motive forces, and saw the delicate cracks spreading and branching out behind the glittering, seemingly pristine facades that were rotten underneath. His heart went out to the oppressed and persecuted—but at the same time he didn't take sides, he held himself back, almost as though he was floating high above everything, full of pride and a sense of his own worth. Since no one forced him to decide, he could continue to avoid taking a position, using as an excuse the fact that he didn't have much time, he had more important things to do. The fool. He had not yet learned from life that a fully satisfactory content always brings with it an appropriate form, which matches it perfectly, leaving nothing left over.

And there was something else too, a mysterious, dangerous art that he had devoted himself to for a year and a half at university already, one that never stopped yielding knowledge, along with an annihilating sorrow: the art (for only in the hands of an artist did it show its true face) of exploring the underlying basis of things, fusing their bodily, psychological, physical, and spiritual qualities in an unbelievably godlike fashion so that any human utterance or action, any event at all, could be seen to have developed from this unified inner source. He was overcome with the desire to look behind the curtain, uncover the great mysteries, and present them to the world naked and unashamed. With this knowledge, he gained great power over other people. But this same knowledge was also what embroiled him in so many doubts and kept him from simply emerging into a happy, healthy lust for life. He was disillusioned, plagued by an excess of knowledge, no question about it—that was the danger that threatened him. Would he see the threat and avoid it? He used to stand in front of the mirror, stare into his own face, and look for traces of age and experience there, but he never found any—nothing had changed, he was still waiting, still at the starting blocks, fundamentally lonely, unhappy, and full of longing. He felt excluded and neglected, disconnected, sometimes even that he didn't belong in the time in which he lived. And then he would feel a wish to be with other people, so strong that he sprang up and went out to where he knew there would always be a big crowd.

One afternoon he ended up in a part of the city that had been seething with unrest for a long time. A lot of things went on in the streets there. When Albrecht arrived, everything was in full swing. It was as if everyone had gone crazy . . . they were standing on the corners, howling and screaming, and every time a police car drove by, with teams of policemen on the running boards, clinging like burrs to the car—holding on with one arm, ready to jump down at once when the order came—the screams only got louder, echoing from one side of the street to the other. Meanwhile, all the ordinary street traffic went on—pedestrians who had nothing to do with the protests, cars driving, horses drawing carts; only the streetcar stops were moved elsewhere and the bicyclists had to dismount. The street had been cleared ten times already, with the police rushing in at full speed, swinging billy clubs in their hands, helmets strapped on tight, first the captain, then his whole squad. They would run down the street and it looked almost fun, running like that in their leather spats, wading like storks, driving people in front of them, beating whoever they could reach—children, women, old men. People stood on front steps or in doorways, lobbies, and basement entrances, frightened and laughing and furious, and they waited until the storm outside had blown over, or moved off to another street, then they started up again, coming out of wherever they'd been hiding, standing back on the streets and the street corners, with cars driving by until the police got another order. It's like in school, Albrecht thought: when the teacher is standing at the front of the class, the back rows make noise, and if he goes to the back of the room, it starts up in the front. Mounted police with guns stood waiting on the square nearby—only in case of emergency. A short man in puttees, wool jacket, and peaked cap walked up the street full of pedestrians. He cupped his mouth and cried out in a monstrously loud voice, and ended what he was saying with a cheer; no one could hear what he'd said in between, but everyone enthusiastically cheered with him. The police blocked off the street on both sides and drove the people indoors. Their guns stayed holstered. Before long, everything was calm. People were standing around together on the streets like before. Then a young fellow broke free from one group, laughed, and walked slowly across the street in a leisurely zigzag with his hands in his pockets. A policeman was standing on the corner—young, still red and out of breath from running, tugging his belt into place with both hands. The fellow headed straight toward him, everyone could see it all clearly since they were on the corner where both streets met at right angles. He quickly touched his cap and asked the policeman a question. His comrades on the street corners elbowed one another and laughed, they had to hold their sides they were laughing so hard. It was too loud to hear what they were saying to one another; the fellow was asking the policeman something, maybe if he happened to know the time or how to get to such-and-such street from here—which was right around the corner—or if he by any chance had a light for a cigarette. The policeman looked at him, grabbed him, and shoved him onto the sidewalk. This wasn't the time for jokes and games. The fellow pointed down at his jacket and said—you still couldn't hear a word, but it was clear enough—that he was only asking a simple question. To which the policeman said (more or less): Was he trying to make fun of him? And he beat him over the shoulders with his billy club. Now the fellow wasn't laughing. He hadn't pictured it turning out quite like this. He stood there, dazed, and a bunch of other policemen came back from one of their expeditions—excited, out of breath—and gathered there on the corner. The first two had heard the last words of the conversation and they started beating the fellow on the head and shoulders and back with their clubs. It all happened very fast. The man was on the street next to the curb, not saying a word anymore. The fourth policeman hit him on the head with his club, and the fifth hit him from behind in the back of his knees. He was still standing upright but swaying badly now. Then the sixth hit him on the head with the shaft of his club. The fellows on the other street corners had long since stopped grinning. The seventh kicked him in the backside, and the eighth knocked him over like a feather. Some first-aid volunteers came and dragged him away. The street was cleared, the hunt went on in the next street over, you couldn't see anything anymore, you could only hear shouts, orders, and innumerable gunshots. Windows were hurriedly slammed shut. The medical volunteers ran toward the sounds as though possessed.

Suddenly the street was blocked off, with no way out in any direction. The people there were all arrested, including Albrecht: loaded into vans and sent downtown to headquarters. There were crowds there already, greeting the newcomers with cries of solidarity. Women, children, men, all shouting and cursing as loud as they could until they were called in for questioning. Albrecht sat off to one side on a bench and waited until it was his turn. An older sergeant took down his information. When he heard the word "student," he stopped and looked questioningly at Albrecht.

"What were you looking for in that district, young man?" he asked. "According to your own information, you live on the opposite side of town."

Albrecht thought carefully. "I wasn't looking for anything," he said slowly, "I just went there."

"I see," the sergeant answered. He stood up. "You just went

there out of curiosity, even though you knew that there was unrest there and it could end up in bloodshed."

Albrecht, confused: "Yes, but why were you shooting?"

The sergeant stayed calm and serious: "And who was shooting down at the streets from apartments and rooftops? Do you
think we like to shoot people dead just for fun? You seem damned
stupid, young man."

Albrecht said nothing. Soon he was allowed to leave, with a
warning and orders not to take part in any demonstrations.

On the way home he thought over the questioning again and
felt that he had acted craven and cowardly. Now, after the fact, a
lot of answers that he could have given came to mind: I am
always on the lookout wherever people are protesting out of
hunger, for work and bread! That one struck him as especially
good. What would the officer have said then? He didn't like to
shoot at his own countrymen, but people were falling under his
gunshots, so the whole thing was a mistake. That seemed like
the best explanation to Albrecht: it was all a big mistake. But he
had seen how people, simply because things were going badly
and the external structure of their lives was shaken, could bring
themselves to commit incredible acts, even risking their lives.
They wanted to change the world and the social conditions ar-
rayed against them. This seemed so monstrous to him that he
shuddered at the thought of his own inner failings, which apparently prevented him from actively taking sides himself. It made
him aware of his solitude, his self-willed isolation. He continued
to value it, he was persistent and lived off what he had gathered
and saved up in years past, but the bloom was off the rose, the
picture's colors were more and more washed-out, less and less
worthwhile. It was no longer clear to Albrecht if he was still willing to vouch for these ideals and devote his young life to them.
He remembered the words that he carried deep inside him ever
since his schoolboy days, about the life of the mind and how
love for the spirit alone makes it possible to act in the world. He
remembered, and powerful regret rose up within him, when he

compared those words to what he had seen today. When he thought about his own life, how he slaved and struggled and wasted his energy on nothing but things that he himself would describe as external, practical, and economic in the dismissive sense of the word, he hardly knew what was right anymore, what had a real claim on him and what didn't—or maybe, on the other hand, a contradiction was being artificially blown out of proportion here that didn't actually exist in the world.

But there was one question he really wished he had asked the police sergeant, just one: Did he think that the people he had to attack were throwing stones off the roof and firing shots out of the windows because *they* enjoyed it, because they liked throwing things and shooting at people down below? Or didn't he think that they too were driven by a need to act, since only in that way, by defending themselves, could they try to survive? And not just defending themselves, but striking back against what threatened to take them down with it when it collapsed. And still more: that, simultaneously with their striking back, they were trying to make, to build, something new in place of the old, something corresponding to their own lives, where they would be allowed to live without struggle, compulsion, and humiliation. If they got tired or stepped out of the rat race for a single second, their lives were over, they could never catch up. They couldn't afford to put their hands in their laps and be tired.

.

After only a few months, Father followed Herr Wiesel's advice, went to see him one afternoon, and took him into his confidence. A while back, he had paid a debt with a bill of exchange. "I couldn't help it," he said as an excuse—he hadn't taken the step lightly, it was the first time in his life he had had to resort to a bill of exchange, and for now it was fine, the creditor accepted it and Herr Seldersen paid it off by the agreed date. So he started to give out more of them without thinking twice.

Herr Wiesel listened to his explanation calmly. "Be careful," he warned him, "I know that everyone's doing it nowadays but I've always avoided it."

"Well, you've never been in a situation when you had to," Father blurted out. "But there was nothing else I could do, I'm usually very cautious, you know that."

Herr Wiesel did know that. If Herr Seldersen was paying with a bill of exchange, that was a significant sign of the times— not just foolishness or laziness, a sign!

Eventually Father burst out with what he wanted to say, and asked Herr Wiesel to loan him a small sum of money that very day, since he didn't have quite enough money on hand to pay off two bills of exchange that were due the next day. He would bring in some more money today, but that wouldn't be enough and he didn't want to return the bills of exchange unpaid.

"But you have three days before the notice reaches you." Herr Seldersen couldn't be in as desperate a hurry as he was making himself out to be.

Yes, he was, the three days had already passed.

Pause.

"That's different," Herr Wiesel said, and he gave Father the money. He could pay it back when he could, no hurry, don't worry about it.

Herr Seldersen was touched, and thanked him, and asked what he wanted as interest, but the other man seemed not to have heard the question.

Then he went home, not knowing whether to be grateful for Herr Wiesel's ready help or hang his head in shame over his own precarious situation, which had made him put Herr Wiesel's promise to the test. There was actually no reason to be worried or discouraged. It had been more than a year since he had made the settlement and paid off a large part of his debts at once. For the time being, he had been relieved of a great burden, even if Herr Wiesel had tried to say after the fact that the settlement had been a mistake and had suggested a seemingly better plan— that didn't change the fact that more than a year had gone by, during which Herr Seldersen had not had to pay much attention to the great sorrows and struggles getting more and more severe day by day all around him. He was practically living on an island, with the tempest raging all around him, thunder and lightning everywhere, but cool and dry and cheerful where he was. He stood downstairs in his shop; people came in and told him their troubles, with endless complaints about their poverty. He listened patiently, and while earlier he would have felt an underlying fellowship with them, never expressed in words, now he didn't really care; he also gave out bills of exchange and had to borrow money from Herr Wiesel to meet them and avoid any unpleasantness. His old way of taking care of business affairs had recently grown a bit sloppy, careless, even devious. He never strayed from the firm bounds of the law even now, but compared to before he did everything less painstakingly—more sloppily, that was the only word for it—like someone gradually losing track of what was going on.

Frau Fiedler came by every now and then too, always with news of her Fritz. "He is in New York," she said, meaning that she didn't know exactly where he was at the moment, but he had recently been in New York. "He met another German and they wanted to go west together, the other man owns a farm and that means good prospects for Fritz to work and earn money. He's already sent back half the money that we gave him to take with him," she said, full of pride. It sounded extremely implausible—she must have invented the story on the spot, to convince the Seldersens of how well Fritz was doing. They were happy, though, and Frau Seldersen said: "Frau Fiedler, I very much hope that your Fritz finally finds a way to settle down. What cares and sorrows he's given you!"

"Yes," she replied, and thought back over the past. "It was hard with him. But now I tell myself that maybe it's a good thing he went to America. Just look at the boys who are graduating these days."

While they stood there talking, Nikolaus the policeman

walked by outside. Suddenly he stopped, peeked into the store, probably to see if Father was alone, then decided to walk in and whispered a few words in his ear. When he closed up shop tonight, he should not forget to roll down the grate over the windows, he said. "Why?" Herr Seldersen asked in surprise. "What's happening tonight?"

"A rally," Nikolaus said in a secretive voice. "The speaker is coming from out of town, and marching from the station in a big procession. We need to be prepared; who knows if it'll go peacefully or not."

Herr Seldersen laughed. "You really think there'll be trouble?"

Nikolaus nodded slowly and deliberately. "Anything is possible; in any case we need to be armed and ready."

That sounded almost menacing. Father didn't believe it, but thanked the policeman for the advice. He'd certainly roll down the grate.

He went back to the two women and told them about his conversation with the policeman, adding what he'd thought of it. Frau Fiedler was nervous anyway, and said she wanted to hurry home and get everything prepared. Herr Seldersen tried to calm her down, but then Frau Seldersen suddenly started saying that she was scared too, you never knew how close danger might be. She always talked about danger. There's unrest in Berlin too, I only hope Albrecht stays careful. Anneliese is a smart one and stays out of harm's way on her own.

When the Seldersens were alone again, Father asked Mother why she had suddenly started acting so frightened. She said what she was afraid of, and Father could refute all her reasons but he couldn't take away her fear with mere words.

"The only reason to be afraid," he finally said, "is if you have something to lose."

She couldn't deny that, but when he went on to explain why that meant she had nothing to be afraid of, she got angry at him. He was wrong, it was sinful. . . . She didn't have anything, or much of anything, left to lose? She was truly outraged, he always put everything in the worst possible light and never missed a chance to shock other people. Later, she thought that maybe he was right about what Nikolaus had said, he must have his reasons and know what he's saying. Herr Seldersen thought about little Kipfer. He had shown up at the store several times recently, but never had much time to talk with Herr Seldersen.

"There's too much to do," he would say self-importantly. His activities kept him constantly busy. He went around organizing, putting together rallies, only rarely speaking himself. He had to watch out for his health and loud speaking put a strain on his sick lungs. Whenever he shook hands with Herr Seldersen, he gave a mischievous little laugh. He never asked: How are you? How is it going?

He knew, and that was enough.

Hoboes, tramps, bums, fallen women, old men, and other down-and-outs came to town on all the roads, walked around, went into the shops, knocked on doors, were embarrassed—and they came into Seldersen's shop too. Mornings, afternoons, creeping around eerily quietly at night, and people gave them something . . . so that they'd go away. Not out of pity, people had long since learned not to feel that. The beggars carefully opened the doors, stayed standing right outside, mumbled their speech—everyone had his or her own, yet they all meant the same thing—and people gave them something without anyone really listening to what they were saying. They were all types of people: the eternally forgotten, the ones who never found their place in the world, the ones who went off the rails, who never got where they were going, blameless, persecuted, betrayed, and damned. They went begging throughout the whole country.

A man walked into the store and Herr Seldersen looked at him and went to the register for a coin. But the man came closer. He was wearing worn-out black pants and a discolored brown jacket, no collar, no tie, a cap on his head—he looked pretty good for a hobo. Herr Seldersen took a few steps back, and then the man took off his cap and said, loud and clear, "Good day, Herr Seldersen." Father walked in a semicircle around him, looking closely at the man.

"So, you don't recognize me anymore?"

"Yes, yes," Herr Seldersen hurried to say, squinting and thinking hard. But at the moment . . . he smiled . . . "You're Herr . . ."

"Wurmbach," the man said with a bow.

Yes, right, Herr Wurmbach. Herr Seldersen remembered now. But where did he know him from?

"I used to work for Herr Dalke," Wurmbach said. "Salesman in the men's department . . ."

"You used to?" Herr Seldersen interrupted him in surprise.

"I'm unemployed at the moment, he let me go—it wasn't my fault, he said it was because business wasn't good. . . ."

"So, his business is that bad?" Herr Seldersen pressed him. That was all he could think of at the moment.

"It's slowing down," Wurmbach said, "the same as everywhere. I'm not the only one who's been laid off. When business isn't as good as it used to be, it's the salesmen, the employees, who are the first to go. Herr Dalke brought me here from Silesia six months ago, he promised me a good job, I assumed that meant long-term. I brought my family, and now here I am."

By that point, Herr Seldersen had had a chance to look closely at Herr Wurmbach from all sides. He hadn't even recognized him at first! Clothes really can change a person! Of course he knew him, he had seen him walking into Herr Dalke's store every day for six months, clean and well dressed. Now, in this outfit, he looked badly down-and-out—and he had been out of work only two weeks, but was worried about his future. At first glance Herr Seldersen had taken him for one of the better sorts of beggar! He was wrong, of course, Herr Wurmbach had come into the store as a customer. He bought things left and right: buttons, needles, rubber bands, thread for sewing and darning, it added up to quite a tidy sum. He had started out on a little business himself and went around to friends and acquaintances, strangers too, to try his luck selling this and that. He couldn't sit around all day, so he came up with this idea and did a little business, at least it would bring in something to the household.

He came by often and bought more, whenever he sold what he'd bought the last time. He didn't make much of a profit. And he was trying to feed his wife and a child.

"If only I had a bicycle," he said to Herr Seldersen one time.

"A bicycle?"

Yes, then he could ride out to the country, to all the villages. He could cover a lot of ground in a day, the villages were all close together; he thought he could earn a lot more that way.

Herr Seldersen approved.

"But not only that," Wurmbach said, taking a deep breath: "I'd also need a bigger selection. . . . But I'll discuss that with you later, Herr Seldersen."

After three days he was back, wheeling a bicycle. And he started right in on an offer he had for Herr Seldersen. Father could give him goods from his store and then he, Wurmbach, would ride around the country and sell them. It wouldn't have to be just buttons and shoelaces, he'd be able to sell all sorts of other things, Seldersen should just try and then see what happened. It wasn't entirely clear to Seldersen how Wurmbach was imagining their relationship—whether he saw himself as an employee, or as someone running his own business, only with Herr Seldersen's stock—but clarification was not long in coming, Wurmbach had thought it all out. "You give me the items," he said, "I'll sell them on the road, and then every evening when I get back I'll tally it up with you and you'll get a percentage of the total amount I've made that day."

Hmm. Father thought it seemed like a possibility.

But then Wurmbach said something about travel costs that he'd need reimbursed, and Seldersen said a vigorous no. Travel expenses? That was too much, he couldn't cover that; the sales wouldn't bring in enough to make it worthwhile; he'd rather forget the whole thing.

Wurmbach looked downcast. . . . "Not even the expenses!" he said, demoralized. "Then it's not worth it for me either." He laid out his calculations of how much he could sell per day, and the upper limit of how much money he might bring in.

It wasn't much; Herr Seldersen could cover the travel costs after all. Wurmbach was gone all day on his bicycle, covering great distances, and came back in the evening, tired and dusty, to settle up with Herr Seldersen and go home with his share in his pocket. Herr Seldersen could see that Wurmbach wasn't making much; he was trying hard but it wasn't easy.

It went well enough for a while, and they got along. Wurmbach no longer showed up every night to settle up; sometimes he was too tired or got back too late, so he would come by the next day. Eventually, he started coming by only twice a week and settling up for all the days put together. Then he'd take some more things to sell. He seemed to have made his peace with his new line of work; he stayed living where he was, apparently he didn't have any better prospects anywhere else, and he kept at his business, which he'd started only as a fallback plan, he had certainly never seen it as anything but a temporary stopgap. . . .

But eventually Herr Seldersen started to get the impression that not everything was entirely aboveboard. Wurmbach showed up once looking sad and said that he hadn't sold anything, there was nothing to settle up. But since he was there he might as well take some more things to sell. Herr Seldersen handed them over without a second thought; he didn't want to leave him in the lurch. At the same time, he advised him only to sell for cash, not on credit, and Wurmbach answered that he knew perfectly well what he was doing, he wasn't a beginner after all, it was just that business was bad, he said with a groan.

Then, the next time Wurmbach settled up, Seldersen couldn't exactly tell how much Wurmbach had actually received from him and how much he had sold. The list Wurmbach showed him could have been entirely correct, or it could just as easily be concealing something, there was no way to tell exactly. Wurmbach brought the money, took out the sum meant for him, and asked for new items, but this time Herr Seldersen hesitated. First he wanted a precise statement, and told Wurmbach to bring one tomorrow. Wurmbach went home empty-handed. Herr Seldersen discussed matters with his wife, who wanted him to wash his hands of the whole thing, Wurmbach had never made much money for them and now the situation was starting to get murky. If he was trying to pull a fast one—well, he was a poor devil; even at the beginning Seldersen should have known that no one could make ends meet with what he was earning from their deal together. He was trying to look out for himself, and if it didn't work to do it honestly, well, he'd have to try some other way. But still, why did he have to walk into Herr Seldersen's shop of all places; it wasn't as though he himself could afford any losses on top of his usual course of business.

Wurmbach came back the next day, but with an itemized list that was even more confusing and opaque than the first one. He spent a long time explaining the calculations to Father, trying to convince him that the statement was all in order: here were the items he had received, here was what he'd sold for this much money, and he still had the rest. Then Herr Seldersen said he would like to see the rest with his own eyes. The whole situation didn't seem so serious to him at that moment; he wasn't actually trying to prove that Herr Wurmbach was guilty of something. But Wurmbach gave a start. All right, Herr Seldersen could see it whenever he wanted, just pick a time, but still, didn't he trust him anymore? He had something to say about that. Maybe it would be better to dissolve their partnership. He, Wurmbach, would conduct his business on his own.

That's probably for the best, Herr Seldersen replied, he was thinking the same thing himself. In any case, Wurmbach should feel free to come by whenever he wanted any items, he just had to pay for them on the spot. Herr Seldersen would only give him things for cash from now on.

Wurmbach gave a mocking laugh. For cash? Please. If he had cash on hand he wouldn't need to do any of this in the first place. After all, it's no small matter to constantly ride around by bicycle every day.

"I know," Father assured him. "It's hard, but I can't let someone pull a fast one on me."

"Pull a fast one?" So he didn't believe him?

"I don't know what to believe," Herr Seldersen said. "You're a poor devil, maybe you're cheating me, maybe not, you're a poor devil."

Wurmbach: "Don't talk to me about cheating. I need to live, simple as that, my wife and child—"

Herr Seldersen interrupted him: "I'm still honest. Whatever you're doing is up to you, but find someone else to do it with."

Wurmbach wanted to answer back, but Seldersen cut him off. Wurmbach stood there embarrassed, not knowing what else to do. Seldersen promised him that he had no intention of reporting the whole affair to anyone, but his own situation was too perilous to let anyone trick him or cheat him, maybe he hadn't made that clear enough at the start. Wurmbach left the shop without saying goodbye and never came back. He continued to ride around the streets of town on his bicycle, with his package tied onto the basket mount. Who knew where he got the goods from? He carried on, and then, after a year, he suddenly disappeared from town.

.

The Seldersens realized that Frau Fiedler had recently started going around quiet and subdued again, the same as when Fritz had disappeared from town the first time. She only rarely dropped by, and when she did, she avoided the subject of America. The Seldersens didn't dare bring it up—they wanted to spare her; you could see that she didn't want to talk about it. Fritz was still in

America, and it had been almost two years since he'd left. Letters home came only rarely and no one knew exactly where he was at any given time. Last they had heard, he wanted to go to the West Coast. Since then, no news—a short postcard from Chicago, and then total silence.

One day, Herr Wiesel came by full of excitement. He had news to tell them, they wouldn't believe it, but his brother who lived nearby, in M., had assured him it was true. Fritz Fiedler was in M.! What did they think of that?

"Impossible!" Frau Seldersen said. "Fritz is in America."

"But he's actually in M.," Herr Wiesel insisted.

"Well, then he's come back," Herr Seldersen said. "I always thought it would turn out that way."

Herr Wiesel agreed; Fritz's plan to go to America was farfetched and ridiculous. The fact that he'd come back home after two years was proof. "America," he said in a sarcastic voice, "everyone thinks they'll make their fortune over there in America, once they've run out of prospects here. Maybe that used to be true, but now America has to look out for itself, why else would it have such strict immigration laws? There's not enough work there for their own people, they need more unemployed immigrants?"

"Exactly," Herr Seldersen said with a nod, then he left Wiesel alone with Mother and greeted a customer who had just come into the store. Frau Seldersen kept talking but without paying attention, only half listening to what Wiesel was saying. After a while, she heard Father tell the customer that he didn't have the fabric at the moment but he would be getting it in a couple of days, if she could wait that long. Or perhaps there was some other fabric he could recommend . . . ? But the woman insisted on what she wanted. Herr Wiesel said goodbye: "I'll come by again later," he said, waving to Father as he left.

Herr Seldersen tried his best, bringing out all sorts of fabrics and laying them out before the customer, but she refused to be talked into anything. She said over and over again that she would pay cash too, so he wouldn't have to be suspicious of anything. "But my dear lady," Herr Seldersen replied—he couldn't think of her name at the moment—"I would give you the fabric anyway, we've known each other a long time, how long has it been now?"—"Almost eight years," she said, "but you still don't know my name."—Herr Seldersen apologized for his bad memory, he laughed, yes, well, when you get older . . . It was meant as a joke, but you could suddenly see a damned lot of seriousness and truth behind it. An embarrassed silence fell over the shop. Frau Seldersen stayed in the background. Eventually, Herr Seldersen tried the last thing he could: he picked up a notepad and asked the customer if he could order the fabric for her. But the woman refused that too—she was in a hurry, about to take a trip and wanting to sew the dress herself. "Maybe I'll get what I'm looking for in another shop; I'm hoping to leave at once."—"It's possible," Herr Seldersen said, his face looking terribly old and sad, "it's possible. Otherwise, feel free to come back, I'll order you whatever fabric you need within two days. You can have it the next day, in the evening, maybe even the next afternoon."—"Thank you very much," the woman said, and turned to go. In the doorway, she turned around and told him how happy she would have been to buy it here. She always shopped here, he knew that. But money is so tight nowadays, and when you buy something you want it to be just the right thing. No one could expect her to take something she didn't want. "Of course not!" Frau Seldersen put in; she had stood the whole time without saying a word, following the conversation, but there was nothing she could do to change the outcome. "Of course, we try our best but we can't stock everything. Well, maybe it'll work out better next time." And the woman left.

"That was too bad, but nothing to be done about it, was there?" Frau Seldersen asked when they were alone again. She was still thinking about whether there was anything else they could have done.

"You saw it yourself," Herr Seldersen said testily. He couldn't stand being criticized.

"It's just," she began delicately, "that's the third time now that we've sent Frau Binge away empty-handed, her name is Frau Binge, you know her name, but now she won't come back, she's realized by now that there's a lot we don't have, and she's not the only one."

"Well, there's nothing I can do about it," Father answered angrily. But suddenly he thought of something and ran out the door, leaving Mother standing in the store. He looked up and down the street until he saw Frau Binge, then he ran after her, with long strides. She was on her way to Herr Wiesel's when she felt him softly touch her on the arm: she turned around, and there was Herr Seldersen. "Frau Binge," he said, with a slight smile: "Frau Binge," he repeated; he knew her name now, "just a moment please, I was mistaken before, my wife just remembered that I have the fabric you were looking for. It's upstairs in my apartment, I set it aside a while ago for someone who forgot to come pick it up, and he could only afford a small down payment. Come back, I didn't think of it before." Frau Binge looked at him as though seeing a miracle take place before her eyes. All these endless apologies a minute ago, and now . . . the fabric was up in his apartment? She was surprised, and didn't even realize that Herr Seldersen had already led her back to the shop. When they walked in, Frau Seldersen was standing at the counter, and before she could get over her shock and say anything, Father said, loudly and with significant emphasis, "You could have reminded me earlier that the fabric is upstairs in the closet; how long has it been there? I just told Frau Binge about it." Mother had no idea what to make of this piece of theater; Father was giving her meaningful looks, though she couldn't figure out the exact meaning. So she said nothing—the only thing she could do. Meanwhile, Herr Seldersen was talking to his shopgirl at the back of the store, whispering instructions and emphasizing his words with forceful, deliberate hand gestures. The girl's eyes widened and she vanished from the shop. Father came back to the front of the store where both of the women were waiting, and started up a conversation with Frau Binge again. He talked and talked! Frau Seldersen couldn't listen anymore and stood in the doorway, where she saw the shopgirl, Lisbeth, on the other side of the street, turning around furtively. She hurried up the sidewalk, crossed the street, and headed straight for Herr Wiesel's shop. Then she disappeared inside. After a while she reappeared hauling a large package, and, again making a detour to the other side of the street and around to the back door of the shop, came in and, sweating and out of breath, handed it to Herr Seldersen, who untied it in front of Frau Binge. He smiled contentedly. Three large bolts of fabric! What a selection! There must be a small warehouse upstairs tucked into the cupboards. Frau Binge looked and soon found the right fabric; she was pleased. "I'm glad you called me back, Herr Seldersen." She couldn't say it often enough, and shook her head when she thought how close he had come to losing the sale. Then she paid and left the shop beaming.

Oof! That was hard going. Father sat down behind the counter, took out the markup, and sent the rest of the money with the unsold fabric back to Herr Wiesel. He couldn't do that more than once or twice a day, his nerves wouldn't stand it. He laid his exhausted head down on the counter, while Frau Seldersen slowly came back from the door—she hadn't left her place, she couldn't bring herself to stand and watch while Father sold goods he had just gone and fetched from Herr Wiesel like thieves' booty. How did he ever think of that? Was this the first time? Who knows how many times he had had to resort to that pathetic trick. She went over to the counter Father was sitting behind.

"Did you at least make some money?" she asked, her voice full of pity.

He shook his head without looking up. "Not much, a few cents. Still, it's better to make the sale. . . ."

"Yes, of course."

Silence.

Finally, Mother said: "You don't need to do that, get things from Herr Wiesel." She still didn't understand.

"Nonsense," he said testily.

She listened, then started talking to him, saying he should try again, maybe get the fabric himself somewhere, keep more in stock, he was always so cautious. But scenes like that one couldn't happen again if the future was to mean anything at all to her. Wasn't he ashamed of himself?

"No," came his answer, in a lost little voice. "I've learned not to feel any shame." He stared into space.

Pause.

Frau Seldersen: "You have no strength left."

He nodded sadly. "No."

"You're not a man anymore."

"No."

Silence.

Suddenly he said: "Where do you think I could have gotten the fabric from? Who would give me anything?" He jumped up, his face tense, and gasped out his words.

"You're exaggerating," she answered calmly.

"Oh, what do you know? Go upstairs."

She didn't move.

He sat back down. "Spare me your advice, just go upstairs."

She took her key, tears in her eyes, and went up. He went too far when he got excited; for a while now, they had been having a lot of bad fights, any tiny little thing could set him off and make the feelings he had kept to himself until then come bursting out. You couldn't truthfully say that he sought out these fights—his personality was fundamentally peaceful and harmonious—but he lost his temper and self-control all too easily now. And no wonder, he had been struggling hard for years without ever being able to relax, every day bringing new stresses and greater challenges than the last.

The situation with the bills of exchange had worked out well and he had quickly paid back the money he'd borrowed from Herr Wiesel. But he had not been able to break the habit—he couldn't avoid it, he again found himself paying with bills of exchange. It helped at first, only later did it add to the tension, the anxious anticipation, and then came the walk to go see Herr Wiesel . . . it ate away at his nerves. Frau Seldersen was right, there were a lot of items missing from his shelves, but did she have to tell him that to his face? Didn't he know it perfectly well himself? Especially now that there were constantly incidents that made his shortages unpleasantly obvious. All in all, it was quite a cross to bear: standing downstairs in the shop, having to wait until someone walked in and wanted to buy, the hopeful joy at first, then the desperate looking around, with fear already lurking in the background, and finally the naked admission. . . . It was all an act, just make-work ending in nothing: no sale, no profit, no pleasure in it, just a cross to bear. No one had a job, no one had money, it all went together; there was no life, no death, just waiting that made you tired and numb. You went around with your eyes closed even during the day, and nothing that happened—no matter how significant, no matter what direction it came from—awakened any particular feelings. It was all idiotic, nothing but meaninglessly putting one foot in front of the other, without thinking about it, without any inner reason for it. . . . Simply idiotic.

Frau Seldersen wrote to Albrecht and told him what she had heard from Herr Wiesel, and added what she herself had observed in Frau Fiedler: she was acting different, things must have been going badly for some time. At the end, she suggested that Albrecht act as carefully as he could and not come to Fritz with too much advice or too many suggestions. Maybe the best thing would be to leave him entirely alone, the poor boy! She wrote only a little about their own situation: that Father was moody and unpredictable, he must be facing insurmountable problems again but he never said a word about them and she couldn't even think about pestering him with questions.

Aside from that, she was about to let the maid go and would then have to do all of the housework herself; she had done the calculations and they would save a lot of money that way. She didn't try to hide that it would be work that she wasn't used to. She had always been able to afford a maid for all the years she had lived there, but now it was just one more extra expense. As long as her strength held up, she hoped she would be able to handle the work.

Albrecht received the letter in the evening mail. He read it and calmly put it aside, intending to read it again later. He had received another letter too: a job offer, for a two-month gig as a musician out in the provinces. It paid well and he decided with hardly any hesitation to sign the contract. In fact, he rushed it a little, and he later regretted his decision; the two months were during vacation, so he didn't miss much, but he too had to start thinking about his exams soon. When he realized that, he remembered his classmates facing the same circumstances, and this common bond made him feel a certain amount of new hope.

Then he read the letter from his mother again.

Albrecht thought it over for a long time, then wrote to Fritz. It was a reserved letter, without any violent emotion, saying just that he had heard about his return and was up to date on all the recent events. What had happened was over and done with, water under the bridge, there was no point brooding about it now. But before Fritz decided what to do next, Albrecht asked him, in memory of their friendly discussions from years past, to listen to what he, Albrecht, suggested and to take it seriously. He advised him to pick up where he had left off years before and make up the time he needed to graduate, so that at least he'd have a diploma in hand. Then, in eighteen months, he could decide what to do. For now, Albrecht offered him his support. Fritz could finish what he'd started in peace and quiet, and for the time being would not have to suffer any more of the setbacks and failures he would be sure to face when looking for a new job. Fritz's answer came back quickly, and you could tell how many times he had rewritten it. "Thank you very much for your suggestion and the personal offer of help," he wrote—he was truly happy that someone was worrying about him. But he couldn't agree to Albrecht's proposal; he had made his choice and there was no going back. "I've changed a lot," he went on, and this open admission was what mystified Albrecht the most—he had no idea what Fritz meant. Fritz asked Albrecht to visit him in M. one Sunday when Albrecht was on his way home, they could discuss everything in person. It all sounded confused and a bit mysterious.

One Sunday a couple of weeks later, Albrecht took the half-hour train ride to M. On the way, he ran into Fritz's parents, with hearty greetings all around—everyone was in a friendly mood. Fritz was waiting for them at the station in M.; more hearty greetings. Fritz seemed outwardly calm but looked pale and smoked nonstop; his fingers were yellow to the nails. The two friends went on ahead and Fritz spoke candidly about how long he'd been there and what he was doing from day to day. He was in a cheerful mood and seemed to be feeling good about himself. He acted as if he had just seen Albrecht two weeks ago. Albrecht, on the other hand, was embarrassed, a little ashamed and nervous—sometimes he thought that Fritz was putting on an act, sometimes he didn't. Suddenly Fritz asked Albrecht in a low voice not to offer any more personal suggestions; his parents and brother-in-law already had more than enough ideas about his future. He didn't say what he thought of their ideas. So, no more personal suggestions: Albrecht had expected as much from the beginning, and promised his friend.

Then they were sitting together around the coffee table: a family again, for the first time after the long separation. Frau Fiedler kept looking across at her Fritz, happy to have him back again; almost everything else was forgotten. Fritz sat there completely quiet, as though he had ended up at the table quite by chance rather than being the central focus of the group. It slowly grew darker; Fritz's brother-in-law brought out cigarettes and then subtly steered the conversation toward the topic of what Fritz might do next, speaking entirely to Albrecht, since he was practically one of the family, he knew everything and in fact had been involved from the beginning when he'd known about Fritz's plans to run away. There was no need for him to be embarrassed about that: if he hadn't said anything about it, it was only because he had to keep his promise to Fritz. Frau Fiedler nodded and looked at Albrecht; she too had long since forgiven him. Albrecht ground his teeth—they were praising him for something that was really the start of a long ordeal. And one which had not yet ended.

Herr Fiedler was at peace with the situation as well. He hadn't been happy about Fritz going to America, from the very beginning. . . . But I couldn't impose my will on him, he said, Fritz had to have his own experiences for himself. Now he was satisfied, he had been proven right.

Fritz's brother-in-law came out with what he had in mind, unfolding his plans carefully and skillfully. "Fritz isn't too old yet," he said; "he can still start over from the beginning again. He had bad luck in Hamburg, when the firm went under and he was out on the street. He lost more than a year there . . . and then America—" But he didn't want to say anything more about that. Times were damn hard, all over the world, even in America. . . . There weren't jobs lying around to be picked up off the street, much less money and luck. Who had time to think about luck these days? Fritz had traveled around, had seen a lot, and now he was back, now he had to start all over again, no matter what he wanted or hoped for personally—he had to put those hopes aside now. "We all do," Fritz's brother-in-law said. He had been married for ten years, but children had been denied him. He wanted to try to find Fritz a position, it would definitely be hard but he had good connections, Fritz only had to have faith. Sometimes it seemed like Fritz had much too gloomy a view of the future. A young person had to muster up all his strength—look at everyone doing battle out there every day.

Everyone had something to toss into the conversation, it was quite a discussion—except it was about someone's whole life. Albrecht felt that this casual spinning out of someone's fate and future was undignified. They drank and smoked, sitting comfortably in a warm room. Was this part of Fritz's brother-in-law's plan? If so, Albrecht was prepared to acknowledge his skill and forethought—it was extraordinary.

Fritz said nothing. He sat perched on the writing desk, smoking and slowly releasing the smoke into the room so that he soon disappeared behind a thick cloud. He listened to everyone's advice about whether he should become a confectioner or an ironmonger, or something else. He could go back to school in the evenings, take courses, learn languages, his father said, happy to see in advance everything coming together so nicely.

And Albrecht? He sat at the table and was allowed to take part in the discussion; now and then he ventured a word or two, carefully testing to see if he was met with understanding or empty stares. He saw the lay of the land only too quickly, and from then on let the others talk, not saying anything unless he was asked a question, in which case he would painfully cobble together a few words and then sink back into his long, thoughtful silence. He couldn't help it, he was horrified. Didn't anyone in the room see it? Fritz's dear mother, with her oversized love, or the brother-in-law, who himself had been knocked around quite a lot in the world—didn't they feel the powerful, deadly exhaustion in the air, and then the other thing, a tremendous fear? Albrecht couldn't come up with the exact word for it himself, but the whole time he sat at that table with Fritz up on the desk, he could not get free of this strange feeling. He turned around many times to see if Fritz was even still in the room. I've already decided, he had written to Albrecht. Decided what? That he wanted to be a confectioner, or an ironmonger? Fritz sat up on the desktop, elevated above the others, and said not a word. Go ahead and rack your brains, he seemed to be thinking with a laugh; you mean well, even if it will turn out to be totally different from what you expect.

It was completely dark by then, and when Albrecht turned around again he saw the shape of his friend gently looming up out of the darkness. The tip of his cigarette glowed more brightly as he inhaled, and Albrecht saw his face for a moment: it was pale and waxen, like a dead man's. Albrecht held his breath.

He stood up to go and said his goodbyes; he wanted to walk home, he thought he could do it in two hours, and the last train was not due until late anyway. Fritz went with him and they walked slowly through the city. Fritz was completely calm, walking slowly with long strides; Albrecht reluctantly forced himself to match his pace. He felt uncomfortable, alone like this with his friend but without his friend's decisive confidence.

"What do you think of their plans?" Fritz asked with a smile.

Albrecht, cold and firm: "They're good; hopefully they'll come true."

"Yes. But it's not quite as easy as they think. Or don't you know that yet either?"

"I do," Albrecht said gently. "I do know a thing or two."

Silence.

Fritz walked alongside his friend, with his slow, loping steps, smiling to himself. Why are you trying so hard, little man? Fritz thought. What's this secret you think you have to keep? Do you really think it's so simple? You haven't seen nearly as much as I have, my boy, you don't have the courage, not even the courage for the truth (but what he meant was: for silent despair).

You're wrong, Albrecht answered, as mute as his friend; you're wrong, I know more than you think—it's all hopeless, everything is completely hopeless. . . .

"Everything would be much easier if I had a goal, what do you think? I mean, do you have a goal like that?"

Albrecht thought, coming back to his senses out of the great, painful confusion he was in. Did he, young and healthy as he was, have a goal for himself? No, he didn't, he ran around thinking only about the next day, making enough money to live on, not being a burden to anybody—he never saw any further ahead than that. Only occasionally did he stop in the middle of all the rushing around to catch his breath. Then he lost the rhythm, everything continued around him for a few days while he lay like a dead man. Before long he was back on his feet.

But I'm at university, Albrecht suddenly remembered.

Is that a goal? Do you think you'll have better prospects because you're in school?

Albrecht, out loud: "I'm about to take a two-month tour in the provinces as a musician."

"As a musician?"

"Yes, that's what I'm doing these days, playing music."

"So, that's how you make your money. Is it enough to live on?"

"Just barely."

"Are you all students?"

"No, some musicians, some merchants . . ." What a stupid, disastrously stupid thing to say!

Fritz, ironically: "Laid-off confectioners and ironmongers!"

How stupid he was! Albrecht wanted to slap himself.

Fritz: "That wouldn't be an option for me, I can't even play the guitar."

"Nonsense!" Albrecht answered testily.

"Nonsense?" Fritz didn't think so, not in the least. That was the way things went, right? You apprentice three years, and when you're done they fire you, and then you go and play music or recite poetry. Right?

Albrecht felt a deep and powerful strength slowly well up within him, and he wanted to say: Yes, that's how it is, if you're lucky! It's rewarding to touch people's hearts. You mustn't think I'm sitting around in a dream world in Berlin, but you wouldn't know anything about that anyway.

Why not? Fritz would have asked in amazement.

Albrecht: "At least you have your parents to fall back on, that's something certain in an emergency."

"I wish my father was poor," Fritz blurted out.

Albrecht stared at him in shock. What did he mean by that? He wished his father was poor—what crazy ideas Fritz had!

"Maybe some of my decisions would be easier that way," Fritz went on.

Pause.

"Why? Is it hard for you to make decisions now?"

Fritz said nothing, but he breathed heavily and stared down at the ground. "I often think," he said quietly, "how good it would be to have enormous pressure bearing down on me, maybe then I could pull myself together. But what's the point? Everything's a mess, a miserable mess. . . . But really I'm doing fine," he went on in a very different tone, "don't you think? If I wanted, my parents would support me even if I didn't earn a thing, I could learn to drive a car, or fly a plane, they'd put up the money. Now they're trying to find me a job, some kind of job. I'll just wait and see."

"So why don't you actually do it?" Albrecht asked.

"Oh, you might as well ask me to climb Mount Everest, it's the same thing."

Albrecht thought about what Fritz meant by this pressure, and already he quietly thought that he understood. Later, when he thought back on this conversation, he had the same feeling. There must be some pressure bearing down on Albrecht too, controlling but at the same time paralyzing him, fixing him in place. Albrecht's understanding did not reach any further than that.

And then Fritz told his friend about America. Not much: Albrecht wanted to hear more but Fritz was reluctant to satisfy his curiosity; he gave a quick sketch and Albrecht had to fill in the picture himself. He hadn't been granted immigration papers, only a tourist visa, which permitted only a short stay in the country. He had to show that he had a certain sum of money, as proof that he wasn't trying to find work and thus take away jobs from American workers. The whole time he was there, he lived in constant fear that the police would catch him and deport him. He did everything that a foreigner illegally seeking work had to do—wash dishes, clean rooms, polish boots, sell newspapers—but no regular job, nothing long-term. How could anyone get ahead like that? He had to be very careful not to be caught before his time was up. He worked for some crooks smuggling alcohol, there was a lot of money to be made like that, but was it really his destiny to lose his life under a hail of police bullets as a moonshine smuggler on Lake Michigan? Then he met another German, who took a lot of money off him. He said he was a farmer, looking for a hardworking assistant, so they planned to go west to work on his farm. Fritz gave the man money for some purchases and never saw him again. And Fritz didn't dare report what had happened to the police.

The crossing? Herded together in a single room with foreigners, mostly Portuguese, Poles, Balkan Slavs, only a little space for each person. And then the women, lying piled on top of one another every night, what were they supposed to do during the whole trip? There was no lounge, no entertainment. The ship they sailed on was one of the newest on the line.

He wasn't telling Albrecht everything, not by a long shot, just a brief taste of what he had been through. The whole story would take days. He had forgotten some of it too, his memory wasn't up to it, he had been through too much in these two years, he didn't even know why anymore. But Albrecht could sense behind this reticence what Fritz wasn't saying: all that wasted effort, the hope that always ended in hopelessness. What could he say to that? It was horrible, something no one would ever try twice.

Fritz was calm and dispassionate as he told his stories. But he had been right in the middle of everything and it hadn't passed over him without leaving a trace, no matter how he tried to act about it. He was disappointed, terribly disappointed. And not only that. There was also utter hopelessness, the painful astonishment at a world that was very different in reality from the way you would have wanted it to be.

The streetlamps were lit and a light rain was falling. They walked on the high road along the promenade.

"And now you have to try all over again," Albrecht said. "There's no other choice."

Fritz nodded mutely.

"You need to be a little more careful," Albrecht informed him in a superior tone, as though he himself were the slyest of the sly.

Silence.

"There's one thing I don't understand," Albrecht went on. Whenever he looked at his friend, this thought went through his head. "There's one thing I don't understand. You've still got your strength, don't you . . . ?" They were under a streetlamp just then, and Fritz stopped. "My strength? You think so . . . ?" With an indescribable casualness he took his hands out of his pockets, slowly raised his arms, spread his fingers, and held his hands in the air. "Look." His hands trembled all the way to his fingertips, as though a powerful current were invisibly passing through them; they wouldn't stop moving, they skittered from side to side, and the more he tensed his muscles, the more they shook. Fritz looked at his hands, those big, strong hands with a powerful grip that shied away from no task, but they trembled, and Albrecht saw it. He smiled a painful smile and, as if wanting to keep up with his friend, held his hands up too: they were much more delicate, there was no comparison—not as strong and clearly much more sensitive, but a young man's hands nonetheless, that could still buckle down to hard work. He held them in the light, and look, they trembled too, maybe a little less, but there was nothing he could do about it either; he stood there and looked at his hands, which gave away everything and told his friend all there was to say. They shared it—that was enough.

"I'm going to walk home," Albrecht said, "I'll be there in an hour and a half." Fritz walked him a little way farther. "We'll see each other a lot in Berlin, of course," Albrecht promised. "You could rent a room near me."

"Hmm . . ."

They parted on the overpass over the train tracks. "Write me right away and tell me what you've worked out; I leave the day after tomorrow."

They hadn't gone ten steps away from each other when Fritz shouted, "Hey," his voice carrying in the wind. Albrecht stopped and walked a few steps back.

"I forgot to ask, are you having any problems with school? I mean, financially."

Albrecht smiled. "Yes, but so what? Why do you ask?"

"I'd be happy to talk to my parents, see if they could—"

"No, it's not that bad, but thanks," Albrecht shouted into the wind.

"Just an idea; okay, see you later."

Each walked off in his own direction.

.

The autumn was beautiful too—strong, manly, bright, glittering in magnificent colors. You could walk across the heath for hours, your gaze practically drowning in the endless distances. The lakes still kept their warmth from the summer and the water still gave off its lovely scent. And then the forests, the endless forests! Calm, capacious, and quiet, like a serious secret. "Here's somewhere a person can live!" Herr Seldersen would say, always with a deep groan. What a life that would be! He walked amid all that beauty, embarrassed and ashamed as though he didn't deserve it. What times these were, that made men so unmanly! He was a father, the head of his family, a position he filled in a way that deserved respect—he had never taken advantage of it, forcing his authority on anyone else, and in the good years he was always steady and self-controlled. But then, when he came back from the war, and in the years after that when the problems piled up and not a day passed without anxieties and worries, his weakness was revealed. Was he still a leader you could trust to overcome all obstacles and find the right path? The truth was, he needed guidance more than anyone—he was helpless, not knowing which way to turn. His awareness of his own lamentable situation was so horribly clear that he forgot to conceal it with words and deeds. He was too honest for that, maybe not smart enough either. Look, everyone, this is how I am, he seemed to be saying, I am a helpless man who can't do anything, who has to wait and let people walk all over me like a doormat. If someone comes to take my belongings out of my apartment or my shop, I have to stand and watch. He had worked his whole life and responsibly supported his family, paid his rent and debts on time, with all sorts of little things left over too. He was trusted and respected. Now he didn't even make enough to support himself and his wife with dignity, not to mention his debts.

The rent came due the first of every month. For as long as Herr Seldersen could remember, he had always handed it over to the landlord punctually on that day. Now it was the fifth and the rent still hadn't been paid. Father waited another three days, then went to see the landlord.

"This is the first time I've ever been late," he struggled to say. It was unpleasant enough for him to have to talk about it at all. The landlord didn't say anything, but there was no reason for him to. Seldersen thanked him for being so considerate.

But the next time it happened, the landlord sent a shopgirl over from his shop four days after the agreed-upon due date, with a bill he had already signed.

"I'll come over in person after we close," he answered the shopgirl. She had stood in the doorway, shy and embarrassed, while he read the letter; she had only reluctantly carried the message.

Later, when Herr Seldersen went to see the landlord, he was deathly pale with rage.

"Just file a lawsuit why don't you, send the courts after me?" he screamed. "Make sure everyone knows that I'm late on my payments, after I've paid every penny on time for twenty-five years! Now you really have reason to worry!"

Now that was over the line; his anger was making him exaggerate. "What are you talking about?" the landlord asked. "I sent a warning, don't you do that to people who owe you money?"

Herr Seldersen realized that he had gone too far; did he really have to scream out his fears to the world and reveal to everyone his real circumstances? So he retreated, but cautiously, since he still had something on his mind.

"Why did you send me that letter?" He held it in his shaking hand. "When I have the money I'll pay the rent, you just need to accommodate me a little."

"Yes, of course, I only wanted to remind you."

"I see, just remind me, nothing more."

These words kept running through Herr Seldersen's head the whole rest of the day. It had gotten to the point that people thought they needed to remind him of what he owed, when he had always paid everything on time for who knows how many years. All of a sudden people were afraid he might simply have forgotten the first of the month for some reason. He thought about the people who owed him money too, how he sent warning letters to them and still they brought their cash to someone else the next time, walking contemptuously past his shop, not deeming him worthy of a single glance—the truth was, they were ashamed.

When Herr Seldersen walked down the street, looked in the shop windows, and then stood in front of his own selection and compared it to the others, he felt as if someone had jumped out at him and was strangling him. He lay awake all night, tossing and turning in bed, until his wife woke up next to him.

"What's wrong?" she asked, still half asleep.

No answer.

After a while:

"I'm going to redo the shop windows tomorrow, I just thought of it."

"And you wake me up for that?" At the same time, she felt bad for him. "Yes, you're right, the display is already three weeks old. You can rearrange everything inside too. But now you should try to get a few hours' sleep."

"Yes."

She turned over onto her other side and closed her eyes. They lay quietly next to each other, each one listening to the other's breathing, but neither one could get back to sleep.

When October was over, Herr Seldersen took up the iron stove and the long pipes from the floor. Now he had something to do for several days. He degreased the stove, cleaned the pipes, and reinstalled the heating himself. He knelt on the floor, stood on a ladder, hammered nails into the ceiling until the plaster flaked off onto his suit, and was too busy with his project to think of doing anything else. Anyone who spoke to him got whatever answer took the least thought. His clothes were dirty, his hands were dirty, he never stopped working even on nights and weekends. He wiped the dust off only in a token way, and wore the rest as a badge of honor from his hard work.

"Everyone can see I've been working," he said. He had such strange ideas.

Frau Seldersen was extremely upset. "Still, you could at least keep clean," she said. "What will people think of me, letting you walk around like that? I won't work downstairs with you anymore, I'm too ashamed."

Herr Seldersen rudely stormed off. Mother stayed home, crying, and talking to herself through her tears: "I think he's losing his mind. . . ."

•

One afternoon, Herr Dalke sent his youngest shopgirl over to Herr Seldersen and invited him over for an evening. His wife was traveling, he was alone in the big apartment and bored, and would love some company. At first Herr Seldersen wanted to refuse; he wasn't in the mood for a night out that would end, he knew, very late. But Frau Seldersen, who was standing there when the shopgirl brought the invitation, conveyed to him that he couldn't say no to Herr Dalke. And what would his reason have been? Father couldn't decide. Yes, he'll be there right on time, best regards, she said to the girl without a moment's hesitation. Many thanks. Herr Seldersen was paralyzed. The shopgirl left the store and crossed the street; Father saw her walk into Herr Wiesel's. So, Wiesel too, there'd be three of them for the evening, it might be fun. But still, he didn't feel any great desire to go. And what made his wife think she could go over his head and accept the invitation for him if he didn't want to go?

"You'll wear your blue suit and go," Mother said, without giving any further explanation. He had to spend a little time with other people, these days he only rarely even tried, he'd rather just shut himself off and stay home alone, brooding over his own thoughts.

That evening, Herr Seldersen brushed his work suit, which had been mended in so many places that it had taken on a strange, colorless appearance. But he refused to let Frau Seldersen convince him to change suits. "It'll be dark anyway," he said, "and no one will be looking at me." And away he went.

The three of them sat at the small round table in a warm room, with cigars on a side table, bottles of liquor set out. Herr Dalke had provided for everything well. Everyone was in a good, social mood. Herr Dalke didn't wait long before he started shuffling the cards—he was a passionate but extremely bad card player. Playing cards brought him extraordinary pleasure. He was so eager! He sat there the whole time with his face flushed, bent over the table, holding his cards so close to his body that he couldn't see them himself without difficult twists and contortions, he always thought people were cheating. He gave a long speech about every card he played, an endless dialogue with himself that Herr Wiesel only nodded at, now and then throwing in a little joke, which only got Herr Dalke more worked up, while Herr Seldersen sat quietly in his chair and said nothing. He held his own cards carefully arranged, straight in front of his face with his elbows resting on the table. He preferred people who played in Wiesel's style: carefully, silently, but dangerously. How carried away Herr Dalke could get! If he lost, he would hunker down in his chair full of sorrow, as though he had just suffered the defeat of his life; he never stopped talking out loud to himself, long explanations of how he could have played better and then won after all. He had a drink and then returned to battle. And so it went until the early hours of the morning. Herr Seldersen leaned back in his chair, a half-smoked cigar in the ashtray, and the hand he held his cards in rested tiredly on the table; he could barely keep his eyes open. He had known in advance that this evening would run late, and now he looked at the clock—he had been here more than five hours, and hadn't spoken three sentences. Herr Wiesel was fading too, he still nodded at all of Herr Dalke's rambling but maybe he was nodding off to sleep, he had to take care not to let his head slip too far down and hit the table. Only Herr Dalke was as fresh and alert as ever. He was losing, and irritation kept him awake. Herr Seldersen added everything up and passed him the sheet of paper for him to check; Herr Dalke only nodded his head to say he was sure it was right, and slid him the money. Thanks—to be honest, Herr Seldersen was embarrassed to take the money, but after all, he had won. Herr Dalke slid Herr Wiesel some money too, but he took it with a laugh: "That means business will be good today, you know what they say," he said to console him, "and now at least I've brought in something." Herr Dalke had to laugh at the joke, but he said, Business will be good, yes. He wished he would be able to say that again. He wanted to tell them something: A high official had come by the day before—he refused to name names, but they would be shocked—and had taken him into his confidence. He needed some things for himself and his family, he had always shopped at Herr Dalke's, he gave a long speech about necessities, how pleased he had always been with the goods and service there, and at the end he said he couldn't pay for it all at once and asked Herr Dalke for consideration. Herr Dalke had agreed. But that was just one example, he could list dozens more.

Herr Seldersen was on tenterhooks. Herr Wiesel said it was the same with him, giving credit almost finishes us off and makes the borrower careless and lazy at the same time. He had stories he could tell too. Now he always added some money on top, to cover the interest he had to pay. Then, when the payments stopped coming and he had to request payment from the debtors, they walked right past his store as if they were insulted, and didn't even give him the courtesy of a single glance. They must be ashamed. Well, Herr Wiesel couldn't worry about that. Or else they just stayed away altogether, went to someone else, and started to get credit there.

Herr Seldersen knew only too well what that shame felt like. Was it fundamentally any different for him? Didn't he also try to keep an eye out for the main chance, didn't he also start dealing with new people while he still had debts with the old ones?

"What are we supposed to do?" he asked casually.

Herr Dalke shrugged. What can we do? Nothing, absolutely nothing, just be careful. "I'd rather lose the sale than let myself in for such uncertainty, suspicions. . . . Once you start with that, you're done for." True, Herr Wiesel agreed. He gave credit and let his customers keep tabs, but only cautiously; he could still be choosy.

Herr Seldersen thought to himself that there were many days when not a single item would leave his store if he didn't give them away—trusting his customers to pay for them eventually. What did the other two men know of the deals he was forced to make?

"It's not easy," Herr Wiesel said, shaking Herr Dalke's hand. "Good night, thanks very much, sleep well."

"Good night, Herr Seldersen."

"Good night."

They walked through the dark streets. The city government

had turned off the streetlights at one a.m.—to save money. Their footsteps were hesitant and tentative.

"Be careful with giving credit, Herr Seldersen," Herr Wiesel warned him. "It doesn't get you anywhere. You heard what Herr Dalke just said."

Herr Seldersen was surprised. Dalke has to give credit too? He couldn't believe it.

"Why not? You think Herr Dalke is an exception? He probably does it more than he lets on."

"He takes a good look at his customers first, though. He can still pick and choose."

But Herr Wiesel had reached his house, and said goodbye.

Herr Seldersen kept walking alone, playing over the conversation in his mind. The whole time, he had had the strange feeling that Herr Dalke and Herr Wiesel were communicating with each other on some kind of secret level. At first his suspicions seemed groundless: the conversation was following a normal track and everyone contributed to it, each saying whatever he thought, not keeping anything to himself. But then—Herr Seldersen couldn't get free of the thought—Dalke and Wiesel started communicating with each other on some secret level, there was a mysterious understanding between them that Seldersen couldn't quite put his finger on. But what? He was hell-bent on figuring it out, and refused to give up until he had gained some kind of clarity. He felt that he owed himself that.

It was all very simple, in fact, and Herr Seldersen's suspicion was in no way a figment of his imagination. The experiences he had had in the past few years had in many ways sharpened his senses, and they weren't leading him astray here. He was right, although he was also exaggerating the consequences for himself and wrong to feel that the other two were that much better off than he was. There was one simple thing they had in common: they all had to give customers things without getting any cash in hand in return; they had to give credit. Herr Dalke primarily to officials, teachers, and members of the upper classes—he could be relatively sure he would get his money eventually. Likewise Herr Wiesel. But the only people who came to Herr Seldersen's store—how could it be otherwise?—were the poor devils, broke and hopeless. There was something in the air that seemed to lure them to Herr Seldersen's store: a kind of smell of decay, of corpses almost, the same kind of complicated, secret bond, in fact, that Herr Seldersen had just picked up on between Herr Wiesel and Herr Dalke. That's what it was, nothing more. It didn't matter so terribly much to those two whether they lost this or that customer, they'd survive either way, certainly for some time and probably for quite a while. Losing a little money here and there wouldn't change anything with them, it wouldn't make the whole edifice sway. But him? He was a poor devil himself, every penny mattered to him, and he had to go into every situation making sure that he would keep every single customer, now and in the future, under any circumstances, no matter what. He couldn't afford to take any decisive measures, he was too embroiled in the whole mess. The others could keep a tab for four weeks, six weeks, two months, six months: it didn't matter to them; they would just dip into their reserves. They could take vigorous and decisive action, send warnings to customers who were overdue, even sue them or repossess their property; in the end they'd come back, they relied on those stores. But Herr Seldersen?

That was what Seldersen learned, in an almost extrasensory way, from his conversation with Herr Wiesel and Herr Dalke.

•

It couldn't go on, with the best will in the world it just could not go on. The end could not be any more terrible than the current situation. It had started with letters back then and it started with letters again this time. The mailman brought the mail twice a day, and carried in worry and care and despair with the letters; they had been through it all before. Things had gone well enough for eighteen months, and Herr Seldersen had known all along that it wouldn't last forever. It was like a night's sleep during a storm. He read the letters, he knew what they had to say, but this time they sounded a lot more drastic: the warnings were blunt and unambiguous, with no prospect for forbearance; the danger of losing their money was too clear, experience had made his creditors cunning and cautious and completely untrusting. Herr Seldersen wrote back, asked for forbearance, the same as before. A few days later he received as his answer a demand from a lawyer to pay the money within a set time, they threatened to take him to court and every step that might follow. But Father had already taken lawsuits into account too, they no longer scared him. He went to Herr Wiesel and borrowed money, he had hardened himself to that too. He satisfied his other creditors with little sums that he was able to send off in the next few days, but it was only cobbled together, a patch-up job, he would never in his life be able to take care of everything this way. The letters and threats piled up, their language grew more and more sharp and presumptuous. But the money, where was Herr Seldersen supposed to get the money?

·

One afternoon, Frau Seldersen secretly took a long walk. She went up to the apartment, took her purse, and then came back down to the store where Herr Seldersen was sitting and patiently waiting.

"I'm going for a little walk," she said, and her voice sounded firm and sure, she wasn't trying to apologize for going out and leaving him there alone. He nodded to her, glad that she had worked up the energy for a walk. He would have liked to go with her. The sun was high in the sky, the air light and warm over the city.

Frau Seldersen left the shop, but she wasn't intending to just take a pleasant little walk—her goal was not the forest outside of town, rising full and magnificent up over the broad valley, or the parks where you could cheerfully wander at your leisure. She directed her steps to where the buildings were cramped and tightly crowded together on bumpy, potholed streets, where people lived in smoky rooms. She climbed a steep, run-down spiral staircase to the top floor, right under the roof, where she knocked on the door and went inside.

The husband lay on the sofa, lazy and heavy, asleep. Flies were buzzing around his face and he swiped at them in his sleep. The wife was sitting at the table; when Frau Seldersen came in, she jumped up.

"Frau Seldersen!" she cried in surprise. She took a couple of steps toward her, greeted her, and sat back down at the table.

"Shh," Mother said, "not so loud, your husband is sleeping. He must be tired. Is he working again? A night shift?"

"Working!" his wife said sarcastically. "He's picked up bad habits, he's tired all the time, he drinks. He came home this afternoon in that state. We can talk to each other in a normal voice, don't worry."

Frau Seldersen felt sorry for her. By then she had recovered from climbing the stairs.

Pause.

They sat across from each other and looked at each other, embarrassed. This unexpected visit was quite a surprise for the woman; she wanted to find out to what she owed this great honor, many thanks, and so on, but Frau Seldersen would not have climbed the four flights of stairs without a specific reason.

"It's a very nice place you've got here, really . . ." Frau Seldersen said slowly as her gaze wandered around the room.

Is that why she'd come, to convince herself of that?

Silence.

Frau Seldersen searched desperately for a way to start.

"And the curtains, it was so hard for you to decide, but you're happy with them?"

The woman nodded. "I just washed them, they're still fresh from the stretcher."

Pause.

Frau Seldersen was still thinking when the other woman came to her assistance.

"I think there's still something on my tab from the curtains," she said haltingly, as though only remembering with difficulty.

Frau Seldersen nodded and suddenly felt the courage to go on.

"Not only from the curtains." She raised her gaze and looked straight at the woman.

"I know," she whispered.

Silence.

"We have bills to pay ourselves," Frau Seldersen said hesitantly. "The money doesn't always come in, we have to make sure. . . ." Her own words gave her courage. She kept talking. The woman understood that she was one of the people Frau Seldersen was talking about. She owed money, she had a whole page in the account book.

"We haven't seen you in the shop for a long time," Frau Seldersen continued. "Have you been sick? I wanted to look in and see how you were doing, and maybe while I was here you could pay a couple of marks of what you owe."

Now it was on the table: she had come to collect money. That was why she had climbed the four flights of stairs and accepted the stress and the pounding in her chest that went with the visit.

The woman on the other side of the table, the customer who had just been warned, sat on a chair in her room and thought it would be better if she were sitting there all alone, or were outside somewhere. Then she remembered that she was sitting within her own four walls after all, nowhere else—not, for instance, in Seldersen's store or before a judge. She blinked across the table at Frau Seldersen and said:

"I was planning to come to the city tomorrow, maybe the day after, soon though. I couldn't in the last few weeks, I'm sorry." The Seldersens needed money too, of course, she understood that. Then she stood up, took her key, and, turning around several times to look at the sofa, opened a small compartment in the cupboard. She rummaged around inside it and pulled out a small cardboard box where she kept money, hidden so that her husband wouldn't find it. She took out a few coins and carefully locked it all up again, constantly worried that her husband might wake up. Suddenly she no longer seemed to believe he was as deeply asleep as she had just said. Then she came back to the table. "Here," she said, giving Frau Seldersen the money.

"Thank you." Frau Seldersen put it straight into her purse, calculating to herself . . . the woman had not been to the shop for four weeks, and now she was giving her five marks, proudly thinking about what a major payment she had managed to pull together. That made a little over one mark per week, not counting interest. Precious little, and nothing to brag about. But the woman felt that she had done a good and honest thing and Frau Seldersen let her go on believing it. She had five marks in her purse and she spent a while longer sitting at the woman's table; she was no longer in a hurry, and above all she didn't want to seem like she had come only for the measly sum of money.

The man continued to lie on the sofa, sleeping off his binge, and the woman stood at the other side of the table, upright, her hands on her hips, looking down at Frau Seldersen. She only half listened to what Frau Seldersen was saying—she couldn't stop thinking about what had just happened. Then Frau Seldersen stood up and said goodbye, and walked quietly to the door so as not to wake up the man. There she turned around one more time and nodded. The woman was still standing by the table, and she looked at Frau Seldersen with wide-open eyes. Frau Seldersen suddenly felt terrible. She had acted confident and self-controlled the whole time, but now her hands shook, her lips trembled, she wanted to say something to excuse herself. She was ashamed. . . . But she opened the door without a word and went down the narrow, winding four flights of stairs.

The woman in the room sat back down at the table. Now they were coming to see her at home to get the money she owed them! That had never happened to her before, but it was strange . . . the whole incident didn't seem to reflect badly, much less shamefully, on her, but rather on the other woman, the one who had climbed the four flights of stairs to get her money. She was the actress the spotlight was trained on. Very strange, the whole thing. She thought she'd have to talk it over with her neighbor one flight down.

Frau Seldersen went around to different customers' apartments; they all lived near one another here, the afternoon was long, she had a lot of visits planned. Children were playing in the street and Frau Seldersen stopped and held out her hand to a little boy or girl. "Hello," she said in a friendly voice, "is your mother home?"—"No," the child answered in a squeaky little voice, "my mother is out in the fields, she'll be home later."

"And your father?"

"Dunno."

"That's not very nice," Frau Seldersen said, "you know who I am."

She moved on. She crossed a courtyard where chickens ran around cackling and clucking and a dog barked furiously, straining at his chain. Mother went up to the window and looked into the room. She gently tapped her finger against the glass.

"Who's that?" called a tired voice from inside. Frau Seldersen said her name. Hurried footsteps came shuffling over and an old woman appeared behind the window curtains.

"What a surprise!" she cried. "Frau Seldersen, come in! How nice!"

Mother went into the room and was heaped with honors: she had to sit down, the old woman brought her a cup (with no handle and a chipped rim), they had a coffee together. The woman was alone; she lived with her married son and his wife wasn't home.

"You were asleep," Mother apologized. "If I had known . . ."

But the old woman brushed it off. "Only because of my heart," she said in a hoarse voice. "I have to lie down a lot. Yes, my heart's almost done."

"That's what I was wondering," Frau Seldersen took the op-

portunity to say. "I wanted to come by and see how you're doing." She didn't have enough courage to say anything else for
the time being. So she asked sympathetically about everything
she could.

"I haven't seen you in a while," Mother suddenly started to
say. Could she do it?

"I don't go out much anymore," the old woman replied. "The
noise, the excitement, all the people, and my heart. . . ." She
gasped a little for breath. "I am a burden to my children."

Frau Seldersen looked at her. She had known her for a long
time, known her husband too; he had been dead for ten years.
She had lost a son in the war and now lived with the other son.
He was getting by without regular work; the old woman was sup-
porting everyone with her tiny retirement pension. Would Frau
Seldersen dare to say something anyway?

The two women talked for a good long time. Mother hadn't
forgotten why she'd come, but she didn't let any hint of it slip
out. An inexplicable shame held her back. And the old woman,
meekly and happily telling the younger woman about her sorrows, felt practically the same thing: the whole time she was
thinking that she was still in the Seldersens' books and hadn't
given them any money for a long time. She had a little bit set
aside in the drawer. Would she dare to bring it up—Frau Seldersen was here on a visit anyway, it was a good opportunity—would
she give her the money? She stood up and walked with unsteady
steps, swaying through the room. Frau Seldersen said she should
lie down, it would be better for her heart. The old woman stopped
and gave up on her plan. Well, maybe she'd be back in the store
again. Frau Seldersen said goodbye, she had already stayed too
long.

The next place she tried, she found no one at home and the
door locked. She turned around on the doorstep. At the fourth
place, the rooms were full of people—neighbors, friends, men,
women, they'd brought their children. A big tussle on the
floor, hellos, noise, tobacco smoke. Frau Seldersen stopped in

the doorway and didn't set foot in the room. Everyone's eyes turned to her. She waved into the room.

"Don't you want to come in?" the men called out. They flung their cards onto the table with a smack. "It's a birthday party." Mother said thank you, she wasn't planning to stay long. The children crawled over to her. One woman stood up from the table and walked carelessly over to her. Greetings. Mother whispered something in her ear. She looked startled, but Frau Seldersen kept whispering, without letting up.

Pause.

The woman walked slowly across the room, her back very straight, everyone could see her; the men interrupted their game, the room was suddenly dead quiet, even the children stopped and watched expectantly. The woman reached the kitchen cupboard and took two small coins out of a teacup on the middle shelf. Then she came back.

"There," she said, holding out her hand to give Frau Seldersen the money before everyone's eyes, the way you get rid of a beggar at the door. Not another word.

"Thank you," Frau Seldersen said. "Hope we see you again soon." The woman promised it, then shut the door. The noise had already started up inside.

Frau Seldersen slowly descended the stairs, her pulse racing, out of breath, dizzy, half unconscious. When she was back outside, she thought darkly that there was still time to pay a visit to several more people . . . but she had had enough for the day. She slowly turned her steps back to the city.

That night, when Herr Seldersen was counting up the day's earnings, she silently put the money on the table next to him. He nodded his head and kept counting. Frau Seldersen, after a while:

"From Frau Arndt and the Mertens."

"So," Father asked, "you ran into them and asked them for it? I wouldn't have dared."

She gave a dismissive snort and said: "I went to their apartments. Old Frau Bach is sick, maybe she'll send her daughter; they just needed a little reminder."

Father took the money and put it with the rest. He didn't say a word, not even a thank-you passed his lips. His face was rigid, immobile, anger and frustration eating away at him. But Frau Seldersen was angry too, and no doubt she had better cause to be. Did he think it was easy for her to bring herself to take such a step? If he only knew. . . . They had fobbed her off like a beggar at the door. Never again would she try to be helpful, try to do something for him, never. All she got in return was ingratitude.

Just ten days later she set out a second time. This trip was more successful, even Herr Seldersen couldn't get around acknowledging her skill and effectiveness. But he still hadn't come to terms with the substance of the thing. This woman!

Frau Seldersen, on the other hand, encouraged by her success, made these collection walks a regular habit. Twice a month at least.

The money was still not enough, though. The creditors would not stop writing and Herr Seldersen didn't know what else to do. He wrote to Albrecht, without telling his wife first.

Albrecht was in one of the larger cities in central Germany, doing his job as a musician and leading his life without any thought for the future. The day was divided in two halves: in one, he worked hard and almost without a break, and in the other he slept. There was nothing in between—no relaxation, no rest, no happiness. When he received his father's letter, he got an advance on his salary and sent the money off that same day. He got back a thank-you letter just as quickly, which brought tears to his eyes—he tore it to pieces and wanted to forget everything about it. After two months, he traveled back home and arrived tired, listless, a little embittered. A couple of days, then his work started in Berlin. He rested and met with no one.

Fritz Fiedler was still stuck at home. He hadn't found anything, no matter how hard his family tried. He lounged around; the days went by without his finding any regular, meaningful work to keep him busy. He was slowly falling to pieces. And he watched it all happen in angry silence. He only rarely went out or saw anyone.

Frau Seldersen had let the maid go and had been doing all the housework for a while now. She added it up for Albrecht: how much they were saving on food, wages, and everything else. In the weeks since the maid had left, Frau Seldersen had lost more than ten pounds; the work was a visible strain on her. But she forced herself to keep at it, bitterly, as though she had never had a maid in her life. Now and then she looked down at her hands— chapped and raw, her fingernails worn and brittle—but never spoke a word of complaint out loud. In Herr Seldersen's view, it was worth doing not only for the money they saved but also because he knew what it meant to stand around all day without any real work to do, in the store or, like Mother, leaning in the doorway keeping an eye out for customers. Any work was bearable, but to live without anything at all to do was impossible.

At first it went well. They were both satisfied with the new arrangement, even if life had become less comfortable. Herr Seldersen stayed downstairs alone in the morning, got the mail, and anything Mother didn't already know about she didn't need to know, as far as he was concerned. But it wasn't long before she started coming down to the store again; she would stop in to see him in the afternoons first, then in the mornings, and finally she arranged things so that she was always downstairs when the mail came. Why wasn't she upstairs? Father asked grumpily. She shook her head; she couldn't, their problems and the painful uncertainty kept driving her downstairs. So then they were standing together in the shop again, getting under each other's skin. Frau Seldersen was perceptive and knew more than Father told her, although not nearly everything. He wanted to protect her, and he didn't tell her what happened each day—the letters, the warnings, and other unpleasant incidents. But precisely this consideration was what she couldn't stand—she didn't know anything but suspected a lot, nothing for certain, just suggestions and suspicions everywhere that weighed more heavily upon her than the truth would have. When she was alone she looked at the account books, calculated the individual balances, and compared them with earlier ones, paging back, back, back through the years. Her head spun and she went around as in a dream.

One day, an acquaintance stopped her on the street and pointed out that her dress had a big worn spot on it. Frau Seldersen was confused, and thanked the woman for letting her know; she hadn't noticed, she wasn't paying as much attention and care to her clothes these days; she was dressing rather carelessly and indifferently, in fact. "Thank you very much," she said, "I wasn't paying attention, there's always so much to think about—" But she stopped short, she mustn't give away too much.

"Yes, I know," the woman answered. "You're not looking so good, you used to look so much younger."

"I have two grown children!" Frau Seldersen protested. She thought that was an excuse. Then she told the woman that she was now taking care of the household by herself: there are only two of us, but still, there's always work to do. The woman shook her hand and kept walking.

Tears came into Mother's eyes during her walk home. Now people could tell how things were with them just by looking at her on the street, not just Father but her too! And she had tried so hard to keep it all hidden, not let anyone know!

Up in the apartment she fell apart and lay down on the bed, sobbing. She stayed there until afternoon, when Herr Seldersen came upstairs for lunch. When he didn't find anything prepared, he grumbled and went back downstairs.

I'd really like to know what that woman does all morning, she can't even have lunch ready when I come upstairs hungry! She doesn't have that much to do. But it's like he always said, she was never very organized.

So ran Herr Seldersen's thoughts, and he worked himself into a greater and greater feeling of resentment. He hadn't noticed that Mother's eyes were red from crying, that she was stumbling around shattered, sick, and suffering. His poverty had made him deaf and blind; he was excessively sensitive only within painfully narrow confines.

.

The days were getting shorter and colder and it was long since time to order the winter clothes for the shop, but Herr Seldersen kept postponing the date. He wrote to his suppliers and told them not to send the items yet; that way the bills would come due a little later. But then, when the time came, a letter arrived: the manufacturer was saying that they could not supply him with the items he had ordered, his payments in recent months had been too irregular and they couldn't take on the risk of another loss at this time. In recent months they had found themselves in several such delicate situations where they'd least expected them, but times were tough and from now on they had to be particularly careful with their decisions. They could send Herr Seldersen a third of his order.

So then winter was upon them; people wanted heated rooms and warm clothes, but the shelves of Seldersen's store were bare. People came in to shop, he gave them a friendly welcome and acted like nothing was wrong, and they told him what they wanted. Just a moment, he said, and he sent Mother or the shopgirl to Herr Wiesel's or Herr Dalke's to fetch the items. Frau Seldersen didn't approve, from the very beginning; for her it meant the end of their last bit of independence—now they were nothing but a branch, a subsidiary, of the other two businesses—but Father showed a disregard he had never shown signs of before. While the customer waited patiently in the store, he said that the items had just arrived and were still in crates in the basement, not yet unpacked. His ability to make up excuses was inexhaustible, and in fact he even seemed to take a thief's pleasure in presenting such stories to his customers. Still, the excuses were sometimes so obvious and transparent that Mother took her key and went upstairs, ashamed to be in the room. Later, when Father saw her, he grinned with delight, but she could see beneath the smile, he couldn't fool her. Now people only rarely came into the store—the news had gotten around that Herr Seldersen didn't have a great selection, everyone could sense how it stood with him. The stories he told them, to explain why he kept them waiting, were ones they never heard anywhere else. They got impatient and refused to be kept waiting anymore.

They would rather shop at Herr Dalke's—his merchandise was no better, and not significantly cheaper, but Herr Dalke still ran a real business: the presentation, the displays, what couldn't you find there! You could forget your troubles for a little while, feast your eyes on the endless products, and aside from that the children would be given a balloon, or some kind of little toy, a flag with Herr Dalke's name on it. A wonderful little treat, and at no cost. Herr Seldersen ordered big paper plates for Christmas and gave them out for free, but they weren't anything compared to the flags and balloons. It was a useless waste of money; better to forgo such expensive advertising ploys in the future. He couldn't compete with Herr Dalke.

.

Herr Seldersen read the letter, his wife standing beside him, and neither of them said a word. They were both thinking the same thing: This is the end. If he wasn't careful now, everything would be all over, but what was he supposed to do?

"You need to go to Berlin at once," Mother pressured him. He shook his head. "Yes, you do," she repeated, "what'll happen if you don't?"

"I don't know," he said. It was all the same to him now—he just let things take their course. Frau Seldersen cried a lot that day.

The next morning, Father took the train to Berlin. He had thought it over and decided to try to talk with the old boss in person; maybe he'd accomplish what he wanted that way. Maybe he should ask Herr Nelken too. It's impossible, he murmured to himself, they can't, in the middle of winter . . . He had to make it through the winter, he could still feel some remnants of ambition inside him.

Herr Seldersen had a lot of trouble being admitted, and it took a long time. He didn't dare to look around, he thought everyone here in the office knew how things were going with him and what had brought him in to see them. At the reception desk, he gave his name. . . .

Herr Seldersen? Yes, of course, they knew who he was, even if he hadn't been by the office for a long time. "Nice to see you, what is this concerning, please?" Father hemmed and hawed a bit, but eventually said he wanted to discuss a certain letter he had received from them recently. They sent him another flight up; he'd be able to talk to someone there. He walked through the roomy hallways, as familiar to him as his own hall at home. It was dead silent. There were a few customers by the stockrooms, with delivery crates full of packages; the salesmen were standing around bored—lots of new faces, Herr Seldersen didn't know the people here anymore. Then he ran into an old colleague. Good to see you, great to see you.

"So, you've come by to see us? It's been a while. How's it going?"

Oh, if only you knew, Father thought, before stammering out a few vague words. . . . "Whenever I need something, I write, the trip is too expensive when just a postcard will do."

"Don't you get visits from us anymore?" the other man asked.

"Of course," Herr Seldersen hastily answered, "but you know how it is with traveling these days, you used to be on the road yourself."

"Yes, yes, I know," he said, lost in his memories.

Father asked why there was so little business here—it was dead, and in the winter season, before Christmas . . . ? He had expected there to be . . .

The other man brushed it off: "Business isn't exactly booming anymore; we feel it here too." Then he said, in a quiet voice, that the big firm Hans & Co. was stopping payments. It wasn't public knowledge yet, but it wouldn't be long now—it was an open secret. Hans & Co.? Herr Seldersen repeated, that's impossible. He shook his head; unbelievable, where would it end? One after the other, and now the big firms too, the ones we always thought were . . . In the end, you couldn't be surprised when . . .

No, you couldn't be surprised, the other man agreed.

"But where will it end?" Herr Seldersen got excited. "Where, I ask you?!"

Pause.

"I don't know, Herr Seldersen. Every day in the papers you read a big list of the ones who've given up. Maybe that's the best thing, I don't know."

"Okay, but then what, what comes after that?"

"I don't know that either," the man finally said. He was almost ashamed to say it. "I don't know, I'm old, I won't live to see it so I try not to think about it."

Herr Seldersen fell silent. Whatever happened, he wouldn't be there to see it, the other man had said, and that was enough. Now Herr Seldersen often wished he could think like that too— for a long time he had felt the longing for peace, for rest, for unconsciousness, stronger and stronger and dangerously close. No one knew.

He said goodbye and went up another floor. Here he had to look for a long time before he finally found one of the directors. Herr Seldersen greeted him and kept looking for the senior director, he knew him personally, he had great hopes for his talk with him. But he couldn't find him anywhere, it was getting late and he hadn't accomplished a thing. He knew the other director too, if only slightly—he had joined the firm only recently, less than five years ago. He was young, vigorous, and decisive. From the beginning, Herr Seldersen had felt an aversion to him. He never had much to do with him in the years when things were going better; he had always timidly avoided contact with him, for who knows what emotional reasons.

Finally he worked up the courage to go up to the young director and politely ask him where he might find the senior director, the old man—he asked for him by name.

"He's not here," he answered. "What is this concerning, please?"

Herr Seldersen explained that he was hoping to talk to him in person. When was he expected in?

"Rarely," the young director replied; "he's rarely in the office—at his age, with the present circumstances. . . . It's better that way."

Father understood. So he had come all this way for nothing. He thought for a moment, then gave a short bow—he was the older man in the conversation, after all, even if he was the one making the request, he mustn't be too obsequious. He told him his name. "I know who you are," the director answered in a friendly voice; before, he had acted like he was talking to a stranger. Herr Seldersen took a deep breath and cautiously revealed the reason for his visit. The director understood immediately; he was already informed about the entire situation. He stayed perfectly polite, expressed his regret countless times, excused himself for a moment to take a call and then came back to continue the conversation, or called a young man into the room and dictated a few sentences that had just come to him; during these pauses, Father stood there not knowing what to do with himself. What he most wanted to do was just run away, but he couldn't do that, so he waited patiently. Herr Nelken turned up too, but stayed unobtrusively in the background. When the young director came back, he picked up the conversation precisely where he had left off. His tone was friendly and accommodating, just what one would expect from a smart young businessman, but that was exactly what made Herr Seldersen feel so awkward.

"Yes, I see," he said, "I admit that our recent history hasn't been good and you have to be careful." The director nodded forcefully . . . he should show him their books sometime, Herr Seldersen wouldn't believe what he saw.

"But if you don't give me any more credit, where will that leave me?"

Silence.

"The fact is, we can't trust you," the director said slowly. "The experiences we've had show that we're right not to trust you."

Herr Seldersen tried desperately to think of a response. "Trust," he whispered, "right. When someone has money it's easy to trust him, but—"

"But Herr Seldersen," the director interrupted him, "we gave you credit, until you settled with us a year and a half ago and we took a big loss. Then we kept giving you credit—not as much as before, that's true, but you still had a chance. Now you're behind in your payments again. Is that our fault?"

"But it wasn't enough before; if you had given me a bigger chance . . . think about it, the competition is tough."

"I don't know," the younger man shrugged. "Even so . . . it would have meant taking on a much bigger risk. You didn't have any backing, and we can't just give out credit wherever we want to. You're a businessman too. Admit it, it wouldn't have been good business."

"But if I'd had wares to sell," Father repeated. He couldn't get past that thought, as though that were the key to the whole situation.

"No, Herr Seldersen," the director suddenly said, and it sounded as if he were kindly wanting to teach Father something, "that wouldn't have helped you. You're wrong if you think it would have. Your costs would have only been higher."

"Higher? Why?" Father asked. He didn't see why.

"Don't you have unemployment in your town too?" the director asked calmly.

Father fell silent. Now he understood, and it made him dizzy. It was the same misfortune everywhere; no matter how you twisted and turned you eventually ended up back where you started. Everything was connected, and who could escape? Not him, not anymore—his path was blocked. And the way the director made his comment about the unemployment, apparently so calm and indifferent, made Father slowly realize that he wasn't just sitting here by himself, alone, laying out his own personal situation—there was something else in him too, which was a feeling he had never had before. He saw in his mind's eye a patient march of sad people coming up to him and saying: We can't buy anymore, we have only enough money to spend on food and that comes first. But Father gave them something. Nothing would ever change, as long as he was there he would hold out and give people credit, otherwise the whole thing just couldn't go on.

And here he was, fighting to get credit himself from someone else—a desperate struggle, he wanted to keep working. . . . "And now you want to leave me in the lurch," he said softly. He wanted to scream, but he couldn't bring himself to do it anymore.

"We'll give you goods, of course," the director answered, politely as ever. "If I remember correctly, you can have a third of your order from us at once, isn't that correct?"

"That's not enough," Father protested. "Especially now, before Christmas; now's when people want to buy."

The director shrugged. Herr Seldersen left, walking with heavy footsteps. When he passed Herr Nelken he looked up, and a thought flashed through his mind. He decided to stop for a moment. Herr Nelken stood there looking down at the floor; maybe he was looking for a pin he had dropped. Father didn't know if he should shake his hand . . . ? He had played his part here to the end, and he left.

That afternoon he saw his children. He seemed to be noticeably calmer and more composed than he had been recently, but they knew how things stood. They sat together for a long time and Father told them why he had come to Berlin, about the conversation he had had, and the result. Long silence. Finally

Anneliese said that they couldn't just leave it at that, something had to be done. He looked at her. "But what?" he asked quietly. "Any suggestions?" Silence. Then he said that he had seen it coming for a long time, but up until then he had never talked about it, so as not to worry them unnecessarily. Now it couldn't last much longer, and it didn't make any sense to keep hoping. Tears ran down his cheeks when he spoke these words, but he didn't notice he was crying. They sat there in total silence. The whole time, Albrecht never stopped staring at his father; he remembered that he had seen him cry once before. Back then, Father had been sitting on a small bench in the kitchen, crying because he had to start going door-to-door again; he didn't see any other way forward, and it seemed so unbearable to him that he was crying. Those tears were for nothing, he hadn't gone door-to-door after all. Everything turned out different— things didn't improve, but they developed more slowly, and terribly, than he could have suspected. Now he was sitting here, crying, and saying that the end had come. They weren't giving him goods to sell anymore, he had irrevocably lost their trust, it was over for him.

But it wasn't yet over, he was wrong. His ignorance was his only excuse for saying such a thing. He had not exhausted every possibility, not yet suffered the deepest shame—that still lay ahead.

The afternoon disappeared in endless reflections, considerations, plans that came to nothing—it was hopeless. Father went home, kissing them affectionately goodbye before boarding the train.

"We shouldn't let him travel alone," Anneliese said. Albrecht shrugged. He was paralyzed himself.

Mother was waiting for him at the station back home. It was cold and windy, she was freezing even in her overcoat. When she saw him at the gate, saw how he handed over his ticket and then looked around to see if someone had come to fetch him, she knew everything. They greeted each other in silence, she took his arm, and they walked home like that, slowly, against the wind. Father haltingly told her about every possible thing—what he'd seen in Berlin, his afternoon with the children, they send their best wishes—but not a word about the real purpose of his trip. Finally Mother asked him. She couldn't hold out any longer, her nerves were shot. . . . "And what did you manage to get?"

"Nothing," Father answered. "Nothing."

Pause.

"My God," Mother whispered. "What now?"

Had Father even heard her? He pulled his cap down hard, covering his face. Mother quietly cried to herself; she'd been worried all day, she'd had a premonition! All for nothing, and now what? The wind whistled and bent back their bodies; they had to crouch and push hard against it to gain any ground at all. They struggled on, bit their lips, and said nothing. They arrived home exhausted. Mother brought out dinner, but neither of them ate and they went right to bed.

.

And now I have to describe a night that is so full of unfathomable sorrow and deepest despair that I can hardly bear to think about it. I intend to tell it carefully and delicately, so as not to reopen any old wounds: the story of the night when it seemed as though destiny had found a terrible way out of the dilemma. I begin:

In the bedroom closet in the front corner, near the window, Herr Seldersen kept a revolver hidden in a drawer under the washcloths. He had brought it home with him from the war; everyone knew it and no one ever mentioned it. No, I have to start over again, I have to go much further back and not leave any of the events that led to this night under the slightest shadow.

A revolver is good; with a gas hose the suffering is only drawn out longer. Behold Herr Seldersen, a man past fifty who made it through the war on the front lines in good health; four turbulent years were unable to put an end to him, and he came back—the way one does from a campaign one has lost: tired, exhausted, worn-out, but he was healthy, with all his limbs intact, his life spared. And now this old man, on whom life has played such dirty tricks, is lying awake in his bed, unable to sleep, restlessly tossing and turning from side to side as though his whole body were one big wound. His wife lies awake next to him. He groans, pleads, and curses, asking for only one thing: to forget, to rest, rest at last. In the dark of night, he slowly sits up in his bed and gently, carefully slips off the blanket, and he is so inflamed by his idea, the thought of what he has decided to do, that he doesn't notice Mother taking off her blanket just as quietly, but infinitely more nimbly, scared that it's too late. Father stands in front of the clothes closet, softly turns the key, and carefully opens the door whose cracked wood he knows will creak. Then Mother is standing next to him in her nightgown, like a ghost, toweringly large and absolutely determined. She grabs Father's hand and slowly pushes it down with a powerful strength that has miraculously emerged from her old, ruined body. Father is so surprised at first that he puts up no resistance and Mother has an easy time of it, but he soon regains his strength and a silent, desperate struggle begins in the dark. "Let me go," he groans, insane with rage that someone is stopping him. She stands there as if possessed, clasping his hand in an iron grip. And silently crying. "Enough," Father says at last; "it's finally over now." He begs her to let him go. Not a word escapes Mother's lips: her whole body is tense with the extraordinary effort, but she is certain of victory. Pause. "No, no," she says softly, her voice shaking in a sob, "no, no." Who could prevail against that? There is a fierce, bitter struggle. Father looks at Mother in the dark room and sees her old face, her hair let down, her body shaking with fear and agitation. "Come here," she whispers softly, "come back and lie down." It sounds so kind, almost seductive. Father has no choice, he obeys and silently lies down in bed. But the struggle isn't over—it is as though he has only now realized his situation, he throws himself from side to side and a storm of sobs comes over him, his body almost bursting from the violent heaves. Mother, lying next to him, stays completely still at first and lets the pain work itself out, without thinking anything, just there for him. Then her hand gently feels for him and she takes his head the way she used to, slides imperceptibly closer, and wraps Father in her arms. All he can do now is cry it out; she feels his quaking body and gradually feels that his great convulsions are coming at longer and longer intervals, and then gradually he calms down. And so sleep, benevolent and liberating, overtakes him at last.

·

Two days later, in the evening. Herr Seldersen has followed his wife's advice and paid a call to Herr Dalke, putting himself through his deepest humiliation. He let the morning go by, then the afternoon, and only when the streets were starting to dim in the twilight and the lights came on in the shops did he feel the courage to do it. Yes, he went to see Herr Dalke, who made as much in three days as he did in thirty, who had backing, people's trust, everything he wanted. Now Herr Seldersen was going to see him. In truth, they were competitors, even if they had a good personal relationship—had he lost all shame?

Herr Dalke was a clever man. He was upstairs in his office, bent over his books, when Father walked in.

"Good evening," Herr Seldersen said softly. "Is now a good time?"

Herr Dalke didn't look at all surprised to see him. He walked over to Father, invited him to take a seat, and then sat down across from him. He asked him—no, he didn't ask much, he knew why Father was there. He skillfully avoided asking, and did not make it hard for Herr Seldersen to get straight to the point; he knew what had made him come see him. A conversation, cheerful enough, went back and forth between them, about everything weighing down on Herr Seldersen, and then it was actually Herr Dalke who made the suggestion to Father:

hesitantly, gently, he didn't want to impose it on Father. He offered him a sum that was just enough to cover Herr Seldersen's purchases for the winter. Father sat in silence; he hadn't expected that, anything but that.

"It's too much," he said, "I can't accept that, I'll have to pay you back later, after all, it would be much too difficult, no."

They agreed on half the amount Dalke had offered. That was enough.

Herr Seldersen was about to stand up and say goodbye, but Herr Dalke had one more item to discuss. He saw further ahead.

"Herr Seldersen," he said, "I'd like to have some kind of security for the money I'm giving you."

Herr Seldersen looked up, but avoided looking at Herr Dalke.

"Security?" he whispered.

Herr Dalke nodded: "Yes, your furniture and whatever valuables needed to total the amount. It's better that way. Bring me a list tomorrow."

Then he offered Herr Seldersen his hand. Herr Seldersen breathed easier.

"Thank you very much," he said, vigorously shaking Herr Dalke's hand. "Thank you!" He had a friend in Herr Dalke too. In all the years they had known each other, there had never been any ill feeling between them, even if they were also competitors, and in truth they were more than competitors. Herr Dalke possessed what Father didn't—others' trust, a large business, savings, backers, reserves, and that was what mattered. He was one of the people standing together in a more and more impenetrable circle and drawing it closer around themselves, not letting anyone else in. An individual couldn't do a thing against them. Yes, in fact Herr Dalke was responsible—not personally responsible, he didn't mean any harm, but he was on the other side. He was a murderer: not in secret, not lying in wait to ambush anyone, but a firmly established force, secure in his position, murdering with his actions. That was Herr Dalke. And a friend too. Herr Seldersen went to Berlin the next day and bought wares with the money Herr Dalke had given him. He went to the firm where he had recently been humiliated—they had said they no longer trusted him, after twenty-five years . . . fine, but in he went, even though he didn't need to, since with cash in hand he could buy goods anywhere. He didn't want to miss out on the chance to feel his triumph.

He spent a long time shopping around; a large delivery crate was packed for him. When the time came to total everything up, the salesman disappeared for a moment, to check with his supervisor. Those were the rules, they had to check about every buyer. When he came back, he wasn't alone: the young director was with him, the same one Father had recently had his run-in with. It was too bad Herr Nelken wasn't there, Herr Seldersen wanted to ask them to summon Herr Nelken too. He wanted everyone to see what was about to happen. The young director started to say, politely but firmly, that he was very sorry but Herr Seldersen must recall their recent discussion . . .

"I'm paying up front," Father interrupted him.

"Excuse me?"

"I'm paying up front, in cash," Father repeated; apparently they had not understood him. "My train leaves in an hour and a half, the items need to be on the platform by then. I'll take them with me. If that's not possible then I'm sorry, but—"

"But of course, at once." So he wanted to pay up front, that's fine, everything will be delivered promptly, he could depend on that.

The young director stood there and didn't know what else to say. In the end, it didn't matter to him where Herr Seldersen had gotten the money from, maybe he had just come into a surprise inheritance, or won the lottery, or stolen it . . . what did he care? Herr Seldersen paid cash, received his goods, and was once again treated with respect: At your service, Herr Seldersen, at your service as always. . . .

When he was back outside on the street, Father spit three

times. He felt like kicking in the window. Anyway, he had what he'd come for, he could feel satisfied about that. But it was disgusting, unspeakably disgusting, he had had enough of all this playacting. He was almost ashamed of having played such a pitiful role in the drama. Still, he really did wish he could have seen Herr Nelken; he had planned a proper slap in the face for him.

.

In December, late on a Tuesday night in a small hotel in the city center, Fritz Fiedler shot himself. When they found him the next morning his body was cold and a thin red stream was smeared across his face from a small wound in his temple. Albrecht heard about his friend's death the next day. When the maid woke him up in the early morning, it was still dark outside. He turned on the lamp on his nightstand and a cheering yellow glow spread through the room. He went over to the window— there was snow again on the courtyard outside, it had fallen overnight. Then he got dressed, sat down at his table, and ate with the sad ceremoniousness of anyone eating alone. The maid slowly came into the room; she was old and had worked there for more than ten years already. She leaned on the doorframe and suddenly asked: "Do you know someone named Fritz Fiedler, or Fiedeler?"

"Yes, Fritz Fiedler, I know him," Albrecht answered. He went on eating. "What about him, how do you know him?"

"Ach," she said, "it's in the paper today, I just read it. Someone named Fritz Fiedler shot himself."

Albrecht leapt up—all sleep and calm had vanished from the room. Fritz, dead! He ran out, picked up the newspaper lying on the desk, and it didn't take long to find the report: ten lines, a short paragraph, the daily suicides. Fritz had shot himself, and not alone: he had killed a girl too—their love had been so strong, no one had known about it.

The day was just beginning and Albrecht had to get through

it. He took the streetcar into the city and went to the morgue; he had to see his friend one more time. When he opened the door to the waiting room, three figures in black turned toward him: Fritz's parents and another member of the family. Albrecht went over to Fritz's mother and held out his hand.

"Don't cry," he said. "He is finally at peace now."

But that only made her cry more.

Fritz's father stood there the whole time and pointed at his own temple with his index finger: "Here's where he put it in." He repeated the same sentence five times, always the same words with the same gesture.

Albrecht registered and asked to be allowed to see the body. Someone led him into the room. They crossed a spacious auditorium with a crucifix on the altar at the front, then went down long corridors to a staircase. Here they ran into four men, solemnly dressed in tails and top hats. One of them said: "I specifically told the driver to bring a coffin, he said he'd arrange it with the carpenter, he promised. Now there's no coffin and people are coming from out of town. All he cares about is how he can make a little money. —Yes, yes."

They arrived at the basement, where large wooden compartments were stacked high on both sides like rabbit hutches. What could be in them? The man guiding Albrecht went over to one of them back in the corner, indicated to Albrecht to step back, and pulled out a long rolling platform.—On it lay the dead man. The guide stepped away and stood by the wall, clasped his hands behind his back, and lowered his gaze to the floor, his duty fulfilled.

On the bier lay Fritz. He was naked and his magnificent body looked unblemished. With his eyes closed—no more eyeglasses— his face looked asleep, as though he were resting. A red stripe ran across his cheek, pale and dried-out. Dead. If that wasn't there, Albrecht thought, he would not have been able to grasp that this was death. He still didn't comprehend it. He saw his friend lying there as though asleep; all he had to do was gently take him by the hand and he would surely wake up. His hand was stiff and cold. And his body, his beautiful, athletic body, lay there utterly unresponsive. Life had run out from the small hole in his head, across his cheek, and vanished. Albrecht knew that body from when it was still warm and flinched slightly at the touch of his hand, knew how it used to bend and tense and release during track and field events. He knew, he saw. But now here was death. What is death? Or at least, the end of life? There was a compartment here and beyond that was nothing, there was no communication between the two sides.

Albrecht stood by his dead friend's bier for a long time. No tears came to him; an icy coldness rose up within him and he stayed hardened, restrained, self-controlled, but nonetheless moved, full of grief, alive. He said goodbye and it was an hour of death and birth in one, although he didn't know that yet. He was saying goodbye to someone, his friend, who once had lived and whose life was nothing but an attempt to stay alive, as a human being, warm and vital and a part of his age, worth as much as anyone else—an attempt to find his way, undertaken in the full-blooded strength and faith of youth. Albrecht said goodbye to everything they had said to each other, all their arguments and the mistakes they had made together. Death was here and it was true, no longer a mistake, and it brought deliverance. It was only later, when Albrecht thought back to this time standing next to his dead friend, that he understood the full meaning of death. It claimed its victims and brought them release at the same time. It extinguished a life and was thus a symbol, a proof, or more: a warning. It was an act that lay inside everyone, in Albrecht too, more or less clearly, but by being there at all it was necessarily conscious, concrete, and comprehensible. And did this act not thereby bring about a kind of healing? Fritz had carried out what had lain darkly inside him, he had dared to commit the deed and had thus taken it upon himself, so now Albrecht's path to a new life was free.

Fritz Fiedler was dead. Albrecht walked on, through the

streets of his hometown—by the next day he had already gone back home. His parents were not surprised to see him suddenly appear in the shop unannounced, and didn't ask much or say much: they felt what had happened too deeply themselves. Now he was back home, in the city that had meant so much to them both—here was where they had begun, and they would always bear a trace of these bygone things within them.

Albrecht was alone. What could he do for his dead friend? He went to the stand on the corner and bought the newspaper that had puffed up the two deaths into a giant love tragedy.

"I'd like every copy of this paper you have."

"No, you can't have more than three," the newspaper seller answered. "Other people want to read it too." He could no doubt see what Albrecht had planned. There was everything in the article: Fritz's running away from school, America, and much more that had happened—a sad little masterpiece of explanation and interpretation. He had shot himself, with a girl, a love tragedy. The public took pleasure in that.

This was all Albrecht could do: buy the newspapers and burn them. His friend was buried the Sunday before Christmas. The snow still covered the city, well trodden and gray, but it lay white and undisturbed over the graves in the churchyard.

Then Albrecht took the train back to Berlin and life went on, with all its incessant stress and excitement. The winter was cold, the poverty and misery were great—it was the third such winter that people had had to live through. How everyone had feared it, complained, the third winter already . . . and now they were right in the middle of it. At first they thought they would never survive it.

.

Late one winter evening, Albrecht left his apartment and went out into the street, driven out by a mysterious disquiet and his infinite loneliness. It was cold outside and the snow, stamped down hard and smooth as a mirror, covered the roads. Albrecht ran through the busy streets with his hands buried deep in his coat pockets, ears tucked under a cap, without a goal in mind or a thought in his head. There were a lot of people out—there always were, day and night, as though they all had a cozy destination they were wending their leisurely way toward. But anyone in a hurry, trying to move fast, had to be careful. Albrecht zigzagged through the gaps in the crowd, stumbling and skidding. Oof, what would that woman have said if he hadn't turned aside at the last second and had hurtled into her? Ha, nice one. I can't let her think that I was trying to land in her pretty lap, sorry, a thousand pardons! Why am I in such a hurry . . . ? It's too cold in my room today, do you understand what I'm saying? What I mean is that when I got home, my room was very hot. I took off my jacket, loosened my collar, it felt nice. But after a half hour it was almost unbearably hot in there, and stuffy too—I couldn't stand it. Fresh air, deep breaths . . . I carefully swung the window open a little bit and lay down in bed, feeling treacherously tired. I usually never feel tired, never get to relax at all . . . but that's another story. When I woke up again, it was dark and cold. I stuck my hand out the window, but it was just as icy outside. A gust of wind must have opened the window all the way, and the cold air was blowing in. The mirror was steamed up, the stove was dripping with moisture in the corner. I did exercises to warm up; pumped my arms and legs; sang; tried to play the violin, but that only warmed up my fingers. My head was burning hot but everything else was as cold as before. I had forgotten to close the window. What was I supposed to do in a freezing-cold room?

At the intersection, the rails had frozen over with slippery ice: whoever stepped on them and didn't keep control of himself would fall, right in front of the streetcar. The driver rang the bell, scattered sand, put on the brakes, but the glaring eye on the front of the car came closer and closer. Quick—stand up again, keep going, careful! A car whizzed out from behind the streetcar, he didn't see it and he jumped back, and the wheels of the streetcar screeched with rage as the brakes dug in and brought them to a stop. Startled back and hemmed in between the streetcar and an automobile, a pale young man stood erect, his breath racing.

The constable's cap is green, with soft earflaps. The lights on the newspaper office are big and yellow, the line underneath them blue, the windows lined with yellow, the newspapers printed in black on gray paper . . . colors, colors everywhere, everyone on the street a different color, but only one color is beautiful: red. And if there's blood as well, just a little, a thin stripe of it across the cheek. When my father is happy he cries, not tears of joy but because that's when he feels his misery the most. Someone leaning against the wall of a building because it's too cold for him to sit on the floor anymore isn't doing it out of pleasure in the new opportunity life has offered him. If he has a wooden leg, he doesn't have to worry about it freezing and falling off someday. But still, that's something to see: a man leaning against the wall with one healthy leg while the other leg is lying in Russia or France somewhere . . . that's something, all right. In a case like that you don't have to wonder where it all started.

A man came up and said something to him, snatching at his hat and murmuring a few words. Albrecht shook his head: No, I don't have any to spare, I can't give you anything. But he didn't move and he looked at the man more closely. He was old and seriously down and out. . . . A few matches? the man repeated, holding the box in his hand. Albrecht answered: "No thanks, I don't smoke." But still he stayed where he was and looked the man up and down. "Are you a father?" he suddenly asked. "Do you have children?" The man nodded sadly, squinted his eyes, and moved off.

Albrecht ran through the streets. . . . Father, he thought, Father. . . . His head was about to burst, his thoughts were rushing around in his head, it was as though he were only half conscious. And then the feeling, the same savage feeling he'd had more and more often recently, that it's horrible to be running around tormenting himself with his personal emotions and his punishing self-analysis while back at home Father. . . . But enough, no more.

He jumped on a streetcar coming his way, without looking at the number or destination. He stood in the front next to the driver in his thick fur coat; he paid and he rode, until they stopped for a long time and he started to feel cold. "Hey, won't you get out?" the conductor asked. "Last stop." —"Oh, I see, I'll ride back with you." "Can't do that," came the reply. "We're taking the car to the depot."

It was late. How would he get home from here? He was somewhere or another very far on the outskirts of the city. The driver pointed the way to the nearest night bus and Albrecht rode home, tired and worn-out. At no point in the evening had he felt any happier than he was when he started.

·

The holidays arrived and Albrecht went home. He had left Berlin without telling his parents beforehand and they were shocked to see him walk into the shop so unexpectedly. They almost didn't recognize him. He was pale, a bit run-down, and his face looked more tired and frail than ever. Albrecht was very happy to see them again, he was home! But when he reached out to shake his father's hand, he knew right then that he was back, being drawn into the cramped little sphere of their cares and worries, which were his too. These were his parents—Father an old man, though not so much old as utterly broken and helpless; Mother's hair glittered gray, her tiny body was like a child's, but she still remained the stronger and firmer of the two; heaven knew what secret soil she drew her strength from. It was all exactly the way Albrecht had pictured it. . . . He stayed at home for the time being, intending to rest a little. His parents tended him with all the love they were capable of, and he repaid them with childlike loyalty and affection.

Life was miserable in his hometown—wherever Albrecht looked he saw only tired faces with poverty and hard times written all over them. Nowhere was there any carefree happiness and enjoyment of life—even Herr Wiesel went around with a hangdog look; he didn't have anything to worry about, but the life he saw all around him, more wretched and desperate every day, made him suffer: he did have a sympathetic heart. Albrecht walked up and down the streets and went to visit the remote, secret places he knew so well in the forest, where he had once played as a child, excited, with such grand dreams. But even there he felt strangely cold and unmoved. Had he forgotten? Had he been untrue to the forest after all? A dull fatigue filled his head; he was wearing a heavy suit of armor; he gasped and groaned under his load but couldn't get free of it.

Once again, his parents' life was at the threshold of a great change, perhaps the last one they would have to face before the end. It didn't come as a surprise, they had expected it for years now; it was only a question of time, there was no way it could turn out any differently. The bankruptcy had gone deep enough now that Herr Seldersen gave up his shop—he didn't go on. He was firmly convinced. He had put off the decision long enough, kept it to himself almost as though he had a powerful weapon in his hands that he could use to exact a terrible revenge. He had endured the situation—a slow death, unstoppable, like an epidemic, spreading everywhere—for long enough. Was he supposed to go back to Herr Dalke again and ask for more money? Or maybe Herr Wiesel this time? No, he didn't go, not to either one, he'd rather go to the judge and declare bankruptcy. Period.

He told Albrecht, trying to break it to him gently. Albrecht said nothing. He no longer expected anything different. If Father thought that this was the best thing for him, and for all of them . . . but a lot of questions remained unanswered, a lot of problems unsolved. Finally, several days after he'd returned home, Albrecht worked up the courage to ask his father what would happen when he closed the shop and lost his job. What would he do? How did he imagine his future? Damned good questions—there was no avoiding them. Albrecht himself was almost frightened by the inescapable path his thoughts seemed to follow.

Herr Seldersen didn't take long to answer: "We'll give up the apartment here and move in with you in Berlin." They were sure of that step.

"All right, and then? What next?"

Hmm . . . Herr Seldersen shrugged. What next? He didn't know, and he seemed never to have even thought about it, but at the same time he didn't look the least bit taken aback or worried. It was hard to believe, incredible—not a thought as to what would come after? No, first he wanted to end things here. Whatever came next couldn't be worse than this, in any case. He was sure of that. No, Herr Seldersen would take it as it came.

Albrecht didn't bother asking any further questions; he would never understand his father, comprehend his indifference. He himself wasn't planning to face his future with such a wait-and-see attitude—on the contrary, he was as tense and anxious as could be, and ready for the fiercest struggle. That said, at the moment he was exhausted, and he lay there unable to come up with any grand plans. He knew, though, that this seemingly external event, this change taking place purely in the economic sphere, was also laying the foundation for a difficult, decisive step in his own life: coming to terms with where he himself stood, and what he would do in the future. In fact, everything was beginning for him, just when the end was waiting for his father. Father was talking the way someone can talk only if he is at the very end, mercilessly robbed of every possible future—with no hope, no consideration or love, totally merciless. It made Albrecht shudder as this realization put its roots down into him, and a strange feeling often came over him when he was talking to his father: He no longer seemed to be talking to a person, old and defeated, in a hopeless position but still living and breathing. Instead it felt like he was standing in front of a monument, the symbol of a bygone era, and in his thoughts he bowed before it with admiration and unspeakable sorrow. The whole time Albrecht had stayed by himself, he had been quiet and reserved, almost irresolute, in everything he did—no one asked or expected anything of him, except himself. Here, back home, things had fundamentally changed: his parents had grown old, life had pushed their backs slowly but surely to the wall, and they felt tired and betrayed. What else could Albrecht do but pull himself together and summon up his last reserves of courage and confidence from a long-lost place in his soul? It was hard for him, damned hard—there were many times he thought it was too much for him, and in those moments he thought longing, sweetly dangerous thoughts about his dead friend. But he persevered—yes, he continued to walk the earth, God be praised, he was young and not the type to lose heart and stay on the sidelines now that he knew better. He had seen and learned a lot in his years of living alone in Berlin. Events were not taking place in the shadows, or sweeping past at a great distance: he was affected too. And he had seen the fateful inability to act, culpable failure, and wasted humanity.

Albrecht also went to see Dr. Köster—his friend and "teacher," as he jokingly called himself. They arranged for Albrecht to come see him; they wanted to spend a whole evening together again, in peace and quiet, indulging in memories and reviving their old friendship. A lot of time had gone by since that lecture for the Literary Society where Dr. Köster had first seen Albrecht, then still a schoolboy in short pants and with a dreamy look in his eyes. After Albrecht had graduated and gone to Berlin, only a fleeting exchange of cards and short letters kept their connection alive. But they met up often when Albrecht was home during vacations, and their relationship had stayed the same as it was during Albrecht's school days.

He went at the appointed time and they sat together in the

big room where Dr. Köster had lived ever since he had moved to this town. Everything was in exactly the same place as Albrecht remembered it being; he recognized everything, the pictures on the walls, the tall two-part bookshelf, the desk by the window, the piano covered with books and music. Still the same familiar chaos everywhere. Albrecht stood in the room and didn't feel quite right for some time, certainly not comfortable and secure, the way he used to feel there. Maybe it would have been better for him not to come, he thought. Dr. Köster showed him books he had bought recently, read him excerpts, and asked him what he thought.

"Good," Albrecht agreed. "Excellently observed, forcefully described, it's good." He said this without really thinking about it; ultimately he didn't feel like what he heard had any connection to him at all, he hadn't even listened carefully, he just wanted to avoid a break in the conversation and letting his friend notice anything. Maybe he didn't want to disappoint him.

"May I lend you the book?" Dr. Köster asked.

"No thanks, I'd rather not take it," Albrecht answered, firmly refusing.

"Why not?" Dr. Köster was amazed and didn't hide it. "Why not?" he repeated.

"I have to take care of my eyes," Albrecht replied, "and anyway, I don't have time."

Dr. Köster looked at him. He didn't like the tone Albrecht was using to explain himself: it was not impolite, exactly, but it held something hidden inside it that Dr. Köster couldn't yet explain.

"As you wish," he said curtly, and put down the book. Then they sat down. Albrecht sat in a deep armchair, sank into the soft cushions, and tried as best he could to answer the questions Dr. Köster asked him. There was a lot he wanted to hear from Albrecht about how it was going in Berlin, they hadn't seen each other much at all in the past few years—what was he doing, how did everything look out there? He himself never left this town, some cursed fate kept him here.

"So tell me, Albrecht, how are you? You look tired, a little pale. Is life in the big city that hard?"

"Oh," Albrecht answered reluctantly—he didn't want to be reminded of everything—"I just need to relax here a bit. I'm already feeling much better. I've only been here a few days, and my parents are going through a difficult time."

Dr. Köster stole a glance at him and felt uneasy about pressing him any further. He had been a student too, though that was many years ago, and Albrecht's case was clearly different.

"I'd rather hear about you," Albrecht said. "How is your work going, are you making progress? Tell me."

What should he say about it? He had already spent five years on his book; at the moment it wasn't making any particular progress, although it also wasn't at a complete standstill: he had started seeing some of it into print already, corrected a few sheets of proofs, and he was continuing to work on it, but everything seemed to be in a strange state of suspension, hanging in the air, so to speak. He often felt disgusted and deeply repelled by his work, to the point where it took a significant act of will to sit back down to it. It was not yet finished and for now the end was not in sight, even though his publisher had already announced it as forthcoming a long time ago. Aside from that, he was out of money and was currently trying to find a new source of income. It was all rather unpleasant, he admitted. Even if the book ever comes out, who will read it? A work so removed from practical matters, about the spirit and everything connected with the life of the mind, who will really read it? No, when he looked at things straight on he felt a deep hopelessness. He said something along those lines. Those weren't his exact words, but Albrecht could read it all between the lines, and he was not a little amazed.

"So it's here too," he said. "The same resignation, everywhere you look."

Dr. Köster nodded. "Call it resignation, exhaustion, as you wish. The only thing to do is live with the sadness and keep quiet."

"What do you mean, 'live with the sadness and keep quiet'?" Albrecht said. "Do you really think there's nothing else to do but take refuge in that?"

"Of course there is, and you'll be able to argue there is just from among the people you know. But I only need look at you, Albrecht, and I am sure of what I'm saying. I'm truly sorry, but I don't believe that there's anything else for us to do, unless we want to follow the path of the thugs and male hysterics." He seemed depressed.

"You're wrong," Albrecht said slowly. "If you're talking about me, Dr. Köster, you are definitely wrong. I'm tired at the moment, I admit that, and sometimes I also feel adrift in the world; I haven't read any books for a long time, and I'm almost proud of it," he added.

"Proud of it? That's ridiculous, Albrecht! You haven't done much with your life if empty accomplishments like that are what you have to be proud of, let me tell you. Haven't read any books—good God, if you'd said something like that back in the old days! But the whole time I've been sitting here with you, and especially when I showed you the books before, I couldn't help feeling that you have started to think and talk dismissively about the things that used to matter to you."

Albrecht calmly heard the charges—for what was this if not an accusation and a call to change his ways!

"I'm not being dismissive or contemptuous, you have to believe me. It may sound indifferent, that I'd accept, but I don't need to defend myself against that, do I?"

"Indifferent? I'd take that as a sign of your resignation and exhaustion."

"I have a much simpler view of it," Albrecht answered. "I really don't have time. The days go by and there's time only for purely practical matters. I take it you know the conditions I'm living and going to school in, they call it working your way through college: that means that along with my studies I work and earn money, or maybe that along with working and earning money I study, I'm often not totally clear on it myself. All I know is that when it comes to money my classes go to hell. My nerves too, but there's nothing to be done about that either." He paused for a moment. Dr. Köster, sitting across from him, was listening closely. Then Albrecht went on: "You think you'll get hold of the life of the mind, investigate the inner spirit of things, but then you run aground on just the outward form, the external details. Everything is about making sure you have the most basic necessities. I know this conflict is nothing new, lots of other people have been through it already and then forgotten it again."

"Forgotten it again? What is that supposed to mean, Albrecht?" Dr. Köster interrupted him. Albrecht thought for a moment.

"Look, I often meet older, mature people, comfortable and secure in their jobs: they mean well, clap me on the shoulder, and tell me how hard it was for them before, how they starved their way through it under the most difficult circumstances—that's what they say, they *starved their way through it*. Maybe they were rebellious back then, revolutionaries in the struggle. Now they've made it, their wives are proud and smug when they describe how capable their husbands are, and as for the husbands themselves . . . ? It's sad, Dr. Köster, sad, I tell you, you'd crawl off in despair if you ever started looking like that. In fact, I don't know anything more disgusting to see than prosperous revolutionaries, a potbellied paterfamilias with rolls of fat who used to be a sprinter and still hands around the photographs he has from those days."

Dr. Köster laughed. "That's a good one, potbellied paterfamilias. . . . But you were trying to disprove what I said before."

"Right. We were at resignation, and I was about to make a confession."

"A confession? Of what, if you please?"

"Not so fast, I'm not in the mood for a confession at the moment. Maybe a little later, or maybe not at all today."

"Fine, Albrecht, as you wish. I'm just surprised, and in fact a bit saddened, that you're ashamed to tell me something. I thought we had gotten past shame with each other."

"Shame is a peculiar thing, Dr. Köster. If you cared to listen I could confess a few things that would certainly be at least as instructive."

"Go ahead, talk, Albrecht, you should say anything you have in your heart, I'll always be happy to hear it."

"Fine," he began. "You know that at university, if you need to pay the fees late, you have to submit an application where you answer certain questions extremely precisely, and submit proof for some of the things you say to the authorities. At the end of the application, there's one more part: an appendix, a long section where you can add a few personal remarks with more detailed explanations, all to spruce up your application and increase your chances for a merciful decision. You have to be smart about it. The first time I filled out the application and I got to the part where I could give various details about my situation, I suddenly couldn't figure out what to say and I had to ask an older schoolmate who was used to the process to help me. He laughed when he saw my helpless face, and dictated a few sentences for me to copy down that were pretty extreme. I was moved myself. 'Well,' he said at the end, beaming with pleasure, 'you can never make things look bad enough, can you?' I felt very awkward, and said that it was a little exaggerated: we weren't exactly doing well anymore, but it wasn't as bad as all that yet either. But if the higher-ups read that, they couldn't help but be moved. 'Please,' my schoolmate said, 'what are you talking about? Other people come up with stories much better than that, they have no sense of shame at all anymore.' *Sense of shame*, that's what he said— he probably secretly felt bad about the fact that he wasn't callous enough yet and could still feel shame, while other people were past that stage. You see, that was my situation too: a sense of shame that I never lost. In fact, I have much more of it; a lot of the time when I'm applying or interviewing for things it feels almost unbearable. Everyone was always accommodating, I got help and support from every side, I can't complain about that, but everywhere I went I acted humble and obsequious, it was the only way I could show I was worthy of their help. I presented my case, and every time, once I was done, I kept a solemn silence and waited until I was asked another question. Then, once the interview was over and I'd been excused and was standing outside the door, I felt overcome with an awareness of the pitiful role I was playing in life—each time, the feeling was stronger than the time before. I ran home with wounded honor and looked at my face in the mirror and felt the deepest loathing for my new trick of going around, begging with my poverty. My situation felt indecent to me, I can't think of another word for it: disreputable, undignified, hypocritical, whatever you want to call it—even though what I was saying was true, it fit the facts! That was the horrible thing about it. I couldn't get past that. I wanted to tell the people I was going to see long stories about my father, who had worked his whole life and now couldn't go on. Yes, but dammit, why was I, his son and that beautiful word, *heir*, running around demoralized and ashamed? We hadn't done anything wrong, it was just going badly for us in these tough times; what does that have to do with shame, goddammit? Do you have an answer for that, Dr. Köster? Please, tell me your views."

"It's simple, Albrecht. You just realized that with your requests, your humble petitions that you yourself called a little exaggerated, you were putting yourself in a dependent position that you did not want to be in. You're proud, and only what you have done on your own counts for you."

"Not entirely, Dr. Köster, that's only part of it. But you're close. Tell me, what do you think those people would have said if I had told them about my father? They would have given me a well-meaning, understanding clap on the shoulder and assured me that they knew exactly what I meant, they heard stories about similar fates every day, but it was the fault of the economic conditions. You can't change the economic conditions, they would have said, I was just an innocent victim, and since I was modest and hardworking they would help me. And they did help me. But that didn't produce any change in me, I went on feeling ashamed, in fact I might almost say that my shame grew in proportion to the help I received. . . . And why? Because I realized I no longer had any respectable way to act. What could I do? It wasn't only me, I was standing lost and confused with an indescribably bad conscience in a place that stank of decline and decay and death. I got through these hours of the most abominable despair with the help of some irony, some patience, and some lethargy—those were what I had to help me, to try to keep my head above the water that was already up to my neck. . . . We were just victims, my father and— But to hell with all this endless complaining and grieving; we're not women paid to weep and wail, and I'm sick of it."

Dr. Köster looked up at him and smiled. "You're talking like someone who wants to start throwing bombs." He watched with great affection and devotion as his friend stood up and talked himself into more and more of a rage. Albrecht could feel the mockery in Dr. Köster's words.

"No," he said, "no bomb-throwing, that kind of big brave action is not for me, I leave it to people who are stronger than I am. Go ahead and laugh, but the truth is, I'm still struggling with things that were never an issue for other people, that were always obvious. I've decided to become political."

"What? Political, Albrecht? You poor boy!" Dr. Köster sprang out of his chair.

"Yes, you're surprised, you think I'm turning my back on my best qualities, don't you."

"It's true. I can't believe it, you wanting to go over to the side of the thugs and male hysterics. That's the greatest resignation I can imagine." He thought for a moment, then said: "Albrecht, I knew you as a strong, healthy, sensitive young man who kept to himself, not a team player. I thought you would quietly follow your own path, and now, when you tell me this, it seems to me as though you no longer know who you are, you are trying to deny yourself. Are you doing it on purpose, out of a desire for some kind of change? I'm sorry, but I see someone trying and straining too hard—and now he has a cramp, he is convulsing in a spasm, if I may put it that way. Albrecht, at the start of our acquaintance I gave you a book. It was more than an ordinary book and I know what an impression it made on you. Now I ask you, Albrecht, do you remember it? Or do you reject even your memories now?"

"Yes," Albrecht responded slowly and awkwardly, "I remember." He did not want to talk about that now. "I remember," he went on softly, "a lot of it is true, a lot describes me perfectly. It's uncanny how often I would sometimes feel as if I would never escape it—it was horrible. I felt trapped inside myself with no way out. You have no idea how it was for me. I went around conscientiously doing my work—a capable young man, people said when they talked about me, meaning my modesty and energy; a capable young man, and they invited me out to lunch. But no one realized that I was actually eating away at myself, living off my own substance, with nothing coming in from the outside to renew or refill my self, nothing to refresh or nourish me. I suffered endlessly from what I saw around me every day, the experience I was gaining and what I knew from the inheritance of my education. I was right in the thick of life and losing more and more of my connection to it, my foothold in it. If I were one of those people who tightrope-walk across every difficult situation, who masterfully dance their way through the minefields, then I could have gotten through everything without caring. But I'm too serious, too old—too humorless, if you ask me—to be able to do that. Don't laugh when I confess that I really believe in words like 'proper,' 'honest,' 'respect,' and 'dignity.' They are more than words for me: they embody for me the only substance I can see in a fully realized life. And all of that was what I no longer had back then, I had nothing but a feeling of shame, and a boundless bad conscience for going around avoiding making a real decision. I could clearly see how I would only grow more and more disconnected and disengaged, and it was easy to tell when the day came that I had finally had enough."

Now there was a short break in their conversation. In the

course of their discussion they had both stood up and were pacing around the room, each lost in his own thoughts. Eventually, Dr. Köster took heart—he was the older of the two—and had Albrecht sit down again.

"Come, Albrecht, have a cigarette, and then we'll talk through your whole situation together. It seems to me that you're acting in a bit of a hurry, not entirely free of conclusions you've drawn under difficult pressure in a difficult situation." He spoke paternalistically, like a teacher to his student, as though they both had to explore together and find the answer that he, the older man, knew already; he spoke gently and delicately, so that the student wouldn't feel the least suspicion that he was being consciously steered toward the goal.

"No cigarette, thank you," Albrecht said. "Let's not make the conversation look sweeter and prettier through a haze of smoke. It's better to say everything straight-out, the way we feel it in the moment, and draw the contrast as sharply as we can."

"All right, Albrecht, as you wish." He lit himself a cigarette. After a while: "So, let's go back to where you said that you've decided to become political. You added that it sounded a little ridiculous and presumptuous to talk about it like a major decision with far-reaching consequences while other people didn't need to take such a big running start, they just accepted it as self-evident. Now, let's leave these other people out of consideration and not worry about what they might or might not be doing. If there was any sense at all in all our discussions over the years, it was to teach you to think for yourself, independently, and always make use of this independence. Even today, we should do that, no? So when you say that you want to become political, I try to fully comprehend what you're saying and arrive at the causes that are bringing you to give up your solitude and throw yourself into the arms of one of the dozens of political parties on offer. Your solitude—I think that's the most essential thing: you feel a need to come together with other people with similar external goals as you. It lightens your load to do that: you feel freer, life itself becomes a little easier for you. But that's not all, by no means. Your current economic situation, which is perhaps not especially rosy and looks to remain rather unclear in the future, is strengthening you in your decision. I know, it's hard, it's damned hard, I realize that and I'm taking it into account—you are worn-out, your nerves are frayed, you feel rotten and everything seems more drastic and threatening than it really is. Take it slow, Albrecht, rest up a bit, then we'll talk. I suspect that now—and I hope you don't hold it against me that I'm speaking to you so directly—I suspect that you're desperately longing to be happy. Admit it, Albrecht, am I right?"

"I don't admit it," Albrecht calmly replied. "No, I have nothing to admit there, especially about any earthly happiness. I don't long for it the way you're accusing me of, or in any other way either. In fact, that was the first thing I learned many years ago, when you loaned me that wonderful book, and I won't deny that it was painful too: that what people generally mean by happiness, 'earthly bliss and pleasures in heavenly fullness,' was not for me. You need to be built out of a different material than I am for that sort of thing to make you happy, and you need to be young, with laughter and a sense of humor, things I fundamentally lack. Believe me, happiness isn't at all what I'm aiming at. Fundamentally, it's the same for me as it is for you, Dr. Köster—I ask you to never forget that in the course of our conversation, even if we sometimes stray very far from it. You and I are interested in the same thing, namely, and listen closely: *the life of the mind*. Remember when we first met, when I was still going to school and inexperienced in the world, you told me: The mind, our love for the spirit, is the only thing that saves us and makes us able to act in the world. You see, I've kept your words in my mind all this time, I remember them perfectly: *The mind is what saves us*. I already understood that, way back then, and I still believe it today, despite everything, even if earlier I seemed to brag about not having read anything seriously for a long time. I have not forgotten what you said. . . . *And it alone lets us act in the world.* Then, when you added that part of the sentence, I thought I had definitely understood what you meant . . . *lets us act.* . . . But now I see that back then I didn't have the slightest idea of what I know now. When things weren't going well for people, when circumstances conspired against them, I saw how they got down to work and did things and brought about decisive changes. I'm sure it was always that way, but what you said made me see it, and your words about the mind and our love for intellectual and spiritual things made it seem incomprehensible to me why people would act that way. I saw a clear line in the sand between myself and anyone who took vigorous action. At the same time, I was one of the people circumstances were conspiring against, I was one of the victims—but still, I kept myself apart, in my little struggles and indecisions, off to the side and lost in observation and self-analysis. Gradually, but then decisively, I started to feel that I was cutting myself off more and more from whatever life is, and I realized—it was a painful shock too—that I no longer felt connected to what was going on around me, I was lost at sea in an endless, nebulous void."

"One might say that you have thereby perceived the deepest truth," Dr. Köster countered. "The situation you just described to me is the situation of anyone who withdraws and thinks in isolation and has gained a certain insight, don't you agree?"

"Yes," Albrecht answered hesitantly, "maybe. . . . But you can't just stay at that point, or at least I couldn't. I still wanted to find some way to take part in life. Can you understand that?"

"I understand," Dr. Köster said thoughtfully, "that you have to work, to make money. Do you mean the energy needed to do that? The spiritual momentum in your soul?"

Albrecht shook his head. "No," he said slowly, "here too you're only half understanding what I mean. It's more than that—I have to dare to join in, take the step of becoming part of something where I think I belong, something that offers me a chance to live. I need to find a new, stable way to live, and something more than just an external structure. I understand it differently now—the mind, I mean. I've felt differently about it ever since I've had to spend all my time living and working, which for me have been basically the same thing."

"Albrecht, what gave you these ideas? And what conclusions are you drawing for yourself in terms of what you told me before, about becoming political? You are taking it further, Albrecht, you're not someone who is satisfied with simply recognizing something, no matter how much you want it or how happy it makes you."

"All right," Albrecht answered seriously, "if you're asking, I'll tell you. But don't try to gloss over it later, or analyze me, or add a commentary or anything. I want you to understand what I'm saying in just the way I say it.

"You accused me before of losing what was most distinctive and special about me, as you put it, with this decision to become political. Either that or I didn't know myself anymore, you said. You brought up solitude as opposed to joining a political party that creates a sense of belonging due to common outward goals. I don't think you want to reject a feeling of connection with others working toward a common goal, or do you?"

"Not in the least, Albrecht, you've misunderstood me. I meant everything that goes along with that decision, unintentionally included in it so to speak, but I don't understand—"

"Not so fast, Dr. Köster, let me say something else first. You may remember I had a friend here, Fritz Fiedler. One day he dropped out of school because he didn't think he could continue to live his life under those conditions. He just skipped town, that was the only way to prove to his parents that he meant it. They were upstanding working-class people who had worked hard and gotten ahead, and at first they simply couldn't get it through their heads that their son had no interest in being an educated, and in their view respected and prosperous, man. But they let him do what he wanted, in the end they had no choice and they made their peace with it. I don't think they ever really understood it. It took me a while too, to realize what Fritz had done. He told me once that he couldn't see any bridge between what they were teaching him in school and the life he saw all around him; there was clearly a deep chasm between the two, and he saw it, our teachers did too, and he didn't know what to do about it. On top of that, he was young and healthy and very strong, and he craved some difficult task to use his strength on. It was as simple as that: he wanted to work. He wanted to live the life that he saw around him—his father worked, his brother worked, he didn't want anything different for himself. You know how it all turned out. First he tried here in Germany, then, after a year, before his apprenticeship was over, his company went bankrupt and he was out on the street. The year he'd spent there counted for nothing. All right, so he could have started over with another apprenticeship. And do you know what would have happened to him, Dr. Köster, if he had successfully finished it? The same thing! He would have been out on the street, with no prospects for the future, a hopeless case like thousands of others. Then he went to America, and when he came back after two years he was done for. He never talked about everything he'd been through there but it isn't hard to imagine. America has enough unemployment of its own. I talked to him then, but I couldn't help him, I was in a difficult situation myself at the time. He puttered around here for another couple of months, trying to find his footing, but it was no use, he couldn't. Then he shot himself in Berlin one day, in a little hotel, together with a girl. For love, of course, that's what the papers all said—after all, what other reason could anyone have to take his life besides being lovesick and sexually frustrated? That or not having enough to eat, but Fritz did. Anyway, his parents are still carrying on, they look at me questioningly as though waiting to hear the useful, pious moral I'll put at the end of this story. And it's true, it's not hard to reflect on something after it happens and make suggestions after the fact."

Pause.

"I understand your friend's situation perfectly, and especially why it ended the way it did," Dr. Köster began. He possessed more than enough understanding and proved it with his words. "Your unhappy friend recognized the deep hopelessness that lies in wait for us all, at the end of anything we try to undertake today. His fate is a powerful tragedy and a tremendous reproach."

"Exactly," Albrecht said excitedly, "that's how I see it too. But there's more. I would go so far as to say—and it may sound ridiculous to say it, now that he's dead and can no longer rise up to begin a new life, but still: there is another path, starting off from the same experiences and painful recognitions but not necessarily leading to the same end. Of course I know there was no other choice for Fritz; otherwise he would have made it. He wasn't in poverty: on the outside he was still doing fine, he could have kept living off his parents and brother, but that wasn't the life he wanted. He was young and strong but he was simply shut out. If he had decided to become political, to think in political terms, or let us say think historically, have a clear effect on the world by toppling what is already teetering and building something new in his thoughts—if he had decided to do that instead of running around alone, lashing out everywhere and denying a part of himself—then I daresay that it would have turned out differently for him. He wouldn't have reached this decision himself; he couldn't have. And everyone failed him—his parents, even though his father used to be political himself and even spent time in jail for his activities; his teachers, especially, failed him. And I did too, since I didn't know enough at the time to help him."

"But now my question for you," Dr. Köster interrupted, "is this: Since you told me at the beginning that you only care about the life of the mind—you even told me to make sure not to forget it—what does all this have to do with intellect and knowledge? Or are you so far gone that you think everything can be explained from purely economic causes?"

"That's a nasty thing to say," Albrecht replied slowly, and with infinite melancholy he stood up. His face turned rigid and suddenly looked ageless. "Don't be angry at me for saying so, but I find that truly nasty. Do you need me to promise you that I won't forget any of the things we used to talk about—the power of the mind, love for intellectual and spiritual things, the soul, everything hanging in eternal balance between heaven and earth, the doubtful nature of all existence, and all the rest that is so delicate and fragile that it would be dangerous to speak out loud about it, it could disintegrate in the cold inhospitableness of existence . . . do I really need to promise you, do you think I ever *could* forget it? No, I will never forget those things, no one who has ever partaken of them can. But now, Dr. Köster, listen to me, now it is necessary to understand something very different: the infinite tragedy that comes from *being condemned to act in the world while the spirit is already redeemed*. Can you understand that? I've learned that lesson, and I've felt it on my own body. There's no mercy. If I don't act, I'm done for."

Dr. Köster stood up and looked Albrecht straight in the face.

"Dr. Köster," Albrecht quietly went on, "it's not a question of which of us is right. No doubt we both are. I'm sure you have the eternal, unchanging truth on your side. Fine, you can have it, along with your resignation and well-tended exhaustion, you can have those too, you can afford to indulge in them and be tired and resigned. The only thing is that this eternal, unchanging truth has let me go, it's dropped me, and I would be a coward, or a suicide, if I kept on pursuing it in my situation now. All the evidence is against it, it seems to me. To be redeemed in the spirit, fine, and at the same time to be condemned to live in the world, that's what you need to learn to understand. Then you're prepared to take refuge even on crutches, as you put it before. But you're wrong there too, you're only judging from your own point of view. Where is there life without crutches? Let me limp around and remain incomplete, if that's what you think I am, as long as I'm still alive. It is only in life that I think I can serve the spirit. When I talk to you about the form of life I was looking for, you should know that there is only this one form for me now: any I ever had before has been shattered, and I need to create a new one, one that guarantees respect, dignity, justice, and humanity. What do you have to say against that?"

Dr. Köster was silent for a long time. He walked over to the window and looked out onto the street, as though an answer might come to him from the nighttime darkness there. His breath came heavily. He could see before his eyes the image of the schoolboy from back then, the short pants, the open collar, the admiring, innocent eyes. Once he had spoken to that person. He stayed in his place by the window for a long while. Then he suddenly remembered the last words spoken, they were still ringing in his ears, and he slowly turned back around and said:

"Not much, Albrecht. I agree that that's what's most important for you now. To put it in your own words: You are condemned to live in the world, of course . . . and only in this one particular way. I understand that too. No, don't shake your head like that, I know what you're thinking: you're thinking that understanding is not enough—that no imagination, no matter how vivid and colorful, is enough to appreciate this truth; only actively living can do it justice."

"You're right," whispered Albrecht.

"One more question, though," Dr. Köster went on, undeterred. "I'll be as frank with you as you've been with me. Do you really believe it? Answer me, do you believe that your goal can be accomplished—that any goal can be accomplished, if I can put it so bluntly? Answer me."

"Yes, I do believe it," Albrecht answered solemnly. "When I look at my father, I believe it."

His eyes shone with conviction and power.

"An extraordinary delusion . . ." Dr. Köster whispered. "And if not . . . ?"

Silence.

"And if not? What if you are alone, Albrecht?"

After a while: "I want to live, since I have to keep living and working. There is nothing more for us to discuss. Goodbye."

.

Bankrupt! One Thursday, Herr Seldersen went before the judge to file for bankruptcy. He had thought through this step very carefully a month before, and set the day for that Thursday. He could still have changed his mind, because he had kept his decision a strict secret from everybody, but two days before his appointment he remembered that his birthday was on Thursday—how strange that they would coincide. Maybe it was destiny, meant to be. His fifty-sixth birthday. He kept the appointment he had made and gave himself the biggest birthday present of all. Mother wished him happy birthday early that morning, and then the day began.

He was away from home for more than two hours, an endless time—the courthouse was only a few minutes away. Frau Seldersen sat downstairs in the shop, very anxious; everything was coming at once: the birthday, the end of the store. It was merciless. Then Father came back, calm and satisfied. Mother was huddled in a corner, crying, and doing nothing else—just crying nonstop. Father sat down heavily on the chair behind the counter, his hands on the green surface of the writing desk—sat in his shop, the shop he had owned for twenty-eight years, until today. Now he was a stranger in it. He had done all he could, now it was up to other people to bring things to their proper conclusion. He was relieved of all responsibility, now and for a long time to come, until everything was over.

There was no light in his apartment, and no gas in the stove—they had turned off the utilities. He accepted that with a smile, it was summer after all. Next he would move to Berlin, and then . . . but it wasn't yet time to think about that. He was satisfied, he had completed something and was no longer involved. He had said so too, for everyone to hear. At the same time, it hadn't been his decision at all, he had been forced into taking this step. He might have been able to postpone it for a little while but there was no way he would make it through another winter, he knew that; he didn't have it in him. He was no longer involved. At last it was over. He wanted his peace and quiet, nothing more than a little peace; he wanted to be able to sleep again at night, like a human being, not a beaten, hounded animal.

He had been left by the wayside, Johann Seldersen had—he had lost the struggle. What the war, the postwar years, the hyperinflation hadn't been able to do separately, they accomplished in long, tenacious collaboration: the war and the postwar years and the inflation together. It was one thing after another, and Johann Seldersen, shopkeeper, had thrown in the towel—exhausted, dead tired, but calmly, without making a big fuss. He had exited the stage of economic life where he had stood for years as a reliable player between the manufacturers and the consumers, knowing his role to the very end. The citizen Johann Seldersen was no longer a citizen—now he had nothing but the clothes on his back and some old furniture to shabbily furnish his room with, and in fact he didn't even own that. And this after thirty years of work. The account had been totaled up, zero to zero. He was leaving the same way he'd come, except that thirty years lay in between, and that said it all.

A letter arrived that same day, from a manufacturer threatening legal action if they weren't paid within five days. Herr Seldersen read the letter carefully and laughed a mocking laugh. Not his problem anymore; it was somebody else's. A trustee was assigned by the court to manage the situation: an upright, well-respected man the same age as Herr Seldersen. They had often discussed business matters before, and he represented Father before the court. He was above reproach and would take care of everything properly. In fact, Herr Seldersen felt sorry that this unpleasant task had fallen to him. But he discharged his duties; it could take weeks before everything was cleared up. Until then, the Seldersens had nothing to worry about. A daily sum was set aside for them to live on—more than they would have dared to spend on themselves when they were still making their own decisions—and a week later the news was in the paper. Who was surprised? Probably not a single person in the city. So now Herr Seldersen too, people said, and they took a deep breath as if to say: Next it'll be someone else's turn. That's how things went; no one expected anything different, and in the end there was nothing you could do about it.

The days were long and warm and the Seldersens went for walks in the evenings, down the roads and paths, slowly, relishing every step. They had walked there for twenty-eight years, practically a lifetime since they had started their life together within these city walls. They had hoped that later, when they were old, they would be able to live out their modest lives to the end in peace, but it didn't work out that way. They were not yet at the end. They were on a huge carousel that turned, turned, without stopping, and anyone who wanted to get off did so at his own risk. The truth was, they were not yet old enough to fold their hands in their laps and lead the quiet life of the elderly, but they were also no longer young enough to start over as young people do and reacquire a place for themselves in the world. And anyway, no one was asking them if they wanted to. It was cruel and terrible, and at the same time irrevocable. Perhaps there was a reason in there somewhere, some iron necessity for it all, but they didn't see it or understand it, since their fate, their sorrow, their tears were clouding their vision and forcing them to pay attention only to what was closest at hand.

Herr Seldersen arranged a huge going-out-of-business sale, with prices so discounted that things were practically free. Everyone who had stayed true to the shop through the unspeakably difficult years came by, for the last time. They spent their money there once more, without words of pity or sympathy—the feelings spoke for themselves—but the prices were good, the stock needed to be cleared out. Little Kipfer came too, and brought his wife and their youngest child, almost a year old now and shriveled-looking, as tiny as a newborn. It screamed pitifully and little Kipfer tried to calm the baby with a touching fatherly helplessness; he carried the baby in his arms since his wife was too weak. They had brought money to buy what they needed most urgently just then—there was never enough, with four kids. Herr Seldersen served them personally, fetching things from the darkest corners of the store and digging up more items everywhere.

"And then this," he said, bringing out a large piece of cloth, "perfect for a dress for you, Frau Kipfer." He put everything in a big pile. The Kipfers felt uncomfortable—they had only brought five marks. Then Father named a price: "Four marks," he said. "Four marks, is that all right with you?"

Was it all right with them? It was a gift! No one said an unnecessary word.

Herr Seldersen packed it all into a box. He had also set aside some toys for the children—his own children had played with the toys before, but now they were grown, the things were just lying around. Little Kipfer came by a couple of days later to fetch them. When he said goodbye, he shook Father's hand and looked at him for a long time. Then he suddenly said, in a halting voice:

"I'm sorry, Herr Seldersen, truly, I'm sorry."

Father looked up, stiff and serious, and shrugged.

"Well," he said with a hand gesture. Then he laughed, relaxed and helpless. Secretly he felt deeply glad that someone understood and sympathized with him. Little Kipfer understood him. But what was going on here? Kipfer seemed moved, shaken, as though it were happening to him personally, but hadn't he predicted, not so long ago, that this would inevitably happen? He wasn't surprised, it was all right there in the teachings he constantly preached with his sick lungs. He had been proven right. *See?* he could have said proudly. Look, a perfect example, I was right. He could have crowed in triumph. But instead he was sorry, and said so straight-out. The truth was on his side, and yet he felt sorry.

The Seldersens went around to their friends and acquaintances and said goodbye. It's not far, we'll come back soon for a visit, they said. And the new, unknown future drew ever closer. Well, they had the children, everything was easier if you could go through it together. But nothing changed the fact that they were leaving, and had to rejoin the struggle again, at their age.

One early morning, at five, the furniture movers came to pack; in three hours the apartment was cleared out and loaded onto two trucks. Herr Dalke had decided to relinquish his claim and leave them their furniture. Thanks!

They walked through the empty rooms. The wallpaper was darker in spots where the pictures had hung; there was dust and cobwebs in the corners; everything was strange, bare, and empty. And this was where they had lived, for how many years? The ceilings seemed twice as high now that the lamps were gone; the floors were scratched and shabby. Their gaze passed over everything as they took their leave. Farewell! Not a goodbye, not "See you later"—well then, just farewell.

Albrecht envied his parents, who were allowed to cry, just cry, without holding anything back. He took them by the hand and they willingly let him lead them away.

.

Now they live in Berlin, somewhere or other, hemmed in between tall buildings and with a view of gray walls, dim courtyards, and a half-withered chestnut tree. The yards of four buildings built close together border one another, with only a five- or six-foot-high wire fence between them; the first beggar singing for spare change comes by at nine in the morning and it goes like that all day long, they hear each one four times over. Thirty renters live in their building, between the front building on the street and the back building in the courtyard; the stairs are bare and narrow, and at night the street noise blasts into their room. The apartment is one room smaller than their old one, and the rooms are not as large; the furniture is the same.

They are all busy. The children leave in the morning and come back late at night. They are never on time, and it's hard for Frau Seldersen to have meals prepared for everyone. Herr Seldersen didn't take a very long vacation. He is fifty-six years old, and who would hire such an old man, he says; he has no hope of that, but he's not embarrassed about doing a little business on the side: shoelaces, stockings, ribbons, buttons, pins, he sells everything. He goes around into the buildings, to the markets, builds himself a booth. He stands there for hours between the noise and the cries, always prepared for when a possible buyer looks his way. He doesn't shout, doesn't advertise his wares loudly. Anyone who comes to him buys. He doesn't bring in much money, certainly not enough to live on—the state needs to help. Often he has only enough to pay for the booth and the streetcar to and from the market, but then there are also days when he brings home a couple of marks. Then he sits on the sofa for the rest of the day, happy, reading his newspaper. His life isn't quite so useless anymore. A couple of marks . . . so modest he has become. He has lost his feeling for his past life, everything lies so immensely far behind him now. And when thoughts come to him, they leave him unmoved. His fate is that of a stranger— yes, yes, it's best that way. Frau Seldersen keeps busy as well, she never has a moment to rest, which is just the way she wants it. She doesn't like going out into the streets—she clearly no longer understands the life going on around her, and tries not to think about it.

And that too is as it should be.

After Father reads the paper, he painstakingly folds it up again and lays it on the table and stays frozen in place for a long time, quiet, with eyes closed. His breathing is calm. Mother comes in and cries, "Music, music, don't you hear it?" She goes to the window and opens it. They can hear quite clearly the squeaking fifes and drumrolls for the march. It comes closer;

now it's turning the corner. In front, at the head of the procession, is a solitary man, and the rest follow behind him in
well-organized rows of four that swell to a larger and larger demonstration. Workers, the unemployed, impoverished middle-
class citizens, students—women and men—all marching at the
same pace, and even though the man in the first row doesn't
know the man in the tenth row, doesn't even know who he is, they
are marching together. A mighty will streams out from them, a
united readiness: they know why they're marching. When the
first group reaches the house, Albrecht leans a little way out of
the window so that they can see him down below, and silently
salutes the marchers. And slowly, as though he first has to throw
off a monstrous burden, Father raises his hand and steps next to
his son—but his arm falls heavily to his side, as though he does
not have the strength, and he sinks his head and closes his eyes.
The two of them stand there like that the whole time, father and
son, saluting the marchers until the last one has finished walking past the window.

Translator's Note

Shortly before Hans Keilson's death in 2011, I corresponded with him about the end of this novel. The last scene seems strangely like a Nazi rally, but surely he intended it to be a Communist march or other left-wing demonstration? He told me that the publisher (in 1933) had made him change the ending of the book, hoping to avoid political difficulties. Originally, Albrecht and his father had explicitly raised their fists in the Communist salute, not their hands in a Nazi salute. In the published version, it was left ambiguous.

Afterword (1984)

After more than fifty years, *Life Goes On* is being reprinted by my old publisher. I have been invited to contribute a short afterword, giving the history of how the book came to be written and its fate in the context of its era. Strangely, I feel like I am writing a kind of obituary, my own. Fifty years is a long time, during which quite a bit more has been lost than merely the naïve hopes of a very young man bringing out his first book with the famous publisher S. Fischer—hopes for success, fame, yes, I might as well say it straigh-out: immortality.

I have in front of me the "Short Self-Portrait" that I wrote for Fischer's magazine *Korrespondenz* in March 1933. I quote: "When I was born, in December 1909, my father drank a bottle of Sekt. He could afford it. It was 'Silver Sunday' in Advent. But I don't believe he did." Do I still not believe it, even now?

"Someone named Loerke called," my mother told me late one afternoon in December 1932, a few days before my twenty-third birthday, when I came home from my job at the hospital. "He called to congratulate us. He's going to recommend your novel for publication."

About three months earlier, I had sat across from Gottfried Bermann Fischer on Bülowstrasse, in the firm's old office, and handed over the manuscript without any preliminaries. We discussed various things, including medicine (he was a surgeon by training; I was in my ninth semester at medical school) and music: he played viola; I played trumpet and fiddle in various bands, at events for the credit unions, fishing clubs, and wrestling societies on Frankfurter Allee, all around Alexanderplatz, in the Zoo Restaurant, at balls for the press and the movie studios and the technical college, and one day a week for Katharina von Oheimb, and even on the sound tracks to various sound films (*Seven Girls in a Boat* and *The Csardas Princess*). We talked about all of that, everything except literature.

I had been met downstairs in the office building by a woman whose features, a bit peasantlike, made a great impression on me. It was Paula Ludwig, though I learned that only later. When I left, I bumped into a short, frail man by the glass door carrying a fat briefcase under his arm; he looked me over sharply through his rimless glasses from a rather creased face with no beard and no fat on it. It was Alfred Döblin. If it was a manuscript of his in his leather case, it must have been *Unser Dasein* [Our Existence].

Not long after that December phone call, I went to see Oskar Loerke in his apartment in Frohnau and we worked on my manuscript together. Loerke wrote about it in his *Diaries*, which Karl Krolow brought to my attention in Amsterdam in the sixties. I was given an advance and for the first time went skiing in the Engadine, near Compatsch, with a group of other medical students from Berlin. The publisher sent me the proofs there. When I came back, the Reichstag was burning. Loerke and Peter Suhrkamp, who had just taken over the editorship of the *Neue Rundschau* from Rudolf Kayser, recommended changing the ending of the novel and they convinced me. The salute of "clenched fists" disappeared. Ultimately, I didn't care about which party was holding the rally, only about the Seldersens making a political decision as such.

We had already discussed the title. I was young and clueless and had proposed *The New Life*, and Loerke and Suhrkamp had refused, obviously. Comparing oneself to Dante . . . Then I suggested *Life Goes On*, and there it was. That was my entrance into German "literature" and my exit from it too. I had, it is true, won third prize in a student contest sponsored by the German Publishers and Booksellers Association, in 1926: "Recommend a Book" (I chose Hermann Hesse's *Demian*). But the piece was printed only in a special pamphlet, with only my initials. With the thirty marks I won, I ordered three books, and it took weeks before the nosy and scandalized bookseller in my small town handed them over to me: *Eros in the Slaughterhouse* by Karl Plättner, a comrade of Max Hölz's in the March 1921 workers' revolt; *First Experience: Four Stories from Childland*, by Stefan Zweig; and the exquisite, leather-bound pocket edition on thin paper of Sigmund Freud's *Lectures* (3rd ed., 1926: Leipzig, Vienna, Zurich). I kept the last of these through all these many years—the best and most encouraging introduction to the profession that I still practice today, if more critically than I once did.

I can still remember what made me start writing the novel. An American friend was studying at the Berlin Psychoanalytic Institute and she inspired me to stop by there one day, sign up, and tell them "my troubles." The analyst I saw—could it have been Sachs?—heard me out in all seriousness and then informed me that he saw no reason for me to enter analysis. I went back home, furious, and sat down to write the opening sentences of this book.

And so, occasionally interrupted by the demands of school and my work as a musician, I started to tell the story of myself and of my parents in the small-town capital of the district of Mark Brandenburg, and later in Berlin—the story of an independent small businessman and his economic downfall, set in the political, social, and economic upheaval of the years after the First World War, the period of the Weimar Republic, the hyperinflation, and the rise of National Socialism. It was a piece of self-analysis within the narrow range of my understanding and abilities, and a description of broader developments insofar as I could grasp them. But it was only one part of my self-portrait.

I wrote the other part, about being young and Jewish in the Germany of that time, only later, in the Netherlands, as the novel *The Death of the Adversary*, which appeared in Germany in 1959. In the United States it was one of *Time* magazine's Best Books of the Year for 1962.

So, in 1933, my book was published. I was able to attend a reception at the villa in the Grunewald—I gave "Tutti" a big bouquet of flowers and shook "Samy's" hand; "We'll bring out one of your books." Aside from that, I stood lost in a crowd of people, most of whom I did not know. A slim, wiry man stalked confidently around the room—it was Leonhard Frank—and there was Hermann Sinsheimer, who wanted to serialize my novel in the *Berliner Tageblatt* (before changing his mind). I met Richard Huelsenbeck there as well: the cofounder of Dadaism, later a psychiatric colleague of mine. The press had published a book of his at the same time as mine.

I stuck close to Joachim Maass and Karl Jakob Hirsch (author of *Kaiserwetter*), whom I'd already spoken to by chance on the way there, and to Kurt Heuser, whom I knew through Stefan Grossmann and his daughter, Maya, a schoolmate (and more to me than that). My book was banned in 1934—the last debut by a Jewish writer from the old S. Fischer Verlag. That same year, I passed my medical exams and was likewise banned from practicing medicine.

I switched over to the other career I had studied for: that of a gymnastics, sports, and swimming instructor state-certified by the Prussian College for Physical Education in Spandau. From that point on I taught at the Landschulheim Caputh, various schools for the Jewish community in Berlin, and the Theodor Herzl School. There, on the Kaiserdamm, I ran on burning hot asphalt in the "Potsdam-Berlin" five-hundred-meter relay race for the Jewish sports club Bar Kochba. In October 1936, my future wife, Gertrud Manz, and I left Germany; the Nuremberg Laws had put us at risk.

Since then I have lived in Holland, where I survived the war and persecution in hiding, working as a doctor (under a fake name) for the Vrije Groepen Amsterdam resistance group. Life did indeed go on, but I was far removed from literature, although I did publish in a few Dutch-language anthologies under the pseudonym Benjamin Cooper, and also started pouring out German-language poems, some of which, to my great surprise, the Dutch literary journal *De Gemeenschap* [The Community] published under the fake name "Alexander Keiland." I sent them to Peter Huchel after the war, and he published the poem "To the Tune of an Old Nigun" in *Sinn und Form*. I wrote the short novel *Comedy in a Minor Key* while I was still living in hiding, and Querido, the German-language émigré press in Holland, published it in 1947. It was practically impossible to import the press's products into Germany, due to currency problems.

It was thanks to the poems published in *De Gemeenschap* that my parents were allowed to come to the Netherlands from Germany after Kristallnacht (the "Night of Broken Glass") in Berlin. My father, as a decorated soldier who had fought on the front lines in World War I, appeared with my mother on a special exchange list in 1943, but no such exchange took place. The lives of both my parents were ended in Birkenau.

After the war, until 1970, I worked with other survivors for Le Ezrat Ha'Jeled (To Help the Children), an organization for Jewish war orphans. I passed my medical exams again, in the Netherlands, as a neurologist and psychoanalyst. In the summer of 1967, I joined the staff of the Amsterdam University child psychology clinic. There, with the support of the clinical psychologist Herman R. Sarphatie and later the mathematician Arnold Goedhart, I began the studies that would eventually become my dissertation in 1979. In 1934, in Berlin, I had been told that if I received my Ph.D. in medicine I would have had to renounce my citizenship, so I decided not to; forty-five years later, I finished what I had started. The Dutch Ministry of Justice and the Interior supported my work, which was published as a monograph in the Enke Verlag's series "Psychiatry Forum" in Stuttgart, in 1979. I spent eleven years sitting at a desk, working on it, which must be why I eventually gave it such a long title: *Sequential Traumatization in Children: A Descriptive-Clinical and Quantitative-Statistical Follow-up Investigation of the Fate of Jewish War Orphans in the Netherlands.* In publishing this book, I finally said the kaddish—the prayer for the dead—that I had been unable to say for so long.

In addition to *Sinn und Form*, I also published poems in *Castrum Peregrini, Neue Rundschau,* and *Die Zeit,* contributed to anthologies, and published academic work in both German and Dutch—not much, all things considered. I wrote countless reports and case studies, though, in the language of my profession, to convince judges and other authorities of the suffering that had befallen the children and adults I treated or studied during the dark years. This is the work that fundamentally shaped my personal relationship to literature.

When I arrived in Holland in 1936, I saw my novel in the public library. Had it hurried on ahead of me, or dragged me along after it? Its title, *Life Goes On*: was it a challenge, a premonition, an incantation conjuring up the future, or just an ironic bon mot? In May 1983, I gave a speech in Osnabrück as the PEN Center's representative for German-language authors in exile, at the opening for the "Week of Burned Books." Written on the wall behind me were all the names of the authors forced into exile. Many of these authors were no longer alive. My name was there too; coincidentally, I was standing directly under it when I gave my speech. I had never been particularly convinced that I belonged on such a list, but I realized on that occasion that it was not just illustrious men and women who had fled the country: the lesser-known authors, the young beginners, left Germany too. Their only fame is to have had their books burned or banned, along with those by Baruch Spinoza, Moses Mendelssohn, Heinrich Heine, Karl Marx, Sigmund Freud, Thomas Mann, and so many others.

Since the war, I have twice been back to visit Bad Freienwalde (now in East Germany) and revisit my memories. It is human nature to forget, and to be forgotten. It is this fact that legitimates days of commemoration.

Literature is the memory of humanity. Anyone who writes remembers, and anyone who reads takes part in those experiences.

Books can be reprinted. The fact is, there are archival copies of books.

Not of people.

HANS KEILSON
Bussum, the Netherlands, spring 1984